I0668895

Broken Stars

BOOK THREE IN THE BLUSHING MOON TRILOGY

KITT LYNN

LUPO PUBLISHING

For Bo. Cuz she's a boss bitch.

CONTENT WARNING

This book contains possibly triggering content.

If you are a survivor and need assistance or support, please call
the National Sexual Assault Hotline at
800-656-HOPE (4673)
https://hotline.rainn.org/

If you are in a dangerous situation and need help or support,
please call the National Domestic Abuse Hotline at
800-799-SAFE (7233)
https://www.thehotline.org/

Please do not struggle in silence. You are not alone.
If you need a more detailed list of the triggers within this
book, please reach out to me at misskittlynn@gmail.com.

I don't want to be the reason for someone to feel hurt, upset,
or traumatized.

- Kitt -

Creature Guide

Hannoth - Large, predatory mammals. They are covered in fur with large claws and fangs. When a hannoth attacks, flaps come away from the sides of its neck, projecting strings of acidic venom.

Kunzite crystals - Found throughout Havre. Pinkish crystals that grow in clusters underground and make everything from the land to the air very cold. But they also give the area a calm and serene atmosphere that anyone walking through them will find relaxing.

Luminite crystals - Bright yellow crystals that emit a tremendous amount of heat. They are harvested and used frequently within villages.

Mountain Men - (aka, Rock men of Gygax). Men made of rocks that live within the mountains throughout Havre. Their origin is believed to be the result of witches and fairy folk that bewitched the mountains to aide during the Great War with the humans.

Rogues - Werewolves with no allegiance to a pack or village. Frequently they are banished from villages, and branded to prevent them from entering any other were-colonies. The actual brand varies based on the village, but traditionally a "R" on the neck or somewhere visible.

Sabbots - Magical humanoid creatures. Tend to tower over alphas. Blue in color with thick scales and barbs that jut out along their spine.

The Enchanted Lands of Havre

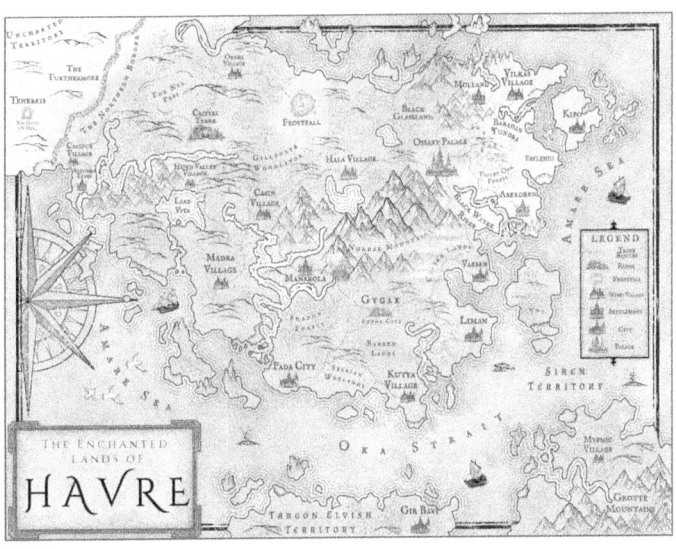

To see a larger version of the map of Havre, visit www.
kittlynn.com.

A Few Days After The King's Camp

Tzidal

"BLUE!" I whispered harshly, trying like hell not to make too much noise. The young male-omega jerked around to me, his vibrant eyes asking me silently what was wrong. "Too far," I mouthed, motioning for him to return.

Blue nodded, then leaned against a tree, waiting for us to catch up. He was so damn eager to get to Ossory he kept rushing off, leaving Lex and me in his tracks.

"Anything from Joon?" Lex asked, gripping my arm as we stepped over an uneven break in the path. He was still weak, limping slowly over the rough terrain.

"No," I breathed a long sigh, unsure if the silence that filled our bond was a good sign. "I woke up the other day feeling such horrible pain radiating from him, but nothing since."

Lex stumbled, and I jerked to help steady him. His

strength had yet to fully return after the beating he took at the King's camp. A lot of the swelling was gone after he fed from my arm, but deep bruises still covered his face, and his ankle was puffy and red.

"Will you heal with time?" I asked, not sure how a Siren's biology worked. "Or do you have to feed?"

"I'll be okay." Lex gave me a smile that didn't quite reach his eyes. I pressed my lips together, letting go of the fact that he didn't answer my question.

"How far do you think we are?" Blue asked, taking a few steps toward us. We had only been traveling for a few hours, but the omega already looked worn and amped at the same time. His bluish-black hair was wild around his face, sticking to the sweat on his forehead. "I think I can see the points of the palace," he said, pointing in the distance.

I narrowed my eyes at the tree line. I couldn't see anything but barren winter branches and a few evergreens. Blue shivered as he glanced all around us. The wind was especially cutting today. I was just thankful it wasn't snowing. Neither Blue nor myself had any shoes.

"Do you think we'll get there today?" Blue's dark blue-green eyes were wide with pent-up energy.

Lex groaned, then sat, plopping onto a downed tree. It was small and sagged beneath his weight, but the poor siren seemed too tired to care. "I need a minute," he whispered, rubbing his ribs.

"I'm not sure how far we are," I said honestly, hoping to temper Blue's expectations. "It could be a few more days. We can't move very quickly," my eyes flickered to Lex, "and we're also traveling pretty far east to avoid the King's camp."

Blue nodded, but I could see it in the way his fingers twisted together: he was brimming with hope. I just prayed he didn't fall apart when it took longer than he wanted.

"Do you think Byriel is okay?" Blue asked, biting his bottom lip. It was the third time he had asked since this morning.

"Strayton won't kill him," Lex said with a lazy wave of his hand. He had said it many times, but I wasn't sure if I agreed. "She needs her people to keep believing in the sanctity of their bloodline. Byriel is probably sitting in a cell somewhere. He's fine."

Blue nodded eagerly at Lex's words, but I already knew he'd be asking again in a few hours. "I just wish I knew where he was," the young omega whispered, twisting the lock of purple hair just next to his ear. I immediately grabbed his hand, stopping him.

"I know it's hard," I dropped my voice to barely a whisper, "But you can't bring any attention to the birthmark on your scalp. People have been hunting and killing wolves with that very mark."

I purposefully left out the fact that Byriel was the one killing them, but that wasn't for me to share. After all, the alpha had suffered and repented for what he had done, and he would never hurt Blue—I truly believed that—but the thought of Byriel knowing about Blue's mark still made me uneasy. Byriel would be devastated, given that he would have killed the poor youngling a year ago if given the chance.

Blue nodded, then jerked his hands away from his hair. "I'm sorry," he said softly. "I keep forgetting."

"Blue," I gave him a pointed look, trying to make him understand just how important this was, "If anyone were to find out about that mark, you'd be killed. And..." I shook my head, cursing myself for letting the young omega come with us. Joon was right. We should have taken him back to his village. "I don't know what will happen when all the marked wolves are killed. The prophecy..." I pushed out a heavy sigh, frustrated and confused. "All I know for sure, is that having that mark is dangerous. So don't touch your hair."

"It's all bullshit anyway," Lex cut in. His usually gray eyes seeped black, his strength waning fast. "The prophecy is shit and doesn't say anything of any use," he snipped. I opened my mouth, ready to scold the siren, but he cut me a quick look. "But," Lex said forcefully before turning his tight energy back on Blue, "if you can't keep your hands off your hair, you'll be staying with me in these woods while Tzidal enters Ossory."

Blue's eyes went wide, fear and panic bursting out of him. "I promise I won't touch my hair again!" he said in a rush of words. "I know this is important." His eyes narrowed, and his voice dropped to a serious, intense whisper. "But I need to look for my Byriel. I can't just sit in the trees and wait."

"I understand," I cupped his cheeks, trying to calm him. "And we'll find him. We'll find Byriel and Joon."

The wind shifted and twisted around me, making me shiver. My black servant's robes were just as thin as Blue's formal green ones. I needed a proper coat. We all did.

"What's the plan once we get there?" Lex asked, placing his hand under his arm and rubbing gently.

I slipped my hand into my pocket, making sure the letter Jonelle gave me was still there. "I have something to deliver to the allies." I pulled it out, showing a small envelope to Lex. The deep green seal was smooth around the edges, displaying the image of a Centaurea flower in the center.

"Do you know who to give it to?" Blue asked, running a single pointed finger over the waxy seal. His complexion was so white it edged almost a soft blue in the cloudy winter sun.

"No," I admitted, realizing Jonelle didn't give me any information other than that the allies needed it.

"Do you know how to get into the palace?" Lex asked. "Or where to go once we're in?"

I bit the inside of my cheek. "No."

Lex pulled a face, rightfully judging me.

I couldn't help but laugh.

We were two omegas and a wounded siren in the middle of the woods with nothing but a bit of parchment and no real understanding of what the hell to do with it.

"I think Jonelle expected to be with me." I tapped the letter against my palm, fighting the urge to open it. "She gave it to me because no one would suspect an omega if we were captured." I flipped the parchment over, caressing the velvety paper. "At least that's what she said."

The wind shifted, and Lex went tight before he spun around. My hand flew to the dagger secured at my waist, and I turned, scanning the cold forest all around us.

"What is it?" Blue whispered, moving slowly to Lex's side.

The siren's chest expanded, pulling in a deep breath, then he shook his head. "Hard to tell." His voice was so soft I could barely hear him. "My nose is struggling." He hovered his hand over the center of his still-bruised face. "Maybe an alpha." His eyes met mine. They were filled with worry, and a trace of fear. There was no way the three of us could fight off even one alpha.

"Are they close?" I asked, pushing the envelope back into my pocket. The rustle of dry leaves pricked my ears, and the hairs on my neck stood up.

"I think it's that alpha that led us away from the camp," Blue whispered, sniffing the wind. "Kenji?"

I turned, looking deep into the black forest. Kenji was probably out there, searching high and low to drag me back to Madra, but I wasn't going anywhere. Not without Joon.

"Come on," I placed a hand under Lex's elbow and pulled him up. "We need to move. At this rate, it'll take a damn week to get to Ossory."

Lex stifled a groan, rubbing his ribs down to his hip. "I'll need to feed soon." He glanced over his shoulder as we walked. "Maybe we should let this Kenji find us. It would be nice for a meal to come to me for a change."

I smiled, pretending it was a joke, but a shameful part of me tucked the idea away. Having a shape-shifting siren would most definitely work to our advantage, but we'd need Lex healthy first. And to achieve that, he would need to eat. Whoever it might be.

THE SUN HAD long since set by the time the gates to Ossory came into view. We stood just within the tree line, staring at the large field that seemed to circle the entire city. I had envisioned rows of armed guards and fierce beasts lining the road leading to the impressive palace, but this was so vast and open. It was empty.

"Is no one patrolling the gates?" Blue asked, scanning the mighty border wall, looking at the very top of the borders. "There," he gasped, pointing up. A few guards could be seen atop the vast structure, glaring at the field with bows slung over their backs. "It's so creepy to have them looking down at you like that."

I had to agree. While it wasn't likely the guards could see us in the shadows within the tree line, it did make me uneasy about stepping out into the moonlit field.

"Would they attack us?" Blue's voice dropped to a whisper as if suddenly concerned someone could overhear us.

"No," I said, but I didn't know.

"The field just helps them see any threats approaching the gate," Lex said. His dark eyes were puffy and tired.

"You know," I said, suddenly remembering. "My village back home had a sizable field leading up to the main gates too.

I never left, so I didn't know just how far it spanned; it always felt massive when looking out from the marketplace."

My mind drifted to the vegetables and wares the merchants would be selling this time of year. It was winter, which meant potatoes, parsnips, and loads of carrots. My mother would be making her winter stew soon, filling my tiny childhood home with the sweet scent of seared meats and spices.

I missed her and my father so much.

They probably thought I was dead—killed alongside Korban just next to that cluster of willow trees.

That felt like a lifetime ago.

"What are you thinking about, puppy?" Lex's big gray eyes searched my face, concern pulling his brows together.

"How hungry I am." I smiled and placed my hand over my stomach. I hadn't thought much about what I looked like since leaving home, but for some reason, I was suddenly very aware of my trim waist and strong legs. I had moved and fought and worked more this last year than I ever had in my entire life.

I wasn't the same omega that left my village almost a year ago. I was strong. I was a fighter. And I missed Joon. My alpha. My mate. And in order to find him inside those massive palace walls, I would need a plentiful meal and a good night's sleep.

"Blue?" A fresh wave of determination flowed through me.

His eyes went wide, eager to help.

"How about you find something for me and you to eat? You're faster and a better climber than I am," I said to the young omega. "I'm sure you'll find something wonderful long before I will."

Blue's chest puffed up a bit with pride, and he gave me a fierce nod. "I saw two big osprey nests not far back." He pulled me close, quickly kissing my cheek. "I'm going to find you the fattest eggs you've ever eaten."

I let out a small laugh, thankful to see him feeling a bit better. Blue let out a muffled squeal, then set off, his feet silent as he rushed through the crisp winter brush.

"That should keep him busy." Lex pushed out a long sigh, then slowly lowered himself onto the ground. It might have been the long shadows thrown by the silver moon, but he looked especially pale. His usual velvety complexion was waxy and gaunt.

"We need to get you a proper meal." I looked up and down Lex's withered form, giving him a teasing smirk. "Because right now, you're downright useless to me."

He snorted, then winced, pressing his palm over his ribs once again. "I just can't seem to catch a proper breath of air."

"How about I take a look?" I touched his side, smoothing my hand over the thin, silky pale blue fabric of his robes. I knew he wasn't actually wearing clothes—this was simply what Lex was projecting at the moment, but it still felt so real. "You don't seem to be struggling to keep your current form," I said, hopeful. "That's good." I pressed gently at a puffy spot next to Lex's fourth rib, and he jerked then winced.

"Careful there, pup," he gritted out, pulling in tight, short breaths. "There's no need to handle me like a damn alpha."

"Sorry," I grimaced, removing my hands from his side. "Will eating heal this?"

"Yes," he panted, moving his eyes around the dark forest. "I'm sorry we have to sleep out here and not within the borders. If I could shift—"

I held up my hand, stopping him. "I've been sleeping on the ground for months now. One more night won't kill me." I smiled, hoping to make him feel better.

"Yeah, but if I could just phase into an alpha, we could just walk right up to the gates tonight." He held up a hand, concentrating very hard on his fingertips. His mouth grew tight, and his brow wrinkled. Slowly, the tips of his fingers deepened into a shocking shade of black, but then just as quickly, the color disappeared, returning to Lex's pale white skin. He groaned, frustrated. "I'm just too weak,"

I stood, then scanned the pitch-black forest around us. "What can I get you to eat? I'm not a great hunter, but can you eat berries or roots?"

"Don't worry about it, Tzi," Lex grabbed the nearest tree, using the trunk to pull himself back onto his feet. "I'll find something. I won't be able to outwit an alpha like this, but some wild game will do. Maybe I can get a rabbit or a—"

Something black and furry flew through the air, landing right at Lex's feet. I stared at the lifeless object, unable to rip my eyes away from it.

"Is that a rabbit?" I whispered, hating that my eyes couldn't properly see it in the dark.

"It's a fox." Kenji's baritone voice drifted from behind me, making the skin along my spine pull tight. "I thought I told you to stay beside the river." He stepped up next to me, glaring hard at my face. The tanned alpha looked tired—his palace uniform was wrinkled, and his feet were covered in mud.

I tightened my grip on my blade and squared my shoulders. "And I told you I'm not leaving my mate."

The alpha's eyes widened for a moment as if shocked I'd speak to him in such a way, then he shook his head, tsking softly. "Fucking omegas." He narrowed his eyes in the distance. "Your kind won't listen even to save your own fucking life." He kicked out at the fox, moving it closer to Lex. "Eat, siren. We both know you need it."

Lex's glassy eyes shifted from Kenji to me, then back again.

"Eat," I whispered to my friend. "You need your strength."

The change in Lex's expression was subtle. It was the ease of tension between his brow and the way the corner of his lips twitched as he eyed the fox. He knew what I was thinking. If we needed to escape this alpha, it would be easier if Lex could fight and shift.

Rolling forward, Lex gripped the fox's tale and pulled it to him. His eyes glazed over, and his mouth opened wide, displaying white, pointed teeth. Then he bit down on the critter's gut, feasting wildly.

"We can head out at dawn," Kenji said, still watching Lex eat. His upper lip curled in disgust, unable to hide his opinion of the siren. Alphas hated them so much. Not that I could blame them. Lex spent his days tracking, tricking, then eating alphas. But I had long since accepted it. After all, if shifters weren't so eager to fuck wild creatures in the woods, they wouldn't meet their end so easily.

"I'll get you something to eat," Kenji said to me. "You'll need your strength for such a long journey."

"I can't just leave my mate." I inhaled deeply, pulling in as much of the alpha's scent as possible. His aroma was deep and woodsy, with not a trace of sweetness. He wasn't mated, but I hoped I could still appeal to some part of him. "Could you just abandon someone you loved?"

Kenji's eyes narrowed, his expression pinched. "Stop being a brat," he ordered. His dominant tone pushed under my skin, and I bristled, not caring for a stranger to speak to me like that. Alphas commanded their mates, their pups, or when an omega was in danger. Kenji was just being an ass.

"I told your mate I'd take you to Madra," he said pointedly.

"And I told Jonelle I'd deliver something to the allies."

Kenji's dark eyes widened, then slipped up and down my body. It wasn't a lustful gaze, but more like he was trying to find what I had hidden. "What are you delivering?"

I crossed my arms and glared up at him through my lashes. Even if he ordered me, I was determined not to tell him.

"What do you have, omega?" he said with the full force of his alpha.

My jaw clenched tight, and my abs flexed hard, but I held firm.

Kenji's narrowed eyes widened slightly, surprised I could defy him. "Omega," he said forcefully.

"Don't!" I flashed my teeth, unsheathing my dagger. "I'm not yours to command."

Kenji eyed my dagger, then the corner of his lips lifted into a small smile. "Fine," he snapped. "Don't tell me. But that doesn't change the fact that I made a promise to your mate to take you to Madra. The best thing you can do for your mate right now is to think happy thoughts and go home."

I pulled a face at his ridiculous instructions. "I promised to deliver a message," I stood a little taller, hoping I looked fierce. It wasn't likely, but I still squared my shoulders and tipped my head back, determined to make the alpha in front of me take me seriously.

"You promised?" Kenji's eyebrows shot up, clearly not believing me.

I nodded, but kept quiet, letting him think it over.

The forest around us was black and silent. There was no way I'd be able to escape this alpha out here in the woods. He could shift into his wolf and track me down in a matter of seconds. But if we could just get inside Ossory, I might be able to give him the slip—and it would be easier to get into the gate with another guard escorting us. We wouldn't even have to wait for Lex to regain his strength. Kenji could pretend he was a prisoner.

"Let me deliver my message," I said to Kenji. "Then we'll go to Madra."

"You'll just go to Madra without a fight?" he asked with a disbelieving lift in his voice. "What happened to saving your mate?"

"My message will save my mate," I said firmly. It was a lie, but if I could just maintain eye contact, this alpha might believe me. I hoped.

Kenji leaned down, pushing into my space. "Tomorrow, I will help you deliver your message. Then we're leaving." His dark eyes narrowed, his scent going sharp. "If you run, I'll tie you up and drag your ass to Madra if I have to. Understand?"

His sharp tone cut into me, making my wolf snarl at his disrespect. "You know," I struggled to keep my tone polite, "I've walked all across these lands, fought horrible creatures, and escaped alphas. I even killed a beta...." My mind drifted to almost a year ago when I left that poor boy at the bottom of that pit. I wonder how long he lasted.

"We've all done things we aren't proud of," Kenji said, his face soft with understanding, but he was still tense as if expecting me to up and run.

I tipped my chin up, refusing to submit and ready to lie my way into the city. "I will deliver my message. Then I will gladly follow you to Madra."

Kenji's eyes stayed glued to my face, but his hand rose, snapping at something in the dark. "Come here, omega!" he barked. "Whatever you have planned will not work." He turned his head slightly, glaring at the tight shadows.

Dried grass crunched, and a few branches shifted. Slowly, Blue emerged, his hands filled with four large eggs. He bowed his head, looking hard at his feet. "I wasn't planning anything," he whispered as his shoulders curled inward.

"He's just a pup," I said, not caring for the way Kenji glared at the young omega. Blue came from a village with no alphas and was still very sensitive to their natural intensity. "There's no need to be so hard with him."

Kenji tracked Blue, watching the youngling slowly walk toward Lex, then sit. Lex's eyes shone brightly in the dim light of the moon, and while there wasn't much visibility out here, I could see the bruises on his face slowly fading.

"I'm feeling a bit better." Lex stood, stretching his arms out over his head. "I think I'll try to find something for dessert." He rubbed his belly. "Maybe something with a sweet disposition." He gave me a quick wink, then stalked off, not waiting for Kenji to respond.

The alpha glared at where Lex disappeared in the dark, not turning back to me until the siren's footsteps completely disappeared. "What purpose does the siren serve?" he asked, spinning back around. He looked alarmed, maybe even scared. "Your mate said he was important to the cause. How?"

I pressed my lips together, fighting the urge to smile. As much as Joon pretended to hate Lex, he made sure Kenji snuck him out of the camp too—my sweet mate.

"The witches say that Lex will help restore balance," I lied. "He's very important to the cause."

The muscles in Kenji's jaw ticked, and his fists curled tight. "I've never seen a siren in person before, but I've heard horror stories of what they're capable of." His biceps flexed, and his abs seemed to ripple with unease.

"Lex won't attack you," I said, not even believing my own words. I was pretty sure Lex would have eaten Joon or Byriel if I had let him. "He's a friend to the alphas that are kind to him."

"Will he stay in Ossory?" Kenji asked, cutting a quick glare into the forest. It was clear this alpha didn't like the idea of traveling all the way to my home village with a siren in tow.

"He'll stay," I said firmly. Blue shifted in my periphery, but I refused to look at him. The poor omega was a shit liar. He wore his emotions like a damn sign. But thankfully, Kenji kept his attention on me. "We just need to drop Lex off, then deliver my message," I said, hoping to ease his worry.

Kenji let out a slow breath, and his fists uncurled. "Get

some sleep." He turned to Blue, and his tone shifted softer, kinder. "I'll keep watch, so you don't have to worry, omega."

Blue's blue-green hypnotic eyes drifted to me, and I nodded, smiling. "We'll be inside Ossory come morning, and then we'll find what we're looking for," I said, hoping he could sense my real meaning. "I promise."

Blue's gaze flickered to Kenji, then back to me. "Okay."

Chained To A Wall

Byriel

I WAS STRUNG UP. Cold, naked, and exhausted. My back and hips ached from being forced to stand for days on end.

My tongue stuck to the roof of my mouth, and my lips were cracked. I couldn't remember ever being this thirsty, not even when I trekked through the deserts of Stone City. I had no idea how much time had passed, and I hadn't been fed in days. Not even a single drop of water had been offered. Strayton was probably giddy with the torture she was lording over me.

The hood on my head kept me from seeing anything, but the thick odors and loud sounds told me exactly where I was. I was in a solitary cell near the stocks. The scent of too much wolfsbane and sewage mixed with the faint aroma of rotted wood and rusting iron. And the occasional bark of a guard or challenging roar of a prisoner cut through the walls making me flinch.

I was just so fucking weak.

A spasm ripped through my shoulders and back. I tried shifting my arms secured over my head, making the shackles cut into my wrists and clank against the cold rock wall. The unrelenting bindings were elvish made. They were forged with mercury, making alphas weak and unable to shift into their wolves. But it seemed my shackles had the added feature of sharp barbs all along the cuffs, pushing the poison into my raw flesh every time I moved.

If I could just get one hand free, I could get the hell out of here and find Blue—my sweet omega.

Where the hell was he?

Was he safe?

Did Strayton lock him up? Hurt him? Kill him?

Or was she unaware of how important he was to me? I prayed that was the case.

But it was pointless to worry. I wasn't going anywhere.

My beast wallowed with me, whimpering and whining loudly as the wolfsbane and elvish-shackles held him in place. My beast's distress and fear for our omega pulsed in every pore of my body, but I held firm, trying like hell not to spiral with him.

Footsteps echoed all around me, growing closer. I jerked at my bindings again, trying to pull the chain out of the wall. A sharp barb slipped into the side of my wrist, cutting me deep. Hot blood trickled down my forearm. If I had to rip my fucking hands off, I would.

"Be careful there, brother."

I turned my head to Strayton's voice, but I couldn't see anything other than the stiff burlap fabric pulled over my head. "Where the fuck am I?" I roared, pulling hard at my chains once again. Pain erupted around my wrists, and thick, hot blood poured down my arms.

"You're not in a position to demand anything from me."

She was closer. So close, in fact, if I could get one hand free, I just knew I'd be able to grab her. "You have disgraced our entire family and killed our father." She sounded so pompous and proud. She was enjoying this. "It will take generations for our people to cope with the pain you've inflicted."

"The pain I've inflicted?" I snarled and jerked.

The bag on my head was ripped away, and I squinted at the sharp lantern shoved into my face. I could barely make out the dark, windowless room, but it was Strayton's wide smile that captured my attention.

"You look like hell," she grinned even wider.

My gaze drifted from my sister to the dark-skinned beta at her side. Arian, the captain of her personal guard, kept his eyes down, showing me respect as a member of the royal family. I had met him in the allied camp, and I prayed he was still a friend to the cause because I needed someone to tell me if Blue was okay. Please, let him be okay.

"What do you want, Strayton?" I seethed, knowing this visit wasn't to simply check on my well-being. My sister wasn't capable of caring about anyone but herself.

"Am I not allowed to look in on my baby brother?" Her black eyes were wide with false innocence. It was a look she had used countless times to gain favor with our father. But he was dead now, and sadly, this annoying habit lived on.

"How are you not yet bored with tormenting me?" I asked, glaring at the she-alpha. "You played us all so well, sister. Father, me, the people of Havre. We're all here to do your bidding. Aren't we?"

Her practiced smile shifted, and something much more wicked took hold. "This isn't a game, Byriel," she whispered, leaning in so I was forced to smell her sharp, woodsy scent. It reeked of our father. "I have great plans for our people. And greater plans still for those that have wronged me."

Arian's head lifted ever so slightly, and his dark eyes cut

sideways at Strayton. I swore I saw a flicker of fear in his uneasy expression.

Had something happened in the days since I was locked up?

I needed to get out of here.

I *needed* to find Blue.

I just prayed Joon got him far away from Ossory. I would never forgive myself if something happened to my sweet omega.

"Strayton, I—"

"You can address me as your majesty or My Queen." Strayton's expression fell into a serious glare, and her eyes flashed with deep pleasure. She was having far too much fun.

"If you're going to kill me, just get it over with," I said, not interested in playing this game anymore. "I can admit when I've been defeated, and this fight is over."

"It is all over," she said with satisfied certainty. "But unfortunately, I can't get rid of you until I'm positive I don't need you anymore. Apparently, witches aren't always right in the things they see or read." She rolled her eyes, letting out a pained huff. "I cannot wait to be rid of witches and their constantly shifting opinions."

"Is that so?" I leaned forward, letting my weight pull at my chains anchored to the ceiling once again. They didn't budge. "I thought you adored the witches. You wouldn't be queen if it weren't for Yasha and her prophecy." I smiled, knowing how much my words would cut her. "You needed them to give you your power."

Strayton's mouth pulled tight, my words grating at her nerves. She was always easy to agitate.

"Sweet brother," she said through gritted teeth. "Tomorrow, when I stand before our people—the most powerful Queen these lands have ever seen—just know I couldn't have done any of this without you." She pushed into my space, flashing her pointed fangs. "You killed so many of our people so that I might get everything I have ever wanted. You sacrificed your soul with the blood of the innocent, and I will thank you with a quick and mostly painless death." Her nose scrunched up as if telling a small joke. "After all, these things are never completely painless, but we'll do our best."

She brought her hand up to my face, then tapped my cheek hard. "I love you, Byriel. Your mindless obedience and absolute predictability have made all my wishes come true." She laughed, then spun on her heel, marching to the other side of the small cell.

Arian's eyes met mine for the briefest of moments before he reached up and slipped the bag back over my head. I didn't fight him. There was no point. But just before he left me alone in the dark, he leaned in and whispered. "Your omega is safe. He's being taken to Madra."

Relief hit me like a mighty wave, and I closed my eyes, finally able to breathe. I might die in this fucking room, but my sweet omega was safe. Blue would surely fight whoever forced him to leave me behind, but at least I could die happy, knowing he was far from me and my wicked sister.

He was safe.

At Dawn

Tzidal

"IS THAT THE PALACE?" Blue whispered in awe, looking up at the massive palace. A whole city sat between us and the pointed towers, but it was so large and intimidating that it felt as if the sleek, black structures were pushing down on us.

"Quiet," Kenji ordered as we approached the main gates. "No talking." His gaze moved over Blue and me, then settled on Lex.

The siren had a night of decent hunting. He wasn't able to find an alpha to satisfy his cravings, but he did find a buck and two small boars. Thankfully, it was enough to allow him to shift this morning. While his transformation into the stocky bald alpha did take him some time, the image was solid and impressive. He was tall with pale skin and a shiny head covered in scars. This alpha's image was very intimidating, and I was worried the siren's frightening appearance might draw too much attention.

"What's your purpose?" An older guard stepped up to Kenji. His face was marred with pockmarks and scars, and his dark hair was gray around his temples. He wore the same black uniform as Kenji, but it was clear from the guard's lack of a weapon or patches that he held a very different position.

I just hoped we'd be able to enter without any issue.

"I'm escorting my new mate to our home." Kenji grabbed me around the waist, slamming me up against his side. My wolf immediately snarled and growled, wanting me to push myself away from the alpha, but I stayed put, trying like hell not to react.

"We're in a hurry," Kenji sighed as if annoyed. "She's with child, and it's been a very long journey. I don't want her to be on her feet any longer than necessary."

The older guard shifted his gaze from Kenji to me. He searched my face before settling on my stomach. I immediately covered my middle with my arms and turned toward Kenji to hide my lack of a belly.

"She's not far along." Kenji placed a protective hand over my hands, shielding my stomach.

My wolf snarled, begging me to jerk out of his hold. This alpha wasn't our mate. But I forced my heels into the cold ground, determined not to move as I shied away from the guard's intense stare.

"And these two?" The pocked-guard looked at Blue. Then they narrowed at Lex. His alpha-form wasn't in a uniform like Kenji but just a pair of simple leather pants.

"What's with all the questions?" Kenji barked at the guard. "What is going on that an alpha can't return home without answering a thousand needless questions?"

The guard's eyes widened. Then he gave the area a sweeping glance, making sure no one could hear him. "How long have you been traveling, brother?" he asked.

Kenji's brow pulled together, tilting his head. "Months. Why? What has happened?"

A heavy sigh pushed from the guard, and he leaned in. "The King has passed."

Kenji gasped, taking several steps back. It was an impressive reaction, given that I knew for a fact he was aware that the King was killed. I had told him not long after it happened.

Big hands gripped my hips, picking me up. Kenji tucked me against his chest, forcing my legs on either side of his hips. His woodsy scent was suffocating, making my wolf growl and whimper loudly. It physically hurt to be so close to him. *This wasn't my mate.*

"Please," Kenji's deep voice vibrated into my chest. I wedged my arms between us, trying to stop the sensation. "I need to report to the palace. Let me drop off my family."

The older guard gripped Kenji's shoulder in a friendly gesture. I leaned away from his hand, wishing like hell I could shove both alphas away from me and run as fast and as far as my legs would allow.

"Be careful," the pocked-guard whispered. "There are rumors there is unrest as to who will take the crown. It's the guards that tend to suffer the most when there's political unrest."

Kenji nodded slowly. "I understand. Thank you."

I held my breath, counting the seconds as Kenji moved us through a crowded street. Once we passed a stall of flowers, I allowed myself to suck in a mighty breath, but it reeked of the alpha holding me. I turned my attention to the building around us, trying to distract my wolf. The market was very different from the small wooden cabins with inviting porches that I was used to back home—it was loud and bustling, with alphas and betas shoving in every direction. I squirmed, wanting down.

"Stop." Kenji placed a large hand over my lower back, keeping me still. "Not until we're around the corner."

Blue stepped up next to me, his wide eyes staring at Kenji's hand on my back and his arm hooked under my ass. It was shameful for an omega to allow an alpha outside of a mate or family to touch them in such a way, and I was sure Joon would want Kenji's blood if he saw me right now.

Desperate to feel a bit of my mate, I opened our bond, seeking him out.

I had kept it closed for the most part, not wanting Joon to feel my fear or worry. A soft pulse of something uneasy—almost uncomfortable—pushed through. I squeezed my eyes shut tight, praying my mate was okay.

We rounded the corner, and Blue grabbed my arm. "You can put her down now," he snipped, tugging me away from the large alpha. Kenji released me, but before I could take a single step, Blue forced me to his chest, hugging me tight. "Are you okay?" the young omega whispered, smoothing a hand over the back of my head.

"Yes," I said, not understanding the young omega's worry. I looked up at Lex's scarred-alpha face, but the siren looked just as worried as Blue sounded.

"You look upset," Lex whispered in a deep voice.

"Omega," Kenji said to me, taking a quick step back. "Did I hurt you? I tried to be gentle. It was not my intention—"

"I'm good," I cut in, smoothing my hands down the front of my black robes and dirty gold sash. I looked rough. We all did.

"Are you sure you're okay?" Blue cupped my cheeks and examined my face. His bright blue-green eyes danced over my features, and his skin grew hazy for a moment.

"Calm down," I whispered, not wanting him to pulse and hurt himself—especially in the middle of the busy market-place. The small road was filled with wolves of every status, rushing in and out of storefronts and haggling loudly with merchants. "There's no need to be worried, Blue. Take a breath."

"You looked like you were in pain," he said, giving me an uneasy smile.

"I'm okay," I repeated softly, pulling Blue's hands off my face. "I just need to deliver my message."

Kenji let out a slow breath of relief, then nodded as if happy to have the matter closed. "I'm aware of one place that might hold a few allies," he whispered. "But they might have moved."

"The guard at the gate didn't seem to know you," Lex narrowed his eyes at Kenji. "Are you not normally stationed in Ossory?"

"I'm not," Kenji said, stepping closer to allow a beta with two pups hanging off her hips to pass. "I normally travel with the King's guard."

"I thought all the guards knew each other," Blue said, his expression as suspicious as Lex's.

Kenji let out a barking laugh. "There are thousands of guards across these lands. How on earth could we all possibly know each other?"

"Byriel knows everyone." Blue crossed his arms, clearly annoyed with the alpha laughing at him. "He knew everyone at the camp."

Kenji let out a heavy, annoyed sigh. "They all know Byriel. He's not only the King's son, but he was also a commander of his majesty's guard. Byriel is someone we *all* know. Now," he turned to Lex, narrowing his glowing red eyes, "is there a problem, siren? Because you're looking at me as if you expect me to stick a blade between your ribs any second."

Lex's fierce face went tight. "I just don't want any tricks from you, wolf. You had better be taking us to the allies."

Kenji's eyes went wide, and his jaw clicked tight.

I jumped between them, desperate to calm both of them down before a fight broke out. "Joon sent Kenji to watch over us," I placed my hand on Lex's muscular alpha arm, "I'm not worried about him hurting us. Just forcing me back to Madra before I can deliver my message."

Lex gave me a tight nod, still looking at Kenji with intense unease.

"I'm not the flesh eater here, siren," Kenji said flatly. "I have no interest in picking a fight. I want to do as promised and take these two omegas to Madra."

"That's fine," Lex bared his pointed alpha-fangs. "But just know that I'm not in the habit of trusting wolves I don't know."

"You don't really have a choice," Kenji said flatly. And it was true. We had no one else to guide us.

"Where to?" I asked, hoping we could just move on already.

Kenji kept his hard glare on Lex as he motioned down the long street. "We'll need to cut through the square and up the east side of the city toward the palace. Blue." He turned to the uneasy omega. "It would be best for you to hold onto Lex as if he were your mate. Omegas are allowed to leave their homes here, but very few are brave enough to wander alone. I don't want to invite any unwanted attention."

Lex let out a deep grunt, then flung his arm around Blue's shoulders, pulling the much shorter omega to him.

Blue let out a nervous laugh and scrunched up his nose. "This is weird," he snorted. "You look like an alpha, but don't really smell like one."

"I can assure you, every inch of me is all alpha, little pup." Lex winked. I rolled my eyes, impressed he was still able to sound so sassy with such a deep and gravelly voice.

Lex had the ability to change everything about him, including his scent. I could only assume he wasn't projecting

25

an alpha's harsher smell to help keep Blue calm....and maybe to keep me calm as well.

Kenji wrapped his hand around my wrist, and I breathed a sigh of relief. I didn't fear this alpha, but I also didn't like being carried by him. It just felt...*wrong*.

We moved quickly, pushing through the throng of wolves. The mix of classes was especially odd, making me think of the allied camp in the forest. There were wolves in elegant robes and flashy jewels and service betas in various colorful uniforms. Even a few young pups with smudged faces played in the dirt gullies in tattered clothes.

Slowly, the crowd thinned as the shops and taverns shifted into tall, busy buildings and impressive manors.

A pretty middle-aged alpha smiled at me from one of the porches. She leaned forward, making her curly red hair fall forward into her face. "Hello, there omega," she said in a throaty purr.

Kenji jerked me hard into his chest, then wrapped an arm tight across my back. "She's taken," he snarled, flashing long, pointed teeth.

Praying the she-alpha wouldn't try to pick a fight, I kept my head down and quickened my pace. I didn't dare to look up until we reached a quiet stretch of road.

"Just up here," Kenji whispered. He kept his arm around my shoulders, and after the she-alpha's lust-filled gaze, I suddenly didn't mind.

Lex let out a gruff chuckle, looking up at the front of a worn, brick building. "Is this...."

"It is." Kenji smiled at the siren, his fingers curling tighter around my shoulders. "Keep your omega close."

I didn't understand their coy smiles. The building was dark with very few windows, and it had a cheery, red bar sign that read '*Spirits for any mood or craving*'. Two sweet-looking betas sat at the end of the porch with their feet propped up on the railing. Their legs were exposed, showing an ample amount of thigh and cleavage. Then it hit me.

"Is this a brothel?" I whispered harshly to Kenji.

Overhearing me, one of the betas giggled loudly. "Be careful there, alpha. This isn't the kind of place to bring your mate."

Kenji gave her a tight smile. "She'll be fine. Come," he tugged me forward, pushing open the flimsy wooden door. It creaked loudly as we entered.

The inside of the brothel resembled a tavern with dim lights and soft piano music. The air was musky and thick, like a thousand bodies pressed against each other. Overwhelmed by the overlapping scents, I pressed my nose to Blue's arm.

I needed Joon.

My head pounded, and a deep burning sensation ran down the back of my skull. A pained hiss left my lips before I could stifle it, and Blue immediately touched my arm.

"What's wrong?" he whispered, his brows knit together.

I shook my head, but before I could answer, Lex leaned down and whispered, "I'm going to piss, then phase into someone else." His deep voice tickled the air, vibrating around me. "This is a perfect place to find something decadent to eat." His dark eyes sparkled with this secret meaning.

My gaze drifted over the busy tavern. Hard alphas drank deeply and groped the blushing betas working the room. "You won't hurt the—"

"I'll pick an alpha," Lex said pointedly, giving me a firm look. "I would never hurt a girl trying to make a living."

I nodded, threading my fingers through Blue's. "Be careful," I whispered. Lex was much stronger after eating last night, but it still took a bit longer than usual for him to phase into this alpha.

"This way," Kenji grunted, stalking across the room.

Blue and I rushed after him, angling around tables and

27

side-stepping servers carrying large trays of ale and whiskey. Kenji didn't stop until we came upon a small table near the back. It was a dark corner of the room with two betas sitting and counting coins.

"Can I help you?" a male omega said to Kenji. His dark eyes drifted to me, then Blue. "We don't do omegas here. If you're looking to sell your kin, we're not that kind of place."

"I'm not looking to sell," Kenji said far too casually.

How was he not disgusted?

Was selling omegas to these kinds of places commonplace?

"I have a message." Kenji dropped his chin, giving the beta a hard look.

The female next to him pulled her nose from a book, finally looking at us. It was clear the pair were siblings. They both had the same rounded nose and hazel eyes, and their curly black hair stuck up at the same spot in the back, even though hers was much longer.

"I was once told to give any information to the twins," Kenji said, eyeing the pair.

The male beta leaned forward, placing his elbows on the table. "We're simply trying to enjoy a few drinks here, alpha. Give your message to someone else." His face was pinched, almost annoyed that we would approach him.

"Now, now, Marx," the female said softly, closing her book. "Maybe this alpha has something fun to tell us." A wide smile split her face, and her eyes sparkled. "What's your message, friend?"

Kenji cut me a quick look, then glanced around the tavern. The noise swelled as a card game near the door got especially lively. "I'd prefer to give my message in private."

Needing to feel the letter, I slipped my hand into my pocket, feeling the velvety parchment and the waxy green seal along the top.

"Look here, alpha," the male beta, Marx, snipped. "My

sister isn't up for sale. If you are looking for someone to entertain you and your omegas, may I suggest—"

Kenji snarled, then lowered his voice to a deep growl, "I
have a very important message. From Jonelle," I quickly
added.

The pair immediately leaned back. Marx still looked skeptical, glaring at Kenji hard. But the female tipped her chin up
as if thinking.

"What do you think, Mary? Marx asked, crossing his arms.

Mary narrowed her eyes at Kenji, then Blue, before settling
on me. Her gaze drifted to my hand stuffed in my pocket.
"What kind of message?" she asked.

Kenji's temper flared, and the corded muscles in his arm
flexed. "Do you fucking want it to not?"

Marx's chin jutted forward, and his voice cut hard. "There
are a fuck ton of wolves out there that want us dead. You get
that, right?" Kenji's fists curled tight, but he didn't speak,
letting the beta continue. "Every asshole with a blade and an
allegiance to the King has had a message from some random
alpha, hoping they've picked someone—"

"I just need to know who to give my message to," Kenji
snarled, pressing his balled-up fists against the top of the table.
His movements were slow, and controlled, but I could scent
his rage bubbling all around us. It was sharp.

My fingers grazed the bumpy seal along the top of the
envelope. "My message is green?" I said with a lift of uncertainty in my voice. "Does that help?" I didn't know if that
mattered, but perhaps the seal meant something.

Mary's eyes widened a bit, then narrowed at my face.
"Green?" she repeated. "Just green?"

The pad of my finger brushed the seal once again, and I
tried like crazy to remember the flower embossed on it. I didn't
want to take it out of my pocket just in case.

"A flower," I whispered. "A centaurea flower."

Marx snorted loudly. "Well, shit." His sister picked up her book, reading once again. For a moment, I thought we'd be forced to leave, but then Marx stood. "Right this way."

The chatter and music within the tavern drifted away as we moved down a long hallway, replaced by the unmistakable sounds of sex. Throaty gasps and deep grunts seeped under the doors as we passed. Blue pushed tight into my side, squeezing my hand so tight my fingers went cold.

"Here." Marx pointed at the door at the end of the corridor. "Go on in."

Kenji nodded, giving the beta an angry glare. Alphas were too damn sensitive.

"Thank you," I said to Marx.

"No problem, omega." He gave me a polite smile. "Stay close to your alpha back here." He pointed at the rooms around us. "The guests can get a little rowdy."

Blue shivered, pushing his nose into my hair.

"We will," I said. "Thank you again."

Kenji didn't move, waiting for Marx to disappear down the hall. Once the beta was out of sight, he marched straight for the door, pulling it open in one swift movement.

Blue and I rushed in after him, then Blue squealed loudly, turning his back to the room.

Dane, the alpha from the ally camp, sat in a lounging chair in the corner with a beta on her knees in front of him. She sucked loudly at his cock, seemingly not bothered in the least at us interrupting them.

"What the fuck do you want?" Dane roared, gripping the beta's brown hair in his fist. She continued to bob her head, taking him deeper and deeper.

"I have a message from Jonelle," Kenji said as if completely unaffected by the shocking sight before us.

Dane's eyes widened, then he tugged the beta up by her hair. "Come back in an hour," he instructed.

She whispered a breathy, "Yes, sir," then stood. Her cheeks were flushed, and the baby hairs that framed her face stuck to the sweat on her brow.

Dane stood, tucking his ruddy cock into his pants. It was shiny and red, and for some reason, it sent shivers down my spine. I turned away, not sure if I was scared or just overwhelmed.

"Are you okay?" I asked Blue, determined to distract my mind.

The young omega nodded, keeping his head down and back to the room. There was a time that I was worried Byriel had taken advantage of him, but it was clear from Blue's bright red cheeks that he was still very innocent.

"Where is this message?" Dane stomped across the room and grabbed a pitcher of water off the side table. He poured himself a glass, drinking deeply.

"Omega," Kenji motioned me forward.

I turned away from Blue and pulled out the letter. Dane took one look at it and laughed bitterly.

"That's what I thought." The alpha held it up, looking disappointed. "I sent this. That's my seal." He broke the wax, scanning the contents of the letter, then held it over a small candle, letting the whole thing burn.

"I don't understand." Kenji's eyes narrowed at my face, clearly pissed. "Why would Jonelle have you deliver a letter to the person that wrote it."

"Calm down, brother," Dane said, plopping back into the worn armchair. It groaned under his weight. "That letter was meant to let our people know the allied camp was moving. I intended to move with them, but then the news hit of the King's death, and it felt more important to be here." His gaze shifted from Kenji to me. "I appreciate what you've gone through to deliver this, omega."

31

"Tzidal," I said, tired of everyone referring to me as a name-less underling. "My name is Tzidal."

"Omega Tzidal." Dane gave me a quick nod of respect. "Thank you."

"Do you know where my mate is?" I asked, praying he just might. "Joon? He was at the King's camp with Jonelle. Do you know where he is?"

"Last I heard he was within the palace," Dane cocked a crocked smile, "I'm impressed he was able to infiltrate Strayton's inner circle so quickly, however I don't know exactly where he is. But I'm sure he's okay, omega. There's no need to worry."

I scrubbed my face, exhausted and achy. The pain in my skull slipped down my back, making my skin feel too damn tight. There were just too many foreign scents in here to focus.

"Alpha Joon will be okay," Blue whispered, caressing my back. "He's strong and smart. He'll be okay."

"I know," I pressed my lips together, suddenly feeling very emotional. I hated it.

"We'll get a room and rest. Then we'll leave for Madra in the morning," Kenji said, leaning down so he could see my face. "It will be okay come morning." I turned away from him, hating the pity in his eyes. I didn't want either of these alphas to see me as weak or pathetic.

"I'll get a message to your mate," Dane said softly. "I'm sure he will be happy to know your escort is returning you to your home, but don't worry about him. Send your alpha happy thoughts through your bond." He smiled as if I were a child, too slow to understand simple english. "Just keep your chin up and keep thinking happy thoughts. Everything will look better once you return to your village."

"I'm *not* going home." I curled my fists, wanting to beat both these alphas senseless. "I'm going to find my mate."

Dane chuckled and Kenji smirked. "She has fire." Dane clapped Kenji on the shoulder. "Good luck with that."

I growled high in my throat, hating how weak and pathetic they clearly thought I was.

"It's okay," Blue pulled my attention away from the alphas. I cut them one more quick glare as they spoke quietly of what was happening within the palace and the unrest around the city, but I couldn't hear them.

All I could think about was Joon.

Was the dull pain in my muscles coming from him?

Was he locked up in a cell somewhere?

Was he being tortured?

I closed my eyes and leaned into Blue's soft clean scent. I wasn't leaving Ossory without my mate, even if I had to kill Kenji to get away from him.

A Fancy Guest Room

Joon

FOUR DAYS.

I have been trapped in this damn room for four days. The doors were locked, and the windows were reinforced. Even the young female beta that delivered my meals each day would run the second she got the cart past the doorway, locking the door firmly behind her.

The thick scent of wolfsbane pushed hard into my nose, and I snorted, trying to push it away. My wolf was so fucking restless, desperate to be released, but he was trapped—just like me.

The lock on the bedroom door rattled, and I launched myself out of the plush armchair, desperate to try to talk to young beta again. I'd have to be calmer this time, soft-spoken.

I gritted my teeth, hating all of this.

The door clicked, then swung open. A male service beta entered, pushing a cart covered in little silver domes. His black uniform was pressed and perfect, just like everything else in this fucking place.

Hope prickled my spine, and I took a deep breath before asking, "Where is Lady Strayton? I need to speak to her. I need to leave."

The male beta's eyes flickered to my face as he slowly pushed the cart so it rested just next to the red armchair in front of the fireplace. The food smelled of spiced, smoked meats and roasted vegetables, but I had no appetite. I needed to get the fuck out of here.

"Her royal highness is busy, sir," the beta hung his head in a submissive display. His black hair pushed into his eyes while he removed the silver domes to reveal my dinner.

Each meal here was more extravagant than the last, but I couldn't enjoy any of them. I was too worried about Tzidal. A faint trace of pain occasionally seeped through our bond, keeping me on edge. She didn't seem to be physically injured, but there was something wrong with her. Something that lingered deep in her mind.

If I would have opened our bond fully, I might have been able to tell, but the last thing I needed for her to feel my growing fear. For now, I would keep our bond firmly closed.

"Why am I being treated like a prisoner?" I whispered through gritted teeth, eyeing the bedroom door.

"I don't know what you mean, sir." He glanced around the extravagant room. I knew what he was thinking. No prisoner was given a lush canopy bed and roaring fireplace as their cell.

"The door and windows are locked, and I can smell guards in the hallway," I growled, and my wolf snarled, begging to break free, but the stench of wolfsbane kept him trapped within me. My voice rose, and I barked, "Why can't I leave?"

The beta shook his head, taking a careful step toward the

door. "Her majesty doesn't like for visitors to roam freely throughout the castle."

I flashed my pointed fangs, then froze. His words hit me like a punch in the gut, and I took a slow step toward him. "Her majesty?"

The beta's eyes went wide, and his mouth hung open as he gathered his thoughts. He seemed shocked I didn't know.

"Yes, sir," he finally whispered. "The, the King. He has passed away, sir."

"When?" I roared, fear pumping hard in my veins. "When did he die?"

The beta hunched his shoulders, slowly edging away from me. "A few days ago, sir. At, at his camp. The Queen hasn't addressed the people yet, but news has traveled fast."

I searched my memories, trying like hell to remember what happened that night at the camp—Strayton's satisfied smirk as she left her father's tent, followed by my sweet Tzidal's terrified expression, and Blue....he had blood on his cheek and hands.

"How did he die?" I asked. Did my little beast manage to kill the King?

"I'm sorry, sir," the beta shook his head. "I don't know. The Queen is still too upset to talk about it."

This changed everything.

I turned away from the dark-haired beta, staring into the fire. The orange flames danced, consuming my vision as I replayed that night. Kenji led Tzidal and Blue through the crowded camp, getting them to safety, but I didn't see my mate actually get away. Was she safe? Was she scared? Was she looking for me?

Why was our bond thrumming hot and achy?

Fierce determination swelled in my chest, and tightened my fists. I spun toward the beta, ready to fight my way out, but it was too late. He was gone. Just the flutter of his black robes peeked through the crack in the door before it slammed shut behind him, and the lock clicked back into place.

"Fuck," I snarled, trying to figure out what the hell to do.

All I wanted was to kill the King for what he did to Fennah, my first mate, and to Tzidal's first mate. And that was done.

The fucker was dead.

My mission was over, and I now needed to get the hell out of here and find Tzidal.

Strayton still wanted that damn star from me and was dead set on going through some kind of gate to get it. I knew the allies were hoping I'd send them information to put Byriel on the throne, but I honestly didn't care anymore.

The next time that damn door opened, I'd kill whoever came through it, then fight my way out.

Tzidal was my priority now, and I needed to find her. Fast.

Still Chained To The Wall

Byriel

"I HONESTLY THOUGHT IT WAS A RUMOR." The voice of my father's most trusted advisor hit my ears, and I slowly lifted my head. With the black hood in place, I couldn't make out anything other than the soft flicker of what I assumed was a lantern, but I couldn't be sure.

"Tibbit?" I asked in a harsh whisper. My throat was so damn dry, and every inch of my worn body hurt. Between being forced to stand for days on end with my arms bound above me and the lack of food or water, I felt as if I was at death's door.

I just wanted this over with already.

"How long have you been in here?" Tibbit's bare feet padded across the stone floor, stopping just in front of me.

I sighed hard, trying to count the days. "When did my father die?" I asked, swaying forward slightly. The muscles in my shoulders burned at the motion, and I grunted hard.

"It's been almost a week," Tibbit whispered.

I wanted to laugh. It felt like I had been strung up in this fucking room for months.

"The Queen hasn't announced the King's death officially," Tibbit said, "but word has traveled fast. She's taking some time to grieve before addressing the people."

I gritted my teeth at the idea of my sister grieving. She was too cold for that. Heartless.

"Do you have any water?" I asked, swallowing hard. The motion was tight against my hollow belly.

Fingers pulled the fabric along my neck, then Tibbit lifted the hood, allowing me to finally see. The room was still the same. Black stone, a few chains hanging from the walls, and a single lantern near the heavy, wooden door, but Tibbit was very different from the last time I saw him.

As far back as I could remember, the beta looked like an old man: long gray hair and beard, a hunched back, and weathered hands that looked like paper. But the man before me looked *ancient*—like a thousand lifetimes had passed since we last saw one another, rather than just a simple few years.

"Drink slowly." Tibbit lifted a glass bottle to my lips, then tipped it. Cool water spread across my tongue and dripped down my chin and neck. I drank deeply, sucking down every last drop. It made my stomach cramp and my body sag against my chains. It gave my tired legs a small break but tortured my wrists once again.

"I need to get you out of here." Tibbit eyed my shackles as a groan sigh of disgust left his throat. The deep lines etched around his eyes were exaggerated in the dim light.

"What is happening in Ossory?" I asked, forcing myself back onto my toes. The tendons along my arches and ankles burned in protest, but there was no helping it—no matter what I did, my arms or legs would suffer.

"Things have fallen to shit in the years since you left."

Tibbit examined the wall behind me, his blue eyes scanning the stone up to the ceiling. I assumed he was searching for some way to unlock me. "Things have been fractured for a while," Tibbit continued. "The King, bless his soul," his eyes pulled in the corners, "he had been falling more and more into your sister's insanity—"

"Let's not blame his madness on Strayton." I gave the elder a pointed look. "My sister is an evil beast, but my father owned his love for violence until the end. That had nothing to do with my sister."

Tibbit's mouth pulled tight, unable to admit I was right. His continued love for my father, even after his death, was admirable, but he had to see the truth. How could he not?

"Byriel," the elder's voice dropped, and he leaned closer to me. He smelled of scented wax and old linen. "Sir. My Lord."

"Don't call me that," I snarled, turning my head away from him. The movement forced a sharp barb into my wrists, making me hiss.

"But it's true," the old wolf said simply. "With Strayton on the throne, you're next in line. The title is yours whether you want it or not, and we cannot let Strayton destroy what little of Ossory remains standing. We need your help, My Lord."

My wolf let out a soft whimper within me, too drained to do anything else. My beast didn't give a shift about Ossory or honor or any of that bullshit anymore. He wanted our omega. *My lovely Blue.* But my omega was far away from here, and I'd spend the rest of my life loving him but never seeing him. It was for the best, even if it killed me and my wolf.

"I'm going to get you out of here, My Lord," Tibbit said with a determined flash in his blue eyes.

"Strayton will kill you." I tipped my head back, trying to stretch my back, but it was no use. Everything fucking hurt.

"The Queen is planning to take a short leave tonight." Tibbit reached up, feeling around my elbows. He was too short to reach any higher. I groaned. Even if he found a key, there was no way he'd be able to reach the locks.

This was pointless.

"Go," I said, resigned to my fate. "Strayton would kill you if she even knew you spoke to me." I eyed the determined beta, watching his long beard twitch with displeasure at my command. "Don't lose your life over a fool like me."

"I'm over a hundred years old, my dear boy," Tibbit laughed, flashing a gummy smile. I remembered him having at least a few teeth. "My life has been spent." His weary gaze slipped over the stone floor, sadness flowing off him. "I belong with your father, my King."

"How could you still have any kind of allegiance to him?" I asked, taking in the deep lines of sorrow pulling on both sides of his mouth. "He was so cruel, even to you. He would—"

"We all have our faults," Tibbit said in a soft, kind voice. "But I made a promise to be loyal to him and Ossory for the rest of my days. I will keep that promise."

"*Faults,*" I snorted, mocking the pathetic word.

"Yes, My Lord. Faults." He tapped the stone, seeming to look for something in the brick behind me, then bent down slightly as if examining the dirty floor. "I've done many things I've regretted in my life, and I'm sure you have too," he paused long enough for his bright eyes to meet mine, "but that doesn't make us unworthy of love. And I loved my King." He stood back up, giving me a pained smile. "I loved my King when he was young and wanted to make Havre a grand place for wolfshifters. And in the end, that was what he still wanted." Tibbit shrugged as if a bit defeated by his memories. "Your father just lost his focus a bit when it came to the execution."

Bitter rage burned through me.

I wanted to scream at the elder—make him admit my father was a monster, then force Tibbit from my cell, but there was no point.

"I understand your anger." He moved away from me, looking at the floor once again. "But there's no point in hating your father anymore. It's Strayton that needs your attention now. Oh! Here we are," his voice brightened, and a quick chuckle jerked from his throat. He grunted, then groaned, seeming to pull at something just at my feet.

I tried to turn to look at him, but it was no use.

"Tibbit," I groaned, too exhausted for this. "Go."

My chains jerked, then suddenly my arms fell, followed quickly by my entire body. I slammed hard into the gritty stone ground. My mind and beast screamed at me to run, but my body was too damn weak.

"I can't unlock you." Tibbit examined the shackles on my wrists. "I'll need a key, but for now, you can at least rest."

Slowly, I curled my back inward, inch by inch, and pulled my knees up, giving my spine one good, long stretch. My muscles were so stiff and tight it hurt. But I still wrapped my arms around my knees, then hugged tight, forcing the stretch deeper.

"Thank you, Tibbit," I panted, unable to think of anything else to say. "Thank you, friend."

The elder patted the top of my head like he had done many times when I was a pup. "Eat to get your strength up." He placed a fresh canister of water just next to my head, followed by something wrapped in brown paper. It was bread. I usually preferred meat, but it had been so long since I had eaten that the salty scent made my mouth water and my stomach rumble.

"I'll bring you more when I can," Tibbit assured me.

I nodded, staring at the bread and water but not daring to touch it just yet. It was a feast.

"I'll be back, My Lord," Tibbit whispered before he slowly stood. His legs were uneasy as he hobbled to the door.

Completely exhausted, I closed my eyes. Every bone and

muscle in my body sagged against the cold stone beneath me. I needed to get up.

I needed to eat, gather my strength, then get the fuck out of here. But before any of that, I needed to sleep.

Before I knew it, vivid dreams took hold, but they weren't the nightmares I was used to. They were of my lovely omega.

My precious Blue and his sweet lips.

A Room At The Brothel

Tzidal

THIS WAS by far the grossest room I had ever been in. And after the Kaska Inn in Stone City, that was quite a feat.

The small twin-sized bed had a sizable divot in the center, showing its obvious, unrelenting use. The bedding was stiff and smelled of musk and sweat, and the floor hadn't appeared to be mopped in ages—if ever.

"Do you think it's safe to use the washbasin?" Blue-eyed the pitcher of dingy water.

"I wouldn't." I opened the wardrobe and then immediately closed it.

Blue's mouth hung open, having already seen the leather straps and paddles hanging within. "Are those to use on alphas or for alphas to use on...." His voice trailed off, his pale complexion going pink.

"It doesn't matter," I waved my hand, hoping not to traumatize the poor youngling. While Blue was an adult, he was still *very* sheltered.

A lust-filled gasp cut through the thin walls, quickly followed by the rhythmic sound of a box spring squeaking loudly. Blue's eyes went wide, and he dropped his gaze to the floor, looking everywhere but at me.

"Do alphas often...rut..." he pulled a face as the word itself was dirty, "...just anyone? Do they not need a connection?"

I grimaced, not sure just how honest I should be. "Lots of alphas are very devoted to their mates. Some are just...lonely." I gave a quick nod, happy with my choice of words.

Another wild moan filled the room, and Blue's shoulders hunched forward, cringing at the sound. He stood so stiff and awkward. It was as if he wasn't sure what to do with himself. I honestly understood his unease. It was weird listening to strangers do something so intimate.

"I'm going to find Kenji," I said, squeezing Blue's wrist. "There has to be a better place for us to stay." I pulled open the bedroom door only to be met with an alpha's bare ass thrusting wildly into a beta he had pinned against the wall. She moaned and screamed, dragging her nails across his back.

"Please, don't leave me!" Blue yelled out in a panicked rush of words.

I slammed the door shut, then turned to the terrified omega. "Yeah," my voice edged a little high-pitched, "We'll just make this place work." I looked around, not sure where the hell to sit. I wasn't going to risk touching that bed.

As if reading my mind, Blue moved to the center of the room, then sat on the small circular rug. The patchwork of red, orange, and yellow thread was aged and frayed. It looked a thousand years old, just like everything else in this room.

Blue rubbed his fingertips over the rough woven material, then nodded. "Sadly, I think it's the cleanest thing in here."

I forced a smile, then sat next to him. "It's better than

sleeping on a rock," I shrugged, trying to make light of our ridiculous situation.

Blue snorted in agreement. "Or in a tree."

A vicious roar shook the walls, and Blue flinched, pushing hard into my side. "What was that?" His voice went high with fear.

I felt bad. I just wanted to laugh at the ridiculousness of it all, but I didn't want Blue to think I was making fun of him. "It was probably just an alpha...." I trailed off, hoping he'd get my meaning, but the young omega just stared at me, waiting for me to finish. "You know." I dropped my voice to a whisper, feeling incredibly awkward. "*Coming*," I whispered.

Blue's brows jutted up, and his mouth formed a perfect 'O'. "You mean that's not fighting?"

"No," I shook my head, realizing just how innocent the poor pup was.

Blue shifted, uncomfortable, rubbing at the chain around his neck. His eyes lingered around my jewelry, the necklace from Joon and the pearl bracelet my first mate gifted me.

"How can you wear metal pressed against your skin all the time?" he asked, adjusting his necklace so it was a bit looser on the back of his neck.

"I don't really think about it," I said, admiring the blue pearl. It shimmered up at me, looking as lovely as ever. Then my fingers drifted up to my necklace. I caressed the pack seal, admiring the embossed wolf and crossed daggers.

I hadn't felt Joon through our bond in a few hours, and it was getting hard to ignore the fear twisting in my gut.

"It's just rubbing the back of my neck." Blue's soft voice cut through my thoughts.

I rocked forward, eager to be distracted from my growing worry. "Do you want me to hang onto it for you?"

Blue bit the inside of his cheek, clearly conflicted. I understood his reluctance. It was a gift from Byriel.

"What if I hold onto it just tonight so it doesn't bother you while you sleep?" I offered.

He pressed his lips together, thinking. "I guess that would be okay."

"Byriel won't mind," I smiled sweetly, lifting the chain over his head. The circular medallion was surprisingly heavy as I slipped it on, making sure the engraved paw print faced outward, hiding the King's seal. I was sure it would invite unwanted attention if seen.

A bed creaked rhythmically down the hall, and a lust-filled scream cut through the halls. I rolled my eyes, annoyed that we'd probably be forced to listen to alphas rut all damn night.

Blue sucked in a quick breath as if he was going to say something, but then he dropped his gaze, staring at his lap. He bit his bottom lip, and his eyes flickered to me for the briefest of moments.

"What's wrong?" I leaned down, forcing his eyes to meet mine. "You can talk to me about anything, pup."

The young omega gripped the hem of his emerald green robes, twisting the fabric repeatedly. I glanced down at my own clothes, noticing that I was just as dirty as the young omega.

My black uniform was wrinkled and covered in grime. My gold–embroidered sash was frayed at the ends, and even the small ribbons that ran the length of my forearms were coming undone. We both needed a proper bath.

"I was..." Blue mumbled at his lap. "I was just wondering...." His face burned red, and he swallowed hard, "Does it hurt?"

"Does what hurt?" I asked, caressing his arm.

Blue's hand moved to his mouth, repeatedly brushing his index finger over his bottom lip. He looked so tired...and maybe even a little embarrassed?

"Mating," he whispered. "Does it hurt?"

Without meaning to, I immediately let out a nervous little laugh. *This was not how I expected my evening to go.*

"Please don't make fun of me," Blue mumbled, covering his face with his hands.

"I'm not," I grabbed his wrists, pulling them away from his bright red cheeks. "I'm not laughing at you. I just find it funny to have this conversation in a *brothel* of all places."

A shy smile pulled at the corner of his lips, and he let out a small laugh. "I know these are the kinds of things mothers tell their pups, but...." He shrugged, unable to finish this thought.

I nodded, understanding. His mother died when he was a babe, leaving him without anyone to talk with about these kinds of things.

"I know the basics," he said as the blush in his cheeks moved down his neck. It made his faint-blue complexion shift a pale purple before flaming red. "I just don't know much else."

Taking his hands, I said a quick prayer, hoping I didn't scare the poor youngling, but I just couldn't lie to him.

"Mating can hurt the first time," I said. "But a good and loving alpha will make sure it doesn't hurt for long."

Blue nodded with wide eyes. He looked like an eager student drinking in as much information as he could. "What about a...." his voice vanished to nothing, and he mouthed, "Knot?"

"Does taking a knot hurt?" I asked, making sure I understood his question. He nodded again, leaning forward as if worried he might miss something. "It can, but it's a good hurt," I said. "It's a hurt you want. You crave."

"Really?" Disbelief and a trace of fear filled his eyes.

"It helps to be in heat the first time you lay with an alpha," I said, trying like hell to figure out how to explain this better. "You get so caught up in that primal state; you don't care what's happening as long as you're filled."

Blue's expression dimmed, and his eyes shifted nervously across the tattered rug. He picked at a loose thread, squeezing it between his fingers. "I've only ever had two heats in my whole life," he mumbled, rubbing the back of his neck.

I couldn't stop the look of shock on my face, and I tried quickly to correct it, but it was too late. He saw.

"I had my first heat when I was thirteen." He crossed his arms tight across his chest, clearly uncomfortable to admit something so personal. "And then the second one just last summer. But nothing since I turned twenty."

"You know," I rested my hand on his knee, wanting so badly to reassure him, "it's actually very common for omegas to miss their heats when they're stressed."

Blue's mouth pulled into a tight line, giving me a look. "Only two heats in seven years is common?" he said flatly.

I pulled a face, forced to admit his point. "You're also part fae," I slipped his purple strand of hair between my fingers, then tucked it back behind his slightly pointed ear. "I'm sure that messes with your system too. Sometimes it's difficult on the young when more than one species cross-breed."

Blue nodded, thinking that over. "Have you ever missed a heat?"

"I actually have," I said, eager for him to see just how normal it was. "My body has been a little off since my first mate was killed. I haven't even had a heat with Joon yet." I said softly. Then my eyes widened at the fact. "I didn't even realize that until now," I laughed.

He snorted, then smiled sweetly. "We've been a little busy."

The doorknob rattled, and Blue jumped about a foot into the air. I pulled the dagger from inside my dirty black robes, then pushed Blue behind me, ready to attack. The female beta from the front room took two steps into our room, then froze. Her dark hazel eyes went wide at the sight of my blade, and her grip on the thick blankets in her arms tightened.

"I'm so sorry," I let out a tight breath, and my shoulders relaxed. "Mary. Right?" I placed my blade back in its sheath.

"Oh!" The beta laughed loudly as if realizing something. "Mary!" She laughed even harder, the sound a little too familiar. "I could have sworn that asshole called me 'Fairy'!" She kicked her foot behind her, slamming the bedroom door shut.

"Lex?" I asked, not entirely sure.

"Of course," the pretty beta winked. She dropped the blankets just next to my feet, and the sweet scent of soap and lavender fanned across my face.

"I thought some fresh linens might be nice." Mary's features melted away, shifting into Lex's familiar smirk.

A soft hum left Blue's throat, staring adoringly at the siren. "I love it when you do that. It's so magical."

"Says the pulsing fae." Lex leaned down, and tickled under the young omega's chin, making him giggle. "I brought snacks." Lex slipped a small burlap bag off his wrist and handed it to Blue.

He gasped and licked his lips. "Boar," he pulled out some dried meat, "and apples and chestnuts!"

"That's a feast," I pulled out an apple, taking a big bite of the crunchy yellow and pink fruit. It was sweet and tart, and the juices ran down my chin. "My stars, that's good."

Blue scarfed down a hunk of meat, then set about arranging the clean blankets on top of the rug. He was clearly creating a small nest of sorts, and I smiled, happy to see him comfortable enough to make one.

"Wouldn't the bed be more comfy?" Lex asked, pointing at the filthy thing.

"Have you smelled it?" I asked, helping Blue place the softest blanket on top.

Lex sniffed the air, then recoiled. "Yeah, the floor might be better."

"Did you find anything out, or did you just eat?" I asked

the siren, popping a handful of chestnuts into my mouth. It had been too long since I had anything salty. I would never complain about the fresh meat Joon and Byriel hunted for us in the woods, but there was something about seasonings and spices that just made you feel good.

"I did both," Lex stepped over the edge of the nest, snuggling in next to Blue. The omega tensed for a moment, and I pressed my lips together, fighting the urge to point out how rude it was not to ask an omega to enter their nest first.

"Did you find out where Jonelle could be?" I asked around another big bite of apple. "Or anything going on inside the palace?"

"No, but," Lex added quickly when my expression fell, "I think the allies that support Byriel are trying to gain favor with those that used to support the King."

Blue pulled a face, stopping mid-chew. "Why on earth would they want the people that supported the King?"

"It's a numbers game, pup," Lex said simply. "The King is dead, and their allegiances will have to shift somewhere. It's better to have them follow Byriel than Strayton."

"I guess," Blue muttered flatly.

I understood the young omega's emotions. Just before Byriel killed the King, the evil wolf had ordered Blue to strip, then he taunted Byriel, threatening to violate the omega. It was all so horrible. I couldn't imagine anyone knowing what a tyrant the King really was and still supporting him.

"I do, however, have it on good authority that Byriel is still alive," Lex said, and Blue jerked forward, grabbing Lex's hands tight.

"Really?" Hope poured from his intense eyes. "Where is he? Is he okay? Can we get to him?"

"Calm down there, little one," Lex laughed. "All I know is there are rumors that there's a prisoner in the underground cells that was visited by the Queen. I can't see her going down

51

there to visit anyone else." He glanced at the door, then dropped his voice to a whisper. "I think we should sneak out right before dawn. If we wait until sun up, Kenji will be on our asses, and I'm pretty sure he will be dragging you," he poked me in the belly, making me snort, "to Madra, whether you want it or not."

I quickly agreed. "We can sleep for a few hours—"

"No," Blue cut in, his posture tight as his eyes glazed over. His shimmering complexion radiated a soft haze of light, and I stiffened, worried he was going to pulse. "Let's go now." He turned to me with such determination. "We *need* to go now."

"Blue," I placed my hand on his arm, "we should—"

"No!" he said forcefully. "You don't understand. We have to go now. I can feel it, just like when I was with you at the river's edge after my village was attacked. I *know* that we need to go. *Now.*"

My brows pulled together, and I narrowed my eyes. "Do you have visions?"

He shook his head, a bit of frustration wrinkling his brow. "It's not like that. It's just a feeling. Tzidal," he leaned in, his hypnotic eyes pleading with me. "We have to go. Please. Trust me. This is how we find Byriel."

I pulled in a deep breath, then stood. "Okay." I turned to Lex. "Let's go."

Lex eyed the plush blankets beneath him before slowly standing. "First chance for a decent night's sleep, and we have to go *now*," he muttered under his breath.

Blue ignored him, rushing to the bedroom door. Then he jerked it open.

Kenji's eyes widened at the sight of all three of us in the doorway. His gaze moved over Blue, then Lex, but they narrowed at me. "What are you doing?"

"Washroom." Blue's voice was a full octave higher.

Kenji tilted his head to the side, letting me know he didn't believe the young omega. "Washroom?" he repeated, his tone skeptical. "All three of you?"

A bit of defeat beat in my chest, but I kept my head high, trying to think of any way we could get out of this. "It's dangerous for an omega to wander around alone," I said, making sure not to look Kenji in the eyes for too long. The last thing I needed was for him to think I was challenging him. "Is there something you need, alpha?"

He stared at my face as if trying to see through my mind to the truth. When I didn't blink or budge, he finally let out a quick breath and said, "Dane has been kind enough to give us one of his men to stand watch outside your door tonight." He lowered his head, studying my face. "I was going to ask if you needed anything before they got here, but I think you're up to something."

I pressed my lips into a tight line, not sure what else to say. There was no point in lying.

"Do you know what?" Lex snipped, his patience clearly gone. "I'm so sorry to do this to you, wolf, but we've got a lot to do."

Kenji's brows pulled together, but before he could ask what Lex meant, the siren grabbed his face, then pressed their mouths together. The change in Kenji's posture was immediate. The alpha's arms hung at his sides, and his eyes went dark and unfocused.

"Go lay down, wolf," Lex whispered, hovering his lips just over Kenji's mouth. "Sleep, alpha. Sleep very, very deeply. And dream of sweet omegas and fluffy bunnies."

Lex's hands slipped from the alpha's face, and Kenji's big body swayed. Then his feet moved, carrying him to the soiled mattress. The alpha's hulking form pitched forward onto the bed, hitting like a sack of rocks, then he went completely still.

"How did you do that?" Blue asked, his mouth hanging open in awe.

"Siren's trick," Lex smiled, holding open the door for us.

"That might be more impressive than shape-shifting," the young omega said. "Why don't you just kiss everyone you meet to make them do whatever you want?

"Well," Lex snorted. "It's hard to kiss someone on the lips mid-battle. I've tried, but dammit, if it isn't impossible."

The Guest Room...Still

〜〜〜

Joon

THE MOON HUNG high in the night sky when the lock to the bedroom door finally rattled again. I stepped away from the vast window and readied myself to rush the first fucker I saw. I probably wouldn't get far—the palace was probably thick with guards—but I had to try.

"Theo?" Strayton's raspy voice sent chills down my spine, and I dropped my fists. There would be no point in trying to attack her. I could only assume the Queen of Wolves had a whole battalion of guards escorting her everywhere.

The heavy wooden door swung open, and I stood tall, ready to greet my captor. "Your majesty," I said flatly as she entered.

Her long red dress was tight, showing off her impressive form, and swishing as she walked. It made her look wild and reckless, and I couldn't help but think it suited the she-alpha well. "Are you enjoying your stay so far?" she asked, flipping her shiny black hair over her shoulder. The movement fanned her sweet cedar scent into the room, making my wolf snarl. "I hope you've been comfortable."

"I'd enjoy my stay a bit more if I was allowed to leave," I said pointedly.

Her eyes widened at my tone, but her small smile stayed in place. "There are many things my father got wrong during his reign, but his inability to trust anyone was probably the only thing that let him live for as long as he did." She clasped her hands in front of her, making her long painted nails clack together. They were red. Just like her dress. "I need my star, Theo."

"I told you at the camp. It's not here. I—"

"Yes," she snipped, narrowing her dark eyes. "You said it was at the base camp." Her gaze dragged up and down my body as if assessing my clothing. I wore only my leather slacks and nothing else, exposing my scarred chest. "You'll need to get dressed," she continued. "We'll get you a coat and boots. I hear Cristal Terre is very cold this time of year, but we'll grab it real quick, and then you can be on your way."

I tried not to react, confused as to how she expected us to just grab something from a city that was a good two months away by foot.

"Let's go, Theo," she spun, marching right back into the hallway. I rushed after her, not interested in staying in this room for one more damn second than I had to.

I was right about the guards that would accompany Strayton. There were probably at least a good dozen of the fuckers waiting for her, including the captain of her guards and an ally, Arian. The muscular beta stood near the wall and gave me the softest nods. I turned away from him, not wanting Strayton to see that I recognized him.

Strayton moved down the hallway, and I rushed after her, hoping to convince the she-alpha to put off the trip until dawn. Now that I was out of my fucking prison cell, I just needed a quick second to slip away.

"Are you coming to Cristal Terre as well?" I asked Strayton, walking briskly next to her. "It seems rather late to start such a long journey."

"First of all," she cut a glare at my bare feet, "you should walk at least three paces behind me. No one walks with the Queen. And second," Her dark eyes narrowed, "you are speaking to me a little too comfortably." Her jaw pulled tight, letting me know she was very serious about these bullshit rules.

"Forgive me," I bowed my head, "I just worry your dress is too thin and not well suited for this kind of trip."

"There's no need to worry about me," Strayton waved a hand as if I was being ridiculous. "But I will be accompanying you," she spoke loudly. "The fact that you didn't bring the star after writing to me and specifically saying you would bring it is very concerning, Theo. Why would you lie?"

I swallowed hard. Strayton's eyes fell to my throat, watching the motion.

"You seem nervous," she said in a low, accusing tone.

Her guards shifted nervously behind her, and I leaned forward, whispering, "I don't think it's a good idea to bring so many with us. The less eyes that see where the star is, the better."

"You're majesty." Arian pushed past the guards, giving me a menacing look. "I must ask once again that you don't leave the palace. We don't know this alpha," he snarled at me, "and I would be failing you if I allowed you to leave with him." He took a careful step toward Strayton and whispered, "For all we know, he's working with your brother."

I wanted to both punch this fucker and smile at his sharp words. Arian was good. Keeping Strayton on her toes and making sure she believed he was on her side. It was a solid tactic, even if it did put me in danger.

"Theo and I have been corresponding for months now," she smiled politely at Arian. "I appreciate that you're just doing your job, but I don't need an escort."

"Please, you're majesty," Arian begged. "We both know how tense things are. Don't go without a proper guard. Let me protect you."

Strayton sighed softly, looking at the floor as if thinking it over. "What do you think, Theo? Should Arian come with us?"

"I don't give a shit what this fucker does, but if he accuses me of treason again, I'll rip his fucking throat out."

Arian's hand moved to the handle of his blade. "I can't let you walk off with this animal, My Queen. We don't know him."

"Listen here, beta!" I growled, pushing myself to full height. Arian was big for a beta, but I was bigger. "I will not let you—"

"Enough!" Strayton yelled, curling her fists tight. "Arian," she turned to the beta with blazing eyes. "You and only you may accompany us. Theo," she cut me a vicious glare, "Arian's family has protected this house for generations." her voice dropped to a dangerous whisper, "Don't threaten him unless you want to anger me."

I bowed my head, giving her a quick apology.

"Now," Strayton marched off. "Let's get this over quickly. I have a lot to do to prepare for tomorrow."

THIS DAMN PLACE was a maze of stone and brick.

I tried to keep track of the many twists and turns as we made our way through the palace, but all the corridors looked the same. Even the enormous paintings that hung from the walls were weirdly similar—long-dead kings and noblemen, painted in battle or in their wolf-form.

By the time we reached the lower levels of the palace, I had completely given up on trying to find my way out. I'd simply need to find a window and jump.

The kitchen was large, and the only window was all the way on the other side of the vast room. A large table, crates of vegetables, and a few kitchen staff stood between me and it. I'd probably never make it without one of the guards grabbing me. I couldn't risk it. Not yet.

A young service beta bowed low, forcing her to walk at an awkward angle as she approached Strayton. The young girl held up a black fur coat, not standing until Strayton let out a curt, "That will do." The black fur was long, brushing over the she-alpha's black leather boots. It resembled a wolf's pelt, and I recoiled slightly, terrified she might be wearing the skin of a fallen enemy.

"It's hannoth fur," she said, noticing the way I eyed the fur. She shook her head, making her silky black hair swish. "I swear the rumors about me are simply ridiculous."

Another beta stepped forward and handed me a long cloak and a pair of worn guard's boots. I put them on, watching as Arian did the same. I should have grabbed my shirt, but there was no helping it now.

Strayton stood with her arms out, letting the female beta secure the ties of her heavy coat.

Feeling this might be my only chance to talk to Arian, I turned to him and whispered, "Where are we going?"

He shook his head, silently telling me either he didn't know or to shut up. Maybe both.

"Theo?"

I jerked to Strayton's throaty voice, fasting the thick, shiny buttons along the front of my cloak. "Yes, Your Majesty?"

She licked her glossy lips, assessing me like I was a spec of dirt. A few days ago, I would have bet good money this woman wanted to fuck me, but today it was clear she'd rather see me dead.

"I know you have an aversion to the gate," Strayton's mouth pulled tight, making it clear she thought I was stupid, "but this is your fault for not bringing me what you promised."

I didn't speak. There was no point. I didn't know what Theo had told her about the gate or even what the fuck the gate was. All I could do was follow.

Strayton motioned us forward, across the kitchen, and down a cold stone passageway. At the end, a heavy cedar door was pulled open by a guard, revealing a long tunnel. Based on my old village, I could only assume this was a wine cellar of some sort, but it was far too narrow to hold any supplies. As we traveled deeper and deeper into the musky tunnel, I realized the ground was sloped, and it was growing sharper by the second.

The darkness around us grew, and the musk of mold and dirt flooded my nose, pushing away all other scents. Arian kept pace just next to me as we followed Strayton, but seeing more than just her outline was getting difficult.

Then we turned a corner, and a shimmering light cut under a massive metal door in the distance. It danced like water, reflecting blue and silver over the damp gray stone at our feet.

"What is this?" I whispered to Arian, trying to figure out what could create such light. I knew it wasn't lumenite, kunzite, or any natural crystals that grew throughout Havre.

Arian shook his head, barely whispering. "I don't know."

"Dynel!" Strayton shouted at a dark shadow next to the door. A large bald alpha stepped forward and bowed low to his

Queen, grunting out a proper greeting. Based on his strained, deep voice, he didn't speak much.

"We are traveling today and will be returning shortly," Strayton said, waving a manicured hand at the door.

The alpha, Dynel, reached for a set of keys on his belt, fumbling to find the right one. They clinked together as he shoved one key into the heavy lock. Then he jerked hard, forcing it to rattle loudly. Heaving, Dynel pulled the metal bar across the door, and it slowly opened. The rusty hinges groaned, bouncing off the stone walls and floor. The sharp sound made my wolf wince and whimper. Between the wolfsbane holding him in place and my stifled connection with Tzidal, my beast was an absolute mess.

The light intensified, and Dynel's stark features came into view as more light poured out of the room. The alpha was pale, maybe even whiter than Lex or Blue, but his skin was waxy and wet—it looked as if he lived down here.

"Come!" Strayton barked, stepping through the doorway.

I squinted as the light swallowed her up. It was so piercing, burning into the back of my skull. I raised a hand to block out the fierce shimmer, but it was pointless. I'd just have to walk and pray I didn't fall to my death.

Taking a deep breath, I stepped into the doorway. The air crackled around me, making the roots of my hair rise and my fingers tingle. It was weirdly warm, smelling almost like singed hair.

Strayton's high-pitched laugh bounced off the stone. "Honestly?" she seemed to be mocking me. "Open your damn eyes, Theo. It's not that bad."

Unsure of what else to do, I obeyed, dropping my hand.

And the sight before me was simply shocking.

A large, circular burst of light was cut into the furthest wall. It shimmered as if made of water, dancing vibrantly as if suspended in place.

I opened my mouth to ask what it was, then snapped it shut. I was Theo, and he knew what this was. If I didn't keep my wits about me, I was going to get myself killed.

Arian stepped up next to me, his eyes just as wide as mine. "My Queen," he whispered to Strayton. "May I ask, My Lady? What is this?"

"It's a gift from the stars," Strayton smiled, moving around the crudely cut room. The small space looked more like a cave with sharp marks cut in the stone like those made from an ax or possibly even knives. It looked as if this 'gate' was discovered here, not placed.

The metal door behind us groaned as it was slowly forced shut. My beast bellowed, and my muscles flexed with an intense urge to run.

"Come." Strayton bunched the coarse gray fur just beneath her chin. "I want this to be quick." She pointed at the gate. "In you go, Theo."

I hesitated, my eyes flickering between the hard she-alpha and the intense light.

"Theo," she gritted out, her patience wearing thin. "Get your ass in there *now*."

A warm presence moved behind me. It had to be Dynel.

Not sure if I could win in a fight between the mighty alpha and Strayton, I forced my feet to move, walking straight to the gate. The liquid-like surface rippled and flickered. The closer I got, the more it seemed to pull me in, urging me closer. Faster. Sucking me inside. I raised my hand, holding my palm up. Then I closed my eyes, preparing myself to touch it.

"Dynel!" Strayton barked.

A large foot connected with the small of my back, and I flung forward, falling face-first into the light. It stung then burned, singeing the inside of my nose and coating my tongue in bitter, acidic smoke.

I opened my mouth, trying to scream or breathe, but my

chest squeezed too fucking tight. Then I pitched forward and smacked hard into cold rock.

My whole body spasmed, and I choked hard, retching onto the cold stone floor.

"Don't move!" the unmistakable voice of a she-alpha roared as the tip of a blade pressed into the base of my skull, keeping me in place.

I kept breathing deeply through my mouth, trying to calm my still-spinning gut.

The air crackled loudly, and light flashed just as a heavy body landed next to me. Arian groaned, pushing himself onto his hands and knees. "Strayton," he rasped, retching hard. "She's—" He coughed, then spit, holding his middle.

"Is she coming?" A softer voice asked. It didn't hold the authority of an alpha, but it didn't sound right for a beta, either. I tried looking up, but the blade pressed harder into my neck, forcing me down.

"I said not to move," the she-alpha growled deep in her chest.

The room filled with light again, but there was no heavy thump this time.

"My lady!" the high-pitched voice gasped as someone stepped out of the light.

"It's your majesty the Queen," Strayton purred, coming to a stop just next to me. The blade lifted from my neck, then fell onto the ground just next to my hand. I resisted the urge to take it, not wanting to start a fight without knowing exactly how many fuckers were in this cave with me.

Tilting my head to the side, I saw two big alphas in heavy furs and an orc. Their kind didn't normally mix with ours. His presence was surprising.

"Please forgive me, My Queen," the person with the soft voice dropped to his knees, giving a full and proper bow. I narrowed my eyes at the male, taking in his pointed ears and pale pink skin. I had never seen a pink elf before, but that didn't mean they didn't exist. "I meant no offense, My Queen. Please," he bowed even lower, pressing his nose against the stone. "Accept my deepest apologies."

"Please rise, Faydon," Strayton waved her hand, casting a pleased look around the cave. Every creature here bowed, continuing to show their respect. "I'm sure it takes quite some time for the news of these things to travel this far, and my father passed only a few days ago. Your ignorance is forgivable."

Arian placed a hand on my shoulder, then he pulled me up. I snatched up the blade that had just been pressed to my neck, glaring at the she-alpha still bowing to Strayton. Her blonde hair was short, shaved along the sides, and long on top, and her biceps were covered in long thick scars that resembled mine—a clear sign that this she-wolf had battled many of our kind.

"How can we serve you today, My Queen?" the pink elf stood, smoothing down the front of his dingy gray robes. Pointed ears peaked out from his long, greasy black hair, and his eyes were wet and black. They reminded me of Lex's natural eyes.

Could he be half-siren?

"I need my star," Strayton said, giving Faydon an intense look.

His eyes widened, and fear flashed. 'My, my Queen," he stammered. "It still can't be carried."

Strayton's eyes flashed red, and she turned to me, anger flowing off her in waves. "Theo," she hissed. "You said—"

"I said that I left it with my people," I cut in, suddenly very aware of how many creatures were cramped into the tight pace —and every last one of them was looking at me like I was a threat.

"If you fuck me over...." Strayton growled, too angry to finish her sentence.

Faydon took a careful step toward me, his black eyes narrowed. Fear slipped up my spine, and my fists curled tight, ready to fight my way out of here if I had to.

"Forgive me, My Queen," his brows furrowed with confusion. "Theo?" He cut me a curious glare, and my heart sank. There were too many here for me to fight off by myself, and I was sure Arian would let this lot kill me to keep his cover. I couldn't blame him. I'd do the same.

"Faydon!" Arian snapped at Faydon, placing his hand on the hilt of his dagger. "Her majesty requested to be brought to her star." His voice bounced off the walls, his anger feeding into every alpha around us. "Do not keep her waiting, you pixie fuck!"

My eyes widen at Arian's outburst, really looking at the pink-skinned creature this time.

Faydon was small, like an omega, even though I've always heard that pixies more closely resembled the size of a child—it made sense, as pups were their main diet. Pixies were vicious, cunning, and smart, destroying villages by cutting off entire generations. This creature might not be able to get the best of me in a fight, but he was not to be taken lightly. A pixie can be just as bad as a siren...maybe even worse.

Faydon's head snapped to Strayton, and he bowed quickly. "Of course, My Queen." But his eyes narrowed at me just before he turned.

This was not going to end well.

Behind the Brothel

Tzidal

"WHERE ARE WE GOING?" Blue whispered, cutting his eyes up and down the wide cobblestone street. It was so dark, it was impossible to see anything outside of the outline of buildings. Not even the Moon helped us tonight, hiding behind thick, angry clouds. I wouldn't be surprised if it started raining.

"Shhh," I pressed a finger to my lips, telling him to keep quiet. With Kenji out of the way, I sincerely doubted anyone was looking for us, but that didn't change the fact that Blue and I were unaccompanied omegas in a vast city *filled* with predators. I tried not to think about the number of dishonorable alphas roaming the dark alleyways that surrounded us.

Blue nodded, pressing both his hands over his mouth. The small bag of snacks slipped further down his arm, settling at his elbow. I'm glad he remembered to bring it, as it might be awhile before we were able to find something proper to eat.

A soft hum drifted from Lex as he waved for us both to come closer. He wore the face of the enormous bald alpha again. I understood why, but I needed the comfort of my friend's usual form.

Keeping my head down, I grabbed Blue's hand and ran across the empty road, rushing into a tight passageway. The walls were made of stone and weathered wood, pressing right up against us. It felt so creepy. It also didn't help that it was so damn cold. Blue shivered, pushing hard into my side and I wrapped an arm around his middle, hoping to warm both of us.

"This way." Lex squinted into the shadows. I prayed he could see *something*, because other than the occasional soft glow of a lantern cutting through dingy windows, I saw nothing.

"Stay close," Lex warned as he circled his meaty fist around Blue's wrist and tugged him forward. I stayed right on their heels, trying to mimic Lex's confident walk. He always looked like he knew exactly where he was going. It was probably how he got away with so much.

A cough echoed up and down the long alley, and I stopped, scanning the shadows behind me. A glass bottle clattered against the stone ground, then it rolled. Fear prickled my spine, and I picked up my pace, urging Lex to walk faster.

"Do you smell that?" Blue whispered, darting his hypnotic eyes all over the place. His pupils were wide with fear, but his scent remained calm. Impressively calm.

Lex pulled to a stop, inhaling deeply. I did the same. I could scent dingy water, the sharp stench of ale, and what could only be a wet dog. If I had to guess, it was probably a drunk alpha passed out in his wolf-form.

"It's someone familiar." Blue's eyes narrowed as they scanned the cobblestone at his feet. Suddenly he froze, and his eyes went wide. "I think we're being followed."

I jerked at his words, spinning to look all around, but I saw nothing. No movement within the shadows or in the street in the distance.

"Is it Kenji?" I asked Lex. A part of me prayed it was. "How long does your trick last?"

"It usually lasts long enough for me to eat." He shrugged his big muscular shoulders. "I've never knocked someone out just for the hell of it."

"It's not Kenji." Blue closed his eyes, listening hard. "It's...."

Silence pulsed all around us and I held my breath, trying to hear whatever had Blue so on edge. But there was nothing. No feet, no chatter, just silence.

Then a deep voice cut through the night air, "Don't move!"

Before I could move a single muscle, Blue flinched hard. Then he bolted.

He ran so fast, the shadows swallowed him up.

"Go!" Lex yelled in his deep alpha voice.

I jerked, running after the young omega as fast as I could. Heavy feet pounded the pavement behind us—more than one person on our heels. I pumped my arms and legs harder, urging my suddenly exhausted body to be faster.

The tip of my freezing toes caught the lip of an uneven cobblestone and I went flying, falling face first onto the ground. I hit with a heavy grunt, but before I could get my feet back under me, Lex gripped the back of my robes, then jerked me sideways, tucking us into a dark doorway.

The siren's hulking body shrunk, shifting from the massive alpha to his usual form, but this time smaller. The top of his head came level with mine, and his robes were black, melting into the dark.

The footsteps grew louder, and Lex hugged me tight, then

spun, shielding me from two figures rushing past us. I held my breath, listening. The feet slowed, finally coming to a stop.

"Calm down there, omega," a deep voice cut through the dark, filling the alleyway. He sounded raspy, like he had spent a lifetime screaming.

I jerked, knowing they were talking to Blue. *He was trapped and alone!*

Lex's arms tightened, and his gray eyes went wide, silently ordering me to stay quiet. I knew it was stupid to rush out there and try to help. After all, if Lex was discovered, all it would take was one roar of an alpha and we'd be swarmed by enraged shifters in seconds, but I still had to do something.

"Where are you friends?" a familiar voice asked. It was Marx, one of the twins from the brothel.

My whole body went tight with fear and confusion as I turned my head, trying to hear better. My wolf was spun, wanting to run and fight, and save the poor youngling.

"Where is your alpha and the female omega you were with?" Marx asked.

Silence filled the dark alleyway, beating hard in my ears.

"Are you sure this is him?" The raspy alpha asked.

"Positive," Marx said firmly. "He and two others were delivering something to Dane. It was weird because it had *Dane's* seal on it." His voice dropped, whispering, "They're up to something."

"Don't touch me!" Blue hissed and growled. He sounded as if he was struggling, maybe even fighting. My body jerked once again, wanting to run to him, but Lex held me in place, refusing to let me go. I understood why, but hated the siren for it.

"There's no need to be scared, omega," Marx said in a weirdly soft tone. "We just want to talk to you."

Blue growled in response, but he sounded almost muffled.

My wolf snarled, wanting to rip into whoever dared to touch him.

"It's okay," Lex whispered in my ear so softly I almost didn't hear him. "It's okay, Tzidal."

"Where is the siren?" Marx gritted out and Blue whimpered.

Lex's whole body went tight, and his grip on my arms lessened.

"How did you know he was a siren?" Blue's voice was quiet, almost a whisper.

Marx tsked, letting out a quick snort. "Back at the brothel, I left my sister in the office, then rounded the corner to see her pull a random alpha into the back alley. It had me spun at first, but it didn't take long for me to realize. We don't usually see water-dwellers this far north. But Dane must be desperate to form an alliance with a bottom feeder."

"You aren't an ally," Blue said as if just realizing. "You're just pretending. Aren't you?"

"I wanted the senseless murders to end," Marx voice rose as his anger built. "The King was killing our people left and right with no end in sight. I couldn't save my mother, but I was going to be damned if I let anyone hurt my sister." He took a calming breath. "But that's over now. Strayton is on the throne and Byriel is gone. Those that want to overthrow the Queen are just kidding themselves." Soft feet padded against the ground, and I imagined the beta stepping closer to Blue. "The fight is over, but if the allies keep pushing for someone else to be on the throne, we'll all end up dead. This has to stop."

I dropped my gaze, wishing I had the strength to beat the beta and his alpha friend senseless. But there was nothing I could do. They were too strong.

"Let me go!" Blue screamed. "Don't—" His words became muffled and the footsteps grew louder.

My hand flew to my dagger, ready to use it, but Lex circled his fingers around mine, shaking his head no. I gritted my teeth, trying to pull my blade free, but Lex's strength was so much more than mine.

Suddenly, two swift shadows passed us: Marx and the massive alpha, and he was carrying Blue.

I just didn't know where.

The Other Gate

Joon

I WAITED for Strayton to follow the pixie before falling in line behind Dynel and Arian. It was clear Faydon knew I wasn't Theo, but I wasn't sure why he didn't say it out loud. But then again, a pixie's reputation was very similar to that of a siren. Faydon was having his fun with me while he could.

Fucker.

Moving slowly, I ducked under the low dip in the ceiling and then stepped out into a hollow cavern. It was vast and tall, like a cathedral, with a few open holes overhead, allowing the moonlight to cut through. Unlike the gate in the palace, this side didn't have a door or any real barrier outside of a few guards to protect it. It seemed anyone wandering around this cave could stumble upon it.

"Watch your step, My Queen." Faydon indicated the narrow path.

We stepped through a crack in the mountainside, which lead to the ruins in the distance.

It was Cristal Terre.

Many still called it the Crystal City, but the name wasn't apt anymore. There was a time when it was a bustling city, but that was hundreds of years ago, before the war with the humans. Now it was just a collection of ruins and rocks with brightly colored gems and stones slicing out of the ground like mighty pillars.

"This way, My Queen," Faydon bowed low as he pointed to a path cut in the rock.

Strayton strolled past the pixie, pausing briefly to let Dynel catch up. She seemed to prefer the large alpha's protection over Arian which was odd considering the beta was her main guard. Watching the way she walked stiffly next to Arian made me pause. Did she know where his alliances really lay?

"*Theo*," Faydon spoke to me as if making a joke. "Are you coming, *sir*?" His brows jutted up as a knowing smirk filled his child-like face.

My beast snarled, and it took everything in me not to punch the fucker.

"After you," I gritted out—the last thing I needed was any of these assholes at my back.

"If you insist." Faydon's tight glare cut up and down my body, lingering on my face. "I just know how much you like taking the lead," He paused, and his grin grew, "*Theo*."

I flashed my pointed fangs, not in the fucking mood. "Go," I snipped, careful not to yell. Once Faydon was done playing with me, he would reveal I was an impostor, but I was hopeful I could slip away before that could happen.

The night air whipped, cutting straight to my bones and actually making me shiver. It had to be below freezing for it to affect me.

I kept my distance from Faydon as we moved slowly out of the cavern and into the open night sky. An odd sensation pulsed in my head, making my skin itch and my beast yelp.

It was Tzidal.

Our bond was too tight—almost closed off—to truly feel her, but something just felt...*wrong*. The sudden and intense urge to turn around and run back to my omega at full speed hit me like a rolling boulder. I stumbled, trying like hell to catch my breath.

"You okay?" Arian paused, narrowing his dark eyes at me.

I nodded, then forced my feet to move. I needed to get out of here, but I couldn't just run for the hills. I needed to wait until Strayton was distracted, then I'd be able to sneak off.

"My Lady!" A she-alpha's voice rang out, and I turned to the sound.

A sizable camp sat at the base of the mountain, filled with small tents and roaring fires—it looked as if a good thirty creatures could comfortably camp there. Alphas, orcs, a few betas, and even a dragon shifter sat around a large pit, roasting what looked like a mammoth elk. A large wagon held an array of tools at the edge of camp: shovels, pick axes, and several trowels.

"We are honored to have you here." A she-alpha with wild red hair rushed toward Strayton, slamming her fist to her chest, then bowing low. "We didn't know you were planning on visiting."

"Yes,..." Strayton pressed her lips together as if trying to think.

"Sarma." The redhead pressed her hand to her chest, introducing herself. "I am Sarma of Hund Valley, and I'm here to serve you, My Lady."

"My Queen," Faydon corrected her excitedly. "The King has passed." His broad grin was so misplaced.

A wave of shock rippled through the camp, followed by

murmurs and shocked gasps. It seemed every creature that lived here was climbing out of their tents and standing at attention. I couldn't place the general emotion, but the scent of rage overpowered almost everything else.

"Is that true?" Someone yelled out over the hushed whispers. "Is the King dead?"

Strayton stood a little taller, clearing her throat to address the small crowd. She looked as if she was loving this. "Sadly, it is true. My father, the King, passed away. I am bereaved but determined to carry on his legacy. Please," she looked all around, addressing her people with restrained excitement, "don't celebrate my reign. Not yet. Mourn my father first."

I scowled, wondering how anyone could buy this woman's obvious lies.

The redhead, Sarma, scanned the crowd then snarled, "Bow to your Queen!"

A sanctified smile filled Strayton's face as several wolf-shifters took a knee and bowed their heads, but it didn't escape me how many simply nodded or even sat down. A few alphas near the back of the camp pulled sour expressions, then wandered off.

Strayton glared at them but quickly fixed her expression, looking lovingly at those bowing low. "Thank you for your loyalty and dedication." She stood a little taller. "I will make you all proud, but first..." she turned to the pixie, giving him a tight look.

A moment of confusion flitted across Faydon's delicate features, then he startled and jumped, addressing the crowd. "Her majesty has business. Part the way!" He pushed into the throng of alphas and orcs, forcing them to shift to the side. "Let her majesty through!"

I stayed rooted to the spot, watching as Arian and Strayton cut through the camp. Arian's dark head disappeared in the sea of much taller alphas, but I kept my eyes on Strayton, waiting.

Concentrating hard, I narrowed in on my bond with my mate, trying to feel her. Once again, I was met with only a soft slip of pain, but it was...*off*? It wasn't physical or even anger or sadness, but more like an itch I couldn't reach—something was bothering her to the point that it made my skin crawl.

Determined to find out what was wrong with my omega, I spun, then froze.

Dynel's hulking form stood right at my back, glaring down at me. I tipped my chin up, looking hard into the pale alpha's face. While I was confident in most fights, I wasn't so sure I could take this fucker down, especially with so many of Strayton's supporters at my back.

"Go," he snarled.

My wolf growled deep in my chest, wanting to rip into him, but it wasn't smart.

"No need to be pissy," I cut, glaring hard at the beast. "I was just looking around."

Dynel's black brows pulled together in an angry scowl, and he flashed his pointed fangs. "Go," he repeated.

Not sure what else to do, I turned, walking through the camp. Most of the shifters had returned to their tents or sat fireside, drinking deeply from small metal flasks. The atmosphere was so odd I couldn't place if half of these men supported or hated Strayton.

As we left the camp, the yellow glow of luminite pulled my attention. A large crystal jutted up out of the earth, radiating a wonderful heat. Two betas sat at the base of it, warming their hands and feet. Both looked underfed, but the broken shackles around their ankles caught my attention. *Was this a prison camp?*

The terrain became more rough, the grass disappearing

into smooth black rock. The cold cut through my boots, making my toes tingle.

The ruins cut high into the air, different kinds of magical crystal throwing off all different kinds of light: warm yellow luminite, freezing pink kunzite, and gray viscerite. The yellowish mist that flowed from the dull stone made the hair on the back of my neck stand on end. If inhaled, it would pull the seams of your organs apart, killing you in the most painful of ways.

We moved toward a cluster of black glass stone. It was surrounded by a large pit of cracked rock and red dirt. A few chunks of amber circled the area with what looked like skeletons encased inside them—they were bodies from long-fought wars. The land simply swallowed them up, preserving their bones forever.

"Where the hell is it?" Strayton snarled at the pixie.

Dynel pushed at my back, forcing me to walk faster. The wind shifted, and the low hiss of a Bethir filled the air. The giant and deadly serpents were strong and smart, easily able to take down several alphas in one go.

"Your star is still within the rock, My Queen." Faydon pointed at the black rock.

Strayton pulled to a stop, turning to face the pixie. "You didn't remove it?" Her dark brows drew together with confusion.

"We couldn't," Faydon said simply. "No one could touch it." His eyes flickered to me, and his energy doubled, bouncing excitedly on the balls of his feet.

Strayton's slim figure slowly turned, facing me. Her dark eyes pulsed red as they narrowed into angry slits. Faydon's expression was lighter. Amused. He was enjoying this.

"What's going on here, Theo?" Strayton's voice was deep. Angry.

"Yes, *Theo*," Faydon chirped. "What's going on?"

I sucked in a quick breath, steadying myself for Strayton's growing rage. I thought of Byriel and his always calm demeanor. It pissed me the fuck off when he acted like that, but I now understood why.

"You said my star was ready," Strayton snarled, flashing her pointed fangs. "You said—"

"I said neither of those things, My Queen." I kept my chin up, keeping all emotion from my face. "I simply said it was here."

Strayton moved with impressive speed, pushing her hand into her robes and pulling a blade from her hip. She closed the space between us, then pressed the dagger to my neck.

Dynel shifted at my side, his fists curling tight. There was nothing like the prospect of blood to work an alpha up.

"If you don't tell me exactly what's happening in the next two seconds," Strayton growled, "I'm going to split you ear to ear and let the scavengers feast on your bones."

The base of my skull pounded, and my vision blurred. All I could think about was Tzidal. My mate. What was wrong with her?

I needed to leave.

"Speak!" Strayton roared, and my wolf growled deep within me.

"Forgive him," Faydon giggled high in his throat. "I'm sure it's difficult for a dead man to share any stories. Isn't that right, *Theo*?"

"What the fuck does that mean?" Strayton snarled at the pixie. "Speak plainly!"

Faydon's black eyes narrowed, and his nose scrunched with excitement. "Theo is dead, My Queen," he giggled. "He touched the star, and the life was ripped out of his eyes. Just like everyone else that touches the damn thing."

The blade against my throat eased for a moment while Strayton took in his words. Then ever so slowly, her glowing red eyes shifted from the pixie-fuck to me. The dagger pressed tighter, slicing ever so slightly into my skin. It stung, but I remained completely still.

Strayton looked hard into my eyes, taking in my every feature. "Who the fuck are you?"

In The Shadows

Tzidal

I HELD MY BREATH, watching the big alpha carry Blue down the dark alleyway. Lex kept his arms wrapped tightly around me, not releasing me until both the alpha and Marx cut around a corner, disappearing.

"Stay at my side," Lex said softly. There was a seriousness in his tight expression that I wasn't used to. It was alarming. "We're going to follow them, but we have to keep our distance." He gave me a pointed look, making sure I understood.

"Okay." I nodded fiercely, eager to go already.

Lex circled his long fingers around my wrist. Then he tugged me behind him. I glanced up at the cloudy night sky, wishing I could see or feel Joon. Was he okay? Was he hurt? Why couldn't I feel him?

Lex paused at the end of the alleyway, cutting a quick look up and down the street. Before I could move to look with him,

Lex stepped out into the road, pulling me with him. He walked with confidence, holding his head high and his back straight. I mimicked him, praying no one would stop us. We probably had a few more hours until dawn, and it seemed unlikely anyone would be out at this hour, but Ossory was a vast city; there were probably many reasons for strangers to roam the streets at all hours of the night.

Keeping my head down, I stayed glued to Lex's side, not looking up until he came to an abrupt stop. Marx quickly crossed a small wooden bridge in the distance, followed by the big alpha carrying Blue. The creek that ran through the city smelled murky, as if it was used to clean dirty laundry or wash sweaty feet.

Marx picked up his pace, walking straight toward a large brick building. It looked out of place. It didn't have any windows or chimney stacks, and the lone metal door was flanked by four alpha guards, each looking more fierce than the last.

"What is this place?" I whispered to Lex. He didn't answer. Instead, he pressed his lips into a thin line as worry creased his brow.

"Let me go!" Blue yelled, followed quickly by the fierce growl of an alpha.

"Stop moving!" the alpha roared.

My knees buckled at his commanding tone, and I fell, slapping my hands and knees against the cold cobblestone.

"Tzi!" Lex gasped as he reached for me. "Are you okay?"

I nodded, even though I wasn't okay. My wolf spiraled and whined within me, urging me to bow to the alpha's stern order. "I'm fine," I gritted out, trying to move my feet, but they wouldn't budge.

Lex's dark eyes fell to my jerky legs, concern wrinkling his brow. "What's wrong?" He grabbed my upper arms.

"I can't...." I grunted and then sniffled, realizing it was no use. My whole body was intent on obeying that strange alpha's command. I had never experienced this before. My wolf was always loyal to our mate, never submitting to an alpha that didn't love or protect me. "I don't know what's happening," I whispered, my throat tight with the threat of tears. "I can't move." My chin quivered.

"It's okay," Lex scooped me up, and I instantly went limp in his arms. "I'll get you help, puppy. Just stay quiet for me."

I nodded against his shoulder, trying like hell to pull myself together, but it was no use. The pain pounding behind my eyes grew, and my whole body shook violently.

I needed my mate.

I needed Joon *now*.

The Cell

Byriel

"Byriel," Blue giggled, running up ahead of me. "Catch me!"

His vibrant smile and soft scent consumed me as I chased my mate through the meadow of lilies and carnations. Their petals were bright white, making the air around me glow.

I picked up my pace, getting so close to Blue I could feel the warmth from his small body. Feeling me near, he glanced over his shoulder, and his gorgeous eyes went wide with excitement at having me so close.

Unable to keep my hands off him for a single moment longer, I reached out and snatched up my omega. He laughed so bright and free, pretending to struggle before flinging his arms around my neck and kissing every inch of my face.

"You cheated," he pouted as I laid him down amongst the flowers. They smelled so sweet, but it was nothing compared to Blue's natural, clean scent. He was downright mouthwatering compared to any other fragrance.

"I never cheat." I leaned down, hovering my mouth over his. His legs fell open as I situated myself between them, loving the way his small form fit beneath me. He was warm and soft, and I had never been happier.

I knew this was a dream, but I didn't care.

Blue's pink tongue pushed out, brushing over his bottom lip. My eyes fell to the motion, torn between wanting to simply stare at my beautiful mate and needing to kiss him.

Leaning down, I brushed my lips over his. Blue kept his hypnotic blue and green eyes on me, tipping his chin up to invite me closer. Then, I slowly pressed my mouth to his.

He tasted so....

I jerked awake as metal banged loudly, ripping me from my dream. I snarled, silently cursing the fuckers that woke me. *If the Moon truly loved me, she'd let me dream forever.*

Heavy feet pounded the stone floor down the hall, slowly growing louder. Awareness pricked my skin as I realized they were coming toward my cell. No one came down here. Outside of one visit by my sister and another by Tibbit, I had been left in complete silence the last week.

Curious, I inched my way toward the heavy wooden door, trying to be mindful of the shackles still on my wrists. There was a small long metal plate on a hinge at the bottom. It was normally used to provide food or drink to prisoners, but mine hadn't been used once.

Pressing my cheek against the cold stone floor, I carefully pulled the metal up and peered into the dark hallway. The thick stench of wolfsbane pushed hard into my nose, and I pulled back, trying not to choke on the awful, bitter scent.

"Be careful," the unmistakable voice of a beta warned. I didn't recognize his voice. "Don't hurt him."

"Calm the fuck down, Marx. He's passed out," an alpha growled in a low, raspy voice. This alpha I knew.

I pushed my face back against the metal plate and lifted.

Three sets of feet stood directly in front of my door, but they all faced the cell across from me.

"Who is he?" Bracken, an older beta guard I knew from my years in command, asked. I was surprised to hear his voice. The old man practically qualified as an elder.

"Maybe someone important," the other beta, Marx, said. "Don't let anyone back here. Terrince," he turned to face the alpha, "we need to make sure none of the prisoners find out an omega is back here. He'd be ripped to pieces by the whole lot if anyone knew."

I jerked at his words.

Placing an omega in these cells was highly uncommon. This space was reserved for extremely violent alphas and traitors. I wondered which one Strayton considered me. Probably both.

"He needs to be in an omega-holding cell," Bracken said. I could practically envision the way he crossed his arms and narrowed his light brown eyes—he looked at all the young guards the same way. Or at least he did back when he was under my command. "This is no place for an omega."

The alpha carrying the omega grunted as he placed the passed-out male on the floor of his cell. I squinted, trying to see his face, but it was no use. Marx's feet blocked my view completely.

"Are there any omega cells free?" Marx asked with a lift in his voice. The very fact that he didn't know meant he wasn't in the guard.

The security here was shit.

"Nope," Bracken said flatly. "The Queen has them filled to the brim with her brother's supporters. No idea what she plans on doing with them, but this omega," he paused, and I assumed he was pointing at the poor creature, "needs to be in the infirmary. Not here."

"He's fine," Marx said far too loudly. "He doesn't need the

infirmary. I just need somewhere to keep him while I figure out what the hell to do with him."

Bracken let out an annoyed huff. "Just pointing it out, kid."

"Yeah, well, keep it to yourself unless you got something helpful to say." Marx took a quick step to one side, and my heart thundered in my chest.

Blue's pale face slipped into my view for the briefest of moments just before his cell door swung shut.

Cristal Terre

Joon

"WHO ARE YOU?" Strayton's eyes flashed red as she pushed the blade harder against my neck.

I bared my fangs, ready to accept my fate, but then my bond with Tzidal burned tight. My mate's fear was so thick, and her presence so clear. She was in danger. I couldn't tell what, just that I needed to be with her as soon as possible.

"I asked you a question." Strayton fisted my hair, forcing my eyes to focus on her face. Her once attractive features twisted with rage, and her fangs punched out. "Who the fuck are you?"

I pressed my lips into a tight line, determined to give this woman nothing.

"My Queen," Arian stepped forward. "If he's not Theo, then how did he get his uniform?" His hand flew to the hilt of his weapon as he spun on the pixie. "Do you have spies in your camp?"

Faydon shrugged, seemingly unbothered by the rage pouring off the wolves around him. "Several have touched the star," he said simply. "Whether it's by accident or dumb determination to remove the damn thing. Once the bodies stop jerking, we toss them on the edge of the forest on the other side of the black glass cavern."

Arian's dark eyes narrowed, tilting his head to one side. "You don't strip them? Burn them?"

"We touch them as little as possible." Faydon crossed his arms. If he didn't look so damn annoyed, I'd swear he was being defensive. "The *only* reason we move them is because it felt dangerous to have that kind of rot near camp."

Strayton slowly turned back to me, looking hard into my eyes as she spoke to Faydon. "What happened to Theo? Where is he?"

"I told you, My Queen." The pixie's voice edged higher, happy the focus was shifting back to me. "He touched the star, and it pulled his soul right out."

Dynel rocked uneasy on his feet, inching away from the black rock and the star hidden somewhere within it.

Unable to help myself, I craned my neck to look over Strayton's shoulder, but she jerked my hair, forcing me to move with her.

"Does the star burn bright red?" she asked forcefully, jerking her blade ever so slightly. The quick motion stung, followed by the slow drip of hot blood down my chest. "Is it alive with energy?"

"Oh, yes," he giggled. "Very much so."

Strayton shook her head as if confused. "Then it should be able to be handled. This makes no sense," Strayton whispered to herself, pushing the blade deeper into my neck as she thought. It seemed as if she didn't even realize she was doing it.

Arian's dark eyes flashed to my throat. I could feel more

blood seep, running hot as it disappeared within my heavy cloak.

I needed to get out of here before she killed me by accident, but I wasn't sure how. Not with Dynel breathing down my neck.

Then in one impressive movement, Arian rushed me, pushing me away from Strayton's blade. The beta fisted the front of my cloak. Then he forced me onto my knees. My wolf roared within me for allowing myself to be handled like this, especially by a beta. But I stayed still, trusting Arian's plan.

"What the fuck is this game?" Arian yelled at me. "What do you know? Who sent you?"

Strayton stood just behind the guard with her blade still in her hand, watching my face with rapt intensity.

"My name is Seonjoon of Casin Village." I tipped my chin up higher, making my challenge of the she-alpha clear. "My mate Fennah, daughter of Arzo, was a mighty beta who was brave and cherished. She was murdered in the name of the King and left to rot. And now I will kill you."

The corners of Strayton's lips lifted, followed by a tight, mocking chuckle. "That's very cute, rogue," she scrunched her nose as if I said something cute, "But I cannot be killed."

I smiled wide, mocking her in return. "You look awfully happy for a Queen who just found out a rogue easily infiltrated your camp *and* your palace. You even invited me into your bed."

The excitement in her eyes dimmed as her grip on the dagger tightened. "You've failed," she spat. "The prophecy has been fulfilled. The King is dead, and the star is bursting with energy. All that's left to do is to claim the power that's waiting for me." A wicked smile split her face. "Then you'll all see," she purred. "You were all wrong to doubt me."

"My Queen," Arian lowered his head, speaking respectfully. "We need to get you back to the palace. This star," he glared at the colorful ruins, "it's far too danger—"

"Quiet!" Strayton roared. "Pixie!" She turned to Faydon. He jerked as if he hadn't fully been paying attention. "The star! I need it now! Show me."

"Right this way," Faydon chirped, leading us down into the pit of red dirt. It was steep, making me pick up my pace to keep from falling forward. Faydon cut around a large pillar and then stopped. A red glow illuminated his face, then I stepped around and saw it too.

Nestled in a shiny black rock, a vibrant red light illuminated the night sky. It made the air warm, and my hair stood on end. It was harsh, making me squint to see it clearly. The red crystal sat precariously in the side of the roughly cut rock. It looked as if one more quick wack with an ax might let it fall away.

"I can't believe it's real," Arian whispered as if in awe. His fingers fell away from my arm, and I tensed, readying myself to run the second I had the chance.

"It's very real, beta," Strayton said softly. Her features were so soft, looking at the red crystal with so much affection. "Dynel," she waved the alpha over, "bring the rogue. Let's see what this pretty stone can do."

Before I could move, Dynel's meaty hand gripped the back of my neck. Arian's eyes went wide with panic, but to his credit, he corrected it quickly, pushing his dagger carefully to my throat.

"Allow me, My Queen," Arian said firmly. "I don't trust anyone outside of myself right now." He cut an accusing glare at Dynel.

"What did you say to me?" The alpha growled in his chest as he released my arm. Then he grabbed the front of Arian's shirt, lifting the beta clear off the ground.

My wolf burst from me, bones grinding from my incredibly fast shift, then I ran. Beating my paws hard into the slick stone, I raced as fast as I could through the rough cut of ruins and crystal, listening carefully for the sound of anyone following, but the only thing I heard was Strayton's enraged roar.

"You fucking fool!" she cursed, her voice echoing all around me.

A flock of black birds took flight, flashing silver, and gold before blending into the night sky.

The gruff snort of another wolf pricked my ears, and I picked up my pace. Nearing the center of the crumbling ruins, I cut right, then stopped short. A large cut of viscerite blocked my path. The yellow mist rolled and billowed, filling the night sky. Before I could correct my course, a large silver wolf slammed into me, pinning me beneath his powerful claws.

I snapped my jaws, trying to get to his neck, but it was no use. Dynel's wolf-form was just as massive as his human. His powerful paws pushed hard into my neck, and his hind legs kicked out, slicing into my belly. I tried to roll and get my paws under me but couldn't move under his impressive weight.

My bond with Tzidal flared once again, and my wolf whimpered long and loud, trying desperately to get away.

Dynel's wicked claws pushed into my throat, then they sliced, puncturing my skin and cutting off my airway. A gargled whimper left my snout, but I remained perfectly still, terrified he'd rip my throat out.

"Don't kill him!" Arian panted as he ran up to us. "The Queen wants him alive!"

Dynel's silver wolf let out an angry growl, then he slowly shifted—rough, pale skin replacing silver fur. "Fight and die," his claws pushed deeper into my flesh, making me yip.

Arian pulled his weapon from its sheath, looming over me. "Don't get any ideas, rogue," he spat at me. "I'll gladly let you bleed out here." He held up his blade, moving it so the moonlight reflected off the shiny metal. "Let's go."

I narrowed my eyes at Dynel, waiting for him to release me.

Moving at a painfully slow pace, the alpha pulled his claws from my skin. Then he stood, curling his fists tight, waiting for me to shift. "Shift," he grunted.

Hot blood soaked my copper fur all along my neck and chest. I stayed in my wolf-form, knowing damn well a wound like this could quickly kill me if I shifted.

"Shift!" Dynel roared, making Arian snarl.

"It doesn't fucking matter," Arian gripped my scruff, forcing me to roll onto my belly. "Wolf or human, you're done."

Trying to be mindful of my wounds, I moved slowly back the way we came. Arian held the tip of his blade pressed against my ribs as we walked while Dynel stayed on my tail. Even if I could outrun him, I'd probably bleed out before I could find a decent hiding place.

Strayton turned to the sound of our footsteps. Her face twisted with rage and triumph as we approached. "Did you really think you'd escape?" she mocked me. "You tried to play me, rogue, but you lost. Accept your fate. Faydon," she spun on the pixie. "I need my star," she pointed at the glowing rock. "I'm not leaving here without it."

The pixie's playful expression fell from excitement to deep confusion. "My Queen," he shook his head, "no one can touch it."

The she-alpha let out an annoyed sigh before narrowing her eyes at me. "Should we make the rogue collect it for me? See what happens when the unworthy tries to touch it?"

Fear ripped through me, and my claws pushed hard into the cold red earth. If I was going to die today, I'd die running.

"My Queen," Arian stepped forward, bowing his head. "If you will allow me to speak." He kept his head down, waiting for her permission.

Strayton tipped her chin up, moving her hard eyes between me and the beta. "You may speak, but make it quick."

"I think we need to question this rogue." Arian raised his head. "The only way he could have gotten as far as he did, is if he knew someone within the palace. We both know there are traitors in the court, and I think this..." he cut me a look as his upper lip curled in disgust, "...rogue could have plenty to share."

Strayton narrowed her eyes into the distance, thinking it over. "No one kills him," she paused, waiting for Arian to acknowledge her command.

"Yes, My Queen," the beta bowed low.

"He's mine," she flashed her pointed teeth. "But I still need my star."

Arian kept his head down, and Dynel went completely still next to me. It seemed everyone was too terrified to move to even breathe.

Then, in one swift second, Strayton let out a strangled growl, grabbed Faydon's hands, then pushed him forward. He tried to struggle, but his slight form was nothing compared to her alpha strength.

The pixie let out a vicious scream as Strayton forced his fingers to touch the glowing red light, then she jumped back as if shocked.

Faydon's whole body locked up, and I jerked, wanting to run and hide. But Dynel grabbed the scruff of my neck, holding me in place.

Faydon's body began to jerk as a horrific scream burst from his throat. The pixie's body arched, and the muscles in his neck and arms pulled tight as a steady glow of red light lit him up from the inside out. Something black and wet dripped from his eyes, and then his skin pulsed with an electric white light. Unable to see, I closed my eyes and turned my head away as the light grew and grew, followed by a horrible high-pitched squeal.

Then it was over.

The light disappeared, returning the shadows and stars once again into view. Slowly, I opened my eyes, staring at the dead pixie that now lay on the ground. His once pale pink skin was covered in a wet, black substance. It made me think of Lex's tar-like blood.

"Fuck!" Strayton yelled long and loud into the air.

Dynel's aggression grew, his meaty fists curling tight. Arian stepped back, carefully watching the enraged she-alpha.

"There's one more marked wolf," Strayton seethed. "There has to be. That's the only explanation." She looked desperate, scanning the red earth at her feet as if it might give her the answers she needed. Her eyes fell to a discarded pickaxe, then her expression shifted. Pure determination fixed her features, and she grabbed the worn handle. Then she turned and swung, burying the pointed metal just at the base of the star.

The air cracked as the star pitched forward, slipping easily from the rock. It fell with a soft thud at Strayton's feet. Her eyes went wide with excitement. I rested my head on my paws, interested to see how she planned on picking it up.

"Dynel!" Strayton snipped. "I need something to carry it in. Quick!"

Confusion pulling at his brows, the big alpha scanned the ground around them. Arian's mouth pulled into a tight line, and he took several steps away from the red crystal. For a moment, I thought he might run.

"Pick it up!" Strayton turned on the beta, pointing at her prize. "I'm not leaving here without it."

A wash of defeat flitted across Arian's face before his shoulders fell. "Yes, ma'am." He moved quietly to Faydon's dead body, then jerked at the pixie's shirt. The dirty black fabric stuck to his pale skin, leaving smears of black blood in its wake.

"Don't even think about running," Strayton snarled at me, her chest heaving and eyes glowing red.

"Help me, Dynel," Arian sighed, moving to the star.

The massive alpha stood at the beta's back, waiting for his instructions. "How?" he gritted out.

Arian spread the shirt flat, then using his dagger, he pushed the glowing crystal. "Grab something to help me move it."

Strayton pushed the pickaxe into Dynel's hands, moving excitedly to the side. "Hurry," she whispered. "I'm eager to leave."

Dynel grunted his understanding, then he got to work, carefully pushing the star into the center of the shirt. Arian picked up the very corners of the shirt, gently tying them around the metal curve of the pickaxe.

"That should do," Arian stood, motioning for Dynel to lift it off the ground. It swayed, the light muffled within the dark fabric.

"Arian," Strayton stood a little taller as she scanned the ruins. I swallowed hard, the motion making more blood push from my wounds. "The moment we get home, I want this rogue questioned."

"Yes, ma'am." Arian bowed his head.

Strayton moved to my side, glaring down at my wolf-form. "If you don't tell my men what I want to know, I'll have you killed, skinned, and stuffed." Her wicked smile returned as she purred, "You're pelt would be so lovely in front of my fireplace."

I bared my fangs at her, unable to do much more.

Arian kept his head down, not moving until she marched off.

Dynel stayed on she-alpha's heels, holding the pickaxe out to keep it from touching his big body.

I settled in my spot, watching Strayton's black hair disappear from my view. It was just so quiet and cold, but I waited, trying to figure out how the hell to get back to my mate.

In Lex's Arms

Tzidal

GROGGY AND A BIT DISORIENTED, I rolled my head to the side, trying to see where we were. It was still night, but the familiar buildings and storefronts told me we were back in the market near the main gate.

"Where are we going?" I mumbled against Lex's shoulder.

"I'm finding you help," he said, picking up his pace.

Fear roiled in my gut, followed by a deep vicious cramp. Then to my absolute horror, slick pushed out of my entrance, soaking my black pants. My whole body shook, and I clawed at Lex's shoulders, trying to remain calm, but how could I?

I was in heat, and my mate was nowhere in sight. If an alpha crossed our paths, they would surely fight Lex for me. Hurt me. Violate me. And I'd probably beg for more.

Hot tears poured down my cheeks, and I muffled a sob, trying not to make too much noise.

"Fuck," Lex gritted out as his fingers curled into my slick-soaked pants. "Is that what I think it is?"

Another wave of pain pushed away my embarrassment and fear. I grunted and shook, trying like hell to keep from screaming out loud.

Lex adjusted me in his arms as he rushed onto a porch, then pounded loudly on the front door. The sound echoed up and down the empty streets, making me shiver again, but this time with fear. If the sound woke any alphas, and they found me in heat....

"I need help!" Lex yelled at the weathered door, slamming his fist even harder. A lavender and sage wreath shook, and I pushed my nose into Lex's neck, trying to hide. "HELP!"

The doorknob rattled, and a quick gust of air fanned across my back as the door swung open. "What the hell do you want?" A man's voice gritted out. I couldn't see his face, but I already knew he wasn't a wolf-shifter. He smelled too plain. Human. Maybe a witch.

"My omega is in heat," Lex said in a rush of words as he hitched me up higher in his arms. "Please, I need help...." he took a deep breath, trying to keep his voice down, "...we don't live here. I have nowhere else to take her." The fear in his voice caught me off guard.

"I'm not a healer."

The man's tone was hard and unforgiving. "I don't do omegas."

Another burst of pain ripped through me, and my back instinctively arched from the force of it. My breath caught, and I opened my mouth, filling the market with a vicious, pained scream.

"Please!" Lex begged.

"I recommend getting her out of here before you wake the whole city." The man's voice edged softer. "They'll rip her to pieces."

Lex's hand disappeared from my back, slapping against the door. "I have something to trade for your help."

A light turned on above the store across the street, and a curtain fluttered. A blonde beta moved on the other side of the glass, narrowing her eyes at me. She looked young, maybe nine or ten. Did she have an alpha father inside there? Could he smell me?

"What do you have?" the man asked, his tone lifting with interest.

Lex swallowed hard, then he whispered, "Siren feathers."

The little girl pressed her forehead to the windowpane, staring right at me. Could she tell there was something wrong?

"Are you...." the man took a step closer, the heat from his slight body warming my back. I wanted to hiss at him to back up, but we needed his help. "Come in," the man ordered, stepping to one side.

Lex rushed into the tiny shop, not stopping until he reached the counter on the far end. The dark room was filled with little jars, wooden boxes, and lush green plants flowing from their pots and onto the floor. It reminded me of the witch's home in the willow tree.

"Where...who?" I tried speaking, but my words were slurred, too muffled for anyone to make out.

"It's okay, puppy," Lex caressed my back, holding me tighter. Fear permeated his usually soft scent, sticking to the back of my throat. It made my already terrified wolf whimper loudly.

"Prove you're a siren," the man said in a low and cautious tone. "I need proof."

Lex turned his body as if to shield me from the man, but it allowed me to finally see him. He was short, maybe my height, with wild gray hair. It stuck up in all directions, making him look more like a feral animal than a human being.

Warmth pushed from Lex's chest as some part of his form

shifted—I assumed his face. I wanted to tip my head up to see what he was doing, but I was too busy concentrating hard on not screaming. The twist of pain in my sex was like nothing I had ever felt before.

"Yes," the man's voice came out breathy and excited. "I'll help you, siren. But I want five feathers."

Lex stiffened, and his arms tightened around my back. "I'll give you one."

The man's mouth pulled tight, clearly not happy. "Five, or you can find someone else to help her. I'm sure there are plenty of alphas out there that would love to ease her pain." His eyes narrowed, his true meaning making my wolf whine and yowl within me.

"Please," I whined, my chin quivering. *I needed Joon.*

"Three," Lex snarled, "and you help her first."

"Three?" The man scratched his chin, thinking it over.

Lex's voice dropped to a dangerous whisper, "And if you hurt her or screw us over in any way, I'll feast on your corpse until there's nothing left for your mother to mourn."

"That's fine," the man said with a dismissive wave of his hand. "Three?" He extended his hand, waiting to shake Lex's.

"I give you my word," Lex shook his hand, sealing his promise.

"This way, siren." The man cut around us, heading into the back of the shop.

Lex followed, but his posture was tight. Too tight. "My name is Lex," he whispered. "It's probably best you not call me siren in case anyone overhears."

The man's big hazel eyes widened as if realizing how true that was. "Excellent point, siren." He snorted, flashing a toothy grin. They were slightly yellow, showing his obvious age. "I mean Lex." His brows shot up with restrained excitement.

I was used to people screaming in terror when they saw

Lex or bowing up for a fight. This man's reaction was so...odd. He had to be a witch. They were all so weird.

"Come," he barked, waving for Lex to follow him into a little office. A lantern sat on a cluttered desk, casting a dim glow over the small space. "My name is Lonzie," he pointed to a narrow cot in the corner, "and while I've never treated an omega already in heat, I've had several of your kind visit my shop over the years."

"Are you a witch?" I asked as Lex laid me on the cot. The pillow smelled almost spicy, like cloves and pine.

"I am, gentle wolf." He smiled wide. His two front teeth overlapped, making him look somehow younger. "When did your heat start?"

Sweat bloomed across my forehead, and I hissed, curling into a tight ball. My pussy felt so open and wet as that familiar feeling took hold. Any second now, I was going to be begging to be fucked by anyone with a cock or an eager tongue.

"Lex," I hissed, squeezing my eyes shut tight.

"She's been achy for a few days," Lex said, falling to his knees beside me. His gentle hands caressed my back and shoulders, trying to soothe me. "But she didn't start slicking until just now."

Lonzie nodded, scratching the gray stubble on his chin. "Okay," he mumbled as if in thought, moving his intense hazel eyes over my face. "I might be able to help." Then he turned and rushed back into his shop.

Lex watched him, looking almost pained as the witch disappeared. "It's going to be okay, Tzi." He patted my back. "It's going to be okay."

I sucked in a quick breath, trying not to scream. Everything hurt. My stomach, my head, my sex. Everything pulsed with a sharp stabbing pain that could only be cured with one thing: an alpha.

"I need Joon," I whimpered, my voice thick with emotion. "Please, help me. I need Joon."

"I know," Lex turned to me, placing several kisses along my temple and cheek. "Is there anything I can do to help?" He pulled his mouth into a firm line, then he grimaced. "I could take his form and—"

"No!" I snapped, a little disgusted at the thought of lying with anyone other than my mate. "Only Joon. I need *only* Joon."

"It was only a suggestion," Lex whispered, smoothing the hair from my face. "I never even met an omega until you, so this isn't exactly something I know how to handle."

I tried to nod, but all I could manage was a deep grunt of pain as I pulled my knees to my chest, hugging tightly.

"Open up, omega." Lonzie suddenly appeared at my side. He held a dark yellow gem to my lips, waiting for me to obey. Not sure what else to do, I slowly parted my lips, and he popped it into my mouth. "That's a good girl," he praised, speaking to me as if I were a pup.

"What was that?" Lex asked, turning to watch the witch work.

"Citrine." Lonzie dropped a few herbs into an old mug, tearing a few leaves and then crushing them with a blunt stick. "It'll ease the pain while I fix her tea." He paused, examining his mixture.

The base of my spine tightened, and I sucked hard at the gem on my tongue. It was smooth and slippery, but it tasted like nothing.

"Is it helping?" Lex pushed the hair out of my sweaty face, then he blew, trying to cool my heated skin.

"I think so," I whispered, noticing that the cramping had slowed, not as sharp. "Maybe."

"Drink this, omega." Lonzie slipped his hand under the back of my head, forcing me to sit. "It's hot, but it has to be.

Just drink it fast, and don't swallow that gem. Keep it on your tongue."

The steam from the cup wafted into my face as I prepared myself to drink. This was going to burn.

And it did.

My eyes stung with tears as boiling water rushed across my tongue and down my throat. It seared my sensitive flesh, making the gem heat in the pocket of my cheek. The second I drained the cup, I doubled over, coughing hard into my lap. The gem flew from my mouth, landing with a soft thump on the worn blanket.

Closing my eyes, I tried to focus on my body, eager to see if the tea worked, and the effect was almost instant. The stabbing cramps in my stomach slowed, and the spasms in my lower back eased.

"Feathers." Lonzie wasted no time, holding up a pair of sharp pruning shears.

"Eager?" Lex snipped, rubbing my upper arms as I tried like crazy to slow my breath. My tongue was raw, my mouth flooded with spit.

"I don't want you going back on your word." Lonzie pulled a wooden chair right next to Lex and patted the seat. "Three feathers." He gave the siren a pointed look, reminding him of their agreement.

Lex pushed out a long sigh, then stood. "Fine." He sat with his back to me. "But my omega cuts them."

Lonzie's weathered face scrunched at the idea, not happy. "Don't you dare try to trick me," he whispered harshly. "I did what you asked. I fixed her," he jabbed a finger at me, "and I—"

"Calm down, old timer," Lex groaned. He looked tired. Worn. "I'd just prefer a friend to do something so personal."

Lonzie stared at me for a moment, his hazel eyes drifting between me and Lex. Finally, he nodded, handing me the shears. "Three," he held out the appropriate number of fingers. "And clip them just at the skin. I want the full stock."

It took everything in me not to gag at his instructions, but I forced myself to sit. Slick gushed from my sex, but the deep ache was gone. Whatever the witch had given me seemed to have worked.

I sat, tucking my feet under me. Then I smoothed my hand over Lex's back as he leaned forward. His intricately decorated robes flashed brightly then the fabric seemed to melt away between his shoulder blades. Pale white skin appeared, then slowly withered, going a deep gray as tiny, rough feathers pushed out along his spine.

It felt so wrong to cut them. They were a part of Lex, the same as cutting off a finger or toe.

As if sensing my apprehension, Lex whispered, "It's okay, puppy. Just do it quickly."

I pulled in a deep breath, then gripped one of the feathers. It was firm, with a thick stock and soft wispy hairs. Feeling the thick stock attached deeply to his skin. I hesitated, wishing like crazy I didn't have to do this.

Lex said nothing as I brought the sheers up, positioning them right up against his skin. Then in one swift movement, I snipped, cutting the tiny appendage from his skin. Lex jerked, and black blood seeped from the rough, broken nub. I placed the feather on the bedding, and Lonzie rushed to it, holding it as if it were a precious jewel.

"Towel," I snapped, watching in horror as blood rolled down Lex's back in thick globs.

"No," Lex gritted out between pants. "Just finish it. Quickly."

I immediately grabbed another feather, this one smaller, and sliced it as fast as possible, making Lex grunt. Lonzie practically ripped it from my hands, holding both feathers protectively to his chest.

"One more," Lonzie said, eyeing Lex. The length of the siren's back was streaked with black, his blood clumping. "We agreed on three."

"Please." I tried to keep my voice calm and even, but inside I was ready to kill this witch for wanting to so eagerly hurt my friend even if it was a fair trade. "Won't two do? He's in so much pain."

Lonzie's eyes narrowed, and his grip on his feathers tightened. "You promised," he snarled at Lex.

"Tzidal," Lex panted as he turned his head slightly to look over his shoulder. "Please. One more. Just make it quick."

Lonzie's mouth pulled into a tight line, clearly eager to have the last of his promised prize.

Defeated, I placed my hands on either side of Lex's spine, trying to gather the courage to cut the last feather. My eyes drifted from the bleeding stocks to my blue pearl. It dangled from the leather strap around my wrist, shimmering in the dim light.

"What about this?" I held my arm out to the witch, hoping the stunning bracelet would entice him. I had never seen another pearl in my travels and hoped it was rare. "It's from the northern sea and can't be found in this part of Havre."

"Tzidal," Lex straightened his back, then jerked as blood dripped from his wounds. "Don't—" He sucked in a harsh breath, panting hard.

"Don't move." I placed my hand on his shoulder, keeping him in place. "How about it, Lonzie?" I held my wrist up higher, turning it slightly so he could see it shimmer. "My pearl for the last feather?"

Narrowing his eyes, the witch leaned down, examining it. "Maybe," he hummed. "Take it off. I need to make sure it's real."

I immediately pulled at the leather bindings, handing the bracelet over. Cool air hit my skin, and sorrow shimmered into my gut. My first mate, Korban, gave me that pearl right before he was killed, and I had worn it every day since. It felt wrong to give it up, but it was even more wrong to force Lex to suffer.

"Two feathers and the pearl?" Lonzie's hazel eyes narrowed, waiting for me to agree.

"Deal." I gave him a firm nod.

The old witch smiled, pleased. "You can sleep here if you want. Those herbs should keep your heat at bay for a few days at the most. Keep that citrine, though," he pointed at the yellow gem, "it might let you at least ignore some of your symptoms for a bit."

I grabbed the gem, pushing it into my pocket. "Thank you," I stood, kneeling next to Lex so I could see both his face and back. His complexion was ashen white, and his eyes were fully black. "How about we lay down?" I whispered, smoothing my hand through his fluffy white hair.

"Yes." he forced a smile, straightening his back a bit. More thick blood seeped, but then just as quickly, the stream stopped, and the mess faded away as the fabric of his robes consumed his back, hiding his injury.

"I'll get you another blanket," Lonzie eyed Lex's back before stepping out of the office. He took his feathers and the pearl with him.

A pained grunt pushed from Lex's throat. He was breathing hard, and I resisted the urge to rub his back. Surely the wounds were still there, just not visible. Instead, I ran my fingers through his hair, trying to push all my love for him into the air.

"Thank you," I whispered, pressing my lips to his temple. "Thank you, my friend."

Lex's long fingers wrapped around my now naked wrist, feeling the smooth skin with his thumb. "You shouldn't have parted with it. It was from your mate."

I shrugged, trying to make light of it. "I still have my memories of Korban. He didn't take those."

Lex's lips lifted into a pained smile, and he leaned forward, resting his forehead on mine. "We'll find Joon."

I grabbed his hands, squeezing gently. "I know." Thick emotion tightened my throat, but I forced it away.

Now wasn't the time for tears.

"We'll find Joon, and then we'll get the hell out of here before your heat picks back up." Lex lifted his head, looking deeply into my eyes. Then he pulled a face, grimacing. "Because I really don't want to have to fuck you."

"Me too," I pretended to gag. "Unless," I held up a finger, giving him a playful look, "can you turn into a dragon shifter? I've heard they have the sexiest smiles and a very impressive wingspan."

Lex snorted and rolled his eyes. "If I had to," he let out an exaggerated sigh, "I guess I could fuck you while breathing fire."

"It's the only way I'd let you mate me," I pulled him onto the bed, snuggling up against his side. Lex immediately melted against me, completely exhausted.

But I laid awake, thinking about Blue and Joon and even Byriel.

I prayed they were all okay and we'd find them soon.

Laying Next To The Door

Byriel

BLUE WAS in the cell across from me.

My omega.

My love.

My mate.

Did I imagine his face?

Was he really here?

My heart thundered, and my wolf jerked awake, feeling restless and alive for the first time in days. Could this be a dream?

I sat up, then examined my chains. The barbs dug deep into my wrists, making fresh blood coat my arms every time I flexed my fingers. Scooting a little closer to the small lantern, I looked over the sturdy metal locked around my wrists. While the cuffs appeared unyielding, the chained links that secured me to the wall were rusted and worn.

"This is good," I whispered to myself, scanning the small

cell for any tool I could use to pry them open. But there was nothing except the bread and water Tibbit had left me. I stood, making my chains clank and rattle.

If I was going to get out of here, I'd need my strength.

I quickly unwrapped the brown paper, then took a big bite of the bread. It was stale and tough, but a bit of sweetness lingered on my tongue as I devoured the entire thing in two bites, filling my empty belly. Then I drank deeply, finishing my water just as quickly. My wolf stretched out within me, feeling stronger already, but my stomach cramped, struggling to accept the scraps of food after being empty for so long. I ignored the stabbing sensation, determined to focus instead on my mate.

But Blue wasn't my mate. *Not yet.*

I gathered my chains, ensuring I had plenty of slack while I worked. Examining the metal links, I realized there was only one that had previously been cut and reforged...and it was right next to my cuffs. I would probably cut myself, weakening my wolf all over again, but I didn't have a lot of options.

Taking a deep breath, I sat down and then focused all my attention on the metals in my hands, trying to pry the weakened link apart. It didn't budge. So I pulled harder, making my weak arms ache and sweat bloom across my brow.

"Fuck," I snarled quietly. Panting hard, I relaxed my arms, trying to think of a better plan. "They forged you well," I stared at the link, realizing I might have better luck slipping the cuff off like a bracelet. It was sure to slice my skin all to hell and would probably mangle my hands, but I wasn't sure what else to do.

Then I heard it.

The softest sniffle hit my ears, followed by the scent of tears. Blue's tears. He was so scared and all alone, and I was fucking around with a pathetic piece of chain.

Fierce determination ripped through me. I gripped the

shackle secured around my wrist, then I pulled. The barbs pushed hard into my flesh, scraping bone as they slowly inched their way down over my knuckles. It hurt, sending waves of hot pain up my arms and deep into my chest.

Then with one last tug, the damn thing slipped free, falling with a loud clang onto the stone floor.

I instinctively held my wounded hand to my chest, cradling it while I tried to focus on reigning in the fierce pain. I cleared my mind and rocked back and forth, breathing deeply through my nose and exhaling through my mouth.

I could control this.

I could focus and push past this pain...for Blue.

Once my heartbeat settled, I allowed myself to look at my wounds.

It wasn't as bad as it felt. Deep cuts exposed a bit of bone along my knuckles, bleeding freely, but I could still move my fingers.

"One more." I closed my eyes, then wrapped my mangled hand around the other shackle. My skin burned, and the tendons in my wounded hand screamed as I tugged, ripping the flesh right off my other wrist, but I was free. "Fuck," I spat as I leaned over, pressing my forehead to the cold ground.

The food in my belly churned, and my mouth flooded with saliva. I focused all my attention on breathing, praying it would calm my stomach. I couldn't afford to lose the only meal I had eaten in over a week.

"It's okay," I whispered to myself, then I smiled. "I must be losing my mind," I straightened my back, trying to stretch out my stiff muscles. "I'm talking to no one."

"Hello?" Blue whispered. "Is...is someone there?"

His lovely voice was like a balm for my soul, seeping into my skin and soothing all my ails.

Worried someone might have overheard us talking, I rushed to the door, pressing my ear against the heavy wood.

There were no sounds of guards patrolling or other prisoners moving about, just the awful silence that consumed this part of the prison—the solitary cells.

"Blue?" I whispered, hoping he wouldn't yell or scream once he realized it was me. "Omega, are you okay?"

A swift gasp pushed from his cell, then feet padded across stone. "Byriel?" he whispered excitedly. "Alpha? Is that really you?"

I wanted to laugh out loud and yell from the rooftops. *He was actually here.*

"It's really me, omega," I assured him, keeping my voice soft and even. I hoped he'd mimic my tone and know to stay quiet. "Are you hurt?"

"No," he said even softer, making me smile. "I was so scared we'd never find you."

"Is Omega Tzidal with you?" I asked, knowing they weren't, but perhaps they were close.

"I lost them in the city. We were being chased, and I ran up ahead and lost them." He went quiet, then sniffled. "It was my fault. I shouldn't have run like I did. I always run when I get scared."

"It's okay," I whispered, wishing like hell I could hold him. "I'm sure they're safe." I prayed he believed me. My need to soothe him was so fucking intense. "I'm going to get you out of here," I promised. "I'm going to get both of us out of here."

"Are you okay?" Blue asked. "Did they...hurt you?"

I glanced at my mangled hands and thin stomach. I had only been chained up for a week or so, but without any food or water, I was already wasting away. It was hard to kill an alpha in such a way, but given enough time, it was an effective and painful death.

"I'm okay," I lied, and my wolf growled at me. He hated that I wasn't being honest with our future mate, but my beast didn't understand how fragile Blue was right now. Once I got both of us out of here, I'd lay myself completely open for him to see. *I'd never lie to him again.*

He deserved to know all the horrible things I've done.

"What are you thinking?" Blue's soft voice pulled me from my thoughts.

I let out a heavy sigh, looking at my shredded hands. A few strips of flesh dangled from the sides of my wrists, flashing hot with deep pain. Until they healed, my hands were pretty much useless.

"I'm not sure how to get out of here without making too much noise," I finally said. "Do you by any chance know what time it is?"

"No."

I pulled my lips into a tight line, careful not to make any sound. The last thing I wanted was for Blue to think I was frustrated with him, but without knowing what time it was, I didn't know how many guards were on shift.

"Please talk to me," my omega whispered. "I can tell something is wrong."

"I'm just thinking," I said softly. "Just thinking." I glanced once again at the dark stone walls looking for a loose brick or... I didn't know what. Hell, I didn't even have a stitch of clothing.

"If I could get my door open...." Blue whispered even softer, "Would it be hard to open your door? Would I need a key?"

"No," I said, hopeful. "For these cells, only a pin secures it to the ground because the prisoners are always chained up. Why?" I pressed my ear to the door, listening for any indication that told me he was escaping. "Do you think you can get your door open?"

"Maybe." But a lift in his voice made it sound like more of a question. "What if it makes a lot of noise?" he asked, uneasy.

I pressed my palms flat to the door, trying to push my trust and love to him. We weren't bonded, and it wasn't going to work, but dammit, I was going to do it anyway. "I know these prisons like the back of my hand, Blue," I whispered. "If you can open your door. I can get us out of here. I can promise you that."

"Okay," he whispered, then pulled in a long, soft breath.

Silence hummed in my ears as I listened, hearing nothing but the wind pushing at the old prison walls. I opened my mouth to ask if anything was wrong, but then the air warmed, and the hairs along my forearms rose. Something electric pulsed all around me, and I carefully stepped away from the door.

The energy that flowed all around me was scary and soothing at the same time. It was as if Blue was dancing in the air, filling the whole room with his lovely, fresh scent.

Then all at once, a deafening boom echoed all around me, followed by something heavy slamming into my cell door. The hinges on my door groaned, and the ground shook, filling my cell with bits of falling ceiling and musky dirt.

I blinked repeatedly, trying to keep the dust surrounding me from getting into my eyes.

"Blue?" I rushed to the cracked door, trying to pull it open, but it was still secured. I immediately dropped to the floor and pushed open the metal plate.

Blue's door was gone. Nothing but fragments of metal and wood covered the ground. I narrowed my eyes through the smoke, finally making out my omega. He was on his hands and knees, crawling toward me. What looked like ash covered his pale face, making him look as if he had just rolled around in a fire pit.

"Byriel?" Blue panted hard as he continued to crawl.

"I'm right here, mate!" I yelled. The guards would surely be coming any second. *I needed him to hurry.* "Come open my door, my love. Come quickly."

Blue's head fell forward, but his knees kept pushing through the debris. His hands reached for something just out of my view, then he jerked up and fell backward, collapsing with the pin to my door in his hands.

I jumped up and wrenched the cell door wide open.

The warning bell sounded, clanging loudly overhead, telling all the guards nearby that a prison break was possible.

I bent and pulled open Blue's robes, looking for the charm I gave him. It would allow me to shift, despite the wolfsbane that filled these halls. My heart sank, and my wolf snarled. *He didn't have it.*

"That's okay," I said to myself as I scooped Blue up in my arms. "It's okay, my love. I've got you." My back strained, and my knees threatened to buckle as I lifted the tiny omega. *I was so fucking weak.*

Heavy footsteps filled the corridor, and I spun, knowing the guards would be here any second. There was only one entrance in and out of this prison wing, but I grew up in this city. I lived in the kitchens, the sparring grounds, and even the trenches—anywhere to escape my father, *including the storm drains.*

I spun and ran as fast as I could deeper into the prison. Loud voices called out after me, demanding I stop. I tucked my unconscious mate to my chest, then sprinted around a corner, racing to the furthest hallway.

While still holding Blue, I gripped the small wrought iron grate at my feet, then heaved. It almost slipped from my bloody fingers, but the hurried footsteps of guards filled me with intense determination. I let out a vicious growl as I pulled, lifting the iron grate free.

Trying to be as careful and quick as possible, I lowered Blue into the hole, stretching my arms all the way down. I said a short prayer. Then I dropped him.

All the breath whooshed out of me as Blue slipped into

the darkness, disappearing from my view. I immediately forced my feet into the hole after him, grabbed the iron grate, then forced it back in its place as I fell in after Blue.

The drop was swift and short, and I was thankful when I didn't land on my mate.

"Byriel?" Blue mumbled, lolling his head from one side, then the other.

The puddle of icy water beneath him was shallow but it still soaked his green robes, and the air was freezing. I wanted to hold him, but I couldn't risk making any sound.

I pressed my still-bloody hand over the omega's mouth, and his eyes flew open. Fear flooded his expressive eyes, but it quickly faded as he focused on my face. I pressed a finger to my lips, then pointed up.

"Where the fuck did they go?" An angry voice boomed above us. It was Bracken, and the beta sounded pissed.

A small cut of light flickered through the holes in the grate as a lantern came into view. Blue went stiff beneath me, not moving a muscle.

"Are you sure he went this way?" a she-alpha barked.

My ears pricked at the familiar voice, and I turned my head to hear better.

"How the fuck did he just up and fucking vanish?" the she-alpha growled low in her chest.

It was Jonelle. An ally from Dane's camp.

Our last conversation slammed into me, and guilt rose in my throat. Jonelle had been desperate for me to take the throne from my sister, and I yelled at her, shaming her for the things she said.

"We have to fucking find them!" Jonelle roared. She was a friend, but was also trying to keep her cover. If they found us down here, I wasn't confident the she-alpha would be able to save Blue from whatever punishment Strayton would dish out.

"Perhaps the explosion pulled a wall free," an unknown alpha said, his tone unsure. He sounded young. "Maybe he didn't turn here, but—"

"Her majesty wants to visit her brother in the morning," Jonelle barked.

Even though I couldn't see her, I could imagine Jonelle's tight expression. Her anger always seemed exaggerated by her spiky black hair and massive form. *The she-alpha was a beast when she needed to be.*

"I want every guard searching this entire fucking prison right now!" Jonelle ordered. "I want the city searched and the border patrolled. Find Byriel before the Queen has all our heads!"

"Yes, ma'am!" A course of voices boomed, then heavy boots pounded the stone once again.

"Alpha," Bracken said in a soft, respectable tone. "I don't want to argue, but I saw him run down here. We need to start the search within the prison. If Byriel—"

A low, rumbling growl vibrated the air, followed by the sharp stench of rage. "Where should I search, *beta*?" Jonelle's voice was a dangerous whisper. "The walls? The floor? How about the fucking ceiling?"

"It's not...." Bracken paused, letting out a frustrated sigh. "I didn't mean—"

"What *did* you mean?" Jonelle snapped. "Because as far as I can see, I have a senior guard standing in front of me, refusing to look for a traitor on the run. Is there a reason you don't want to search for Byriel?"

The silence that followed was thick with tension, making Blue's bottom lip quiver. He was so sensitive to other's emotions. Gentle and kind, not one to listen while others suffered.

Not sure what else to do, I pressed my forehead to his, wishing I could purr for him.

"I'm sorry to have overstepped, alpha." Bracken's tone was tight. Offended. "I'll immediately join the rest of the men and begin looking."

"Good," Jonelle snapped.

"Jonelle!" someone yelled down the hall. "We've found how they escaped!"

A single set of feet moved, turning the corner before disappearing into the chaos of noise in the distance. Blue shifted beneath me, but I shook my head. There was at least one more person above us, waiting quietly.

"It's shit nights like this that make me wish I worked in the greenhouse," Jonelle whispered as if talking to herself. "Not enough people visit the gardenias." The she-alpha stood completely still, then, moving very slowly, she began to walk, strolling down the hall and into the distance.

The Palace

᠀

Joon

TWO TARGON ELVES, an elder omega, and the already rotting corpse of an alpha were chained to the walls all around me.

I stared at the elves' pale green skin covered in dark bruises, trying to figure out what they had done to be chained up *inside* the palace with me. Usually, when other creatures offended our kind, we just killed them. It wasn't unusual to see a Targon elf chained up, they were vicious and cunning. A threat to my kind. But they weren't something you normally saw in a were-village, let alone a palace.

Trying to distract myself from the growing fear in my gut, I stared at the intricate tapestry at the end of the large room. It was the only piece of art in the whole vast room. The embroidery showed a bold black wolf with its fangs bared and claws ready to attack. The intricate thread work was impressive, clearly meant to remind everyone here that shifters were mighty and vicious.

Restless, I gave the long, empty room another look, trying to find something that could be used as a weapon. But there was nothing in the long empty room but chains on the walls, dying elves, and a small table next to the only door. Even the ceiling was steepled, and the few windows were situated high up all the walls. Too high for escape. If it weren't for the elves chained to the walls, I'd swear this was a temple of some kind.

"Tibbit," Strayton said to an elderly beta while glaring down at me. Her glossy lips curled with disgust. "Make him shift."

The beta's bright blue eyes widened as he turned to her. "How, My Queen?" His long gray beard bobbed as he talked, the tip swaying just at his waist. "Is there a way to force an alpha back into their human form?"

Exhausted, I laid my big furry head on my paws, trying to move as little as possible. The journey back through the gate was harsh, popping my joints and squeezing my still-raw wounds to the point that they were once again bleeding freely. But I was hopeful the tight collar around my neck was helping. Strayton clearly thought it was demeaning to have me locked up like a dog, but the added pressure to my injury felt good.

Arian stepped forward, narrowing his eyes at me. He looked as if I were a complete mystery. "I think the real question is *how* is he in his wolf-form with so much wolfsbane in the hall?" He pointed to the only table right next to the door. A small bundle of dark purple flowers sat in a vase, the petals wilting and falling onto an intricate box just next to it. It seemed no one was tending to the wolfsbane now that the King was dead.

"It only prevents an alpha from shifting into their wolf."

Strayton rolled her eyes, acting as if Arian were a simpleton. "It doesn't force a wolf to shift back into their human."

"Perhaps the witch can help?" Tibbit whispered, clearly trying to keep his advice quiet in the presence of Arian. Strayton's eyes widened, clearly liking that idea. "In the morning—"

"No. *Now*." She cut a hard glare at Arian. "Find out the status of my brother."

Arian bowed his head. "I'll have someone—"

"No!" Strayton barked, stepping a little closer to the guard. Her long red robes brushed over the cold stone, exposing one long, toned leg. "I want *you* to find out."

Arian's brows pulled together with confusion. "My Queen?" His dark eyes flickered to me. "I don't feel comfortable leaving you with this rogue without proper—"

"Go!" Strayton barked, her fierce energy filling the vast empty room and bouncing off the walls.

Arian's jaw clenched, but he moved, walking briskly across the empty room and out the door. I stole a glance just before the door shut behind him, noticing three guards standing at attention in the hallway. I was sure there were more.

"Tibbit," Strayton turned on the elderly beta.

Tibbit lifted his head a little higher, but his back remained hunched. It seemed he couldn't straighten his spine at all. "Yes, My Queen."

"Bring me Yasha," Strayton crossed her arms, pushing out her impressive cleavage. "Take the passageway. I don't want anyone to see her."

"Yes, My Queen." Tibbit gave a jerky bow before walking toward the tapestry at the far end of the room. His withered fingers gripped the colorful fabric, then he pulled, disappearing behind it and into the wall.

There was another exit.

"I assume you're with the alliance." Strayton strolled toward the only door, pausing next to the vase of wilting wolfsbane. "The real question is, did you support my father or my brother? Because my father is dead, and my brother will soon join him." Strayton's full lips lifted into a vicious smile.

I tried like hell not to react, but I couldn't help the twitch in my upper lip, exposing the tip of my canines.

"So you support my brother." Strayton's face brightened, both happy and a little surprised. "But you said your mate was murdered *in the name of the King*." Her voice edged higher, mocking my words. "I assume your mate was a marked wolf?" Her dark eyes narrowed, watching my expression carefully. "You do know, my dear brother killed the marked wolves. Right? You support the alpha that murdered your love?"

A restless growl pushed from my chest, and claws curled into the ground. I knew *exactly* what Byriel was, and I'd never forgive him for what he'd done, but I no longer craved his blood. Byriel was a monster for what he did, but at least he felt like shit for it.

"What a fool." Strayton chuckled, lifting a small metal box off the side table. The sweeping design etched in the metal closely resembled vines, twisting and curling in a delicate pattern. "So, let me make sure I understand you," Strayton's voice was bright and teasing, "Your mate was killed by my *brother*, on my *father's* orders. So you decided to come here all the way from Casin, and kill *me* for something I had no part in?"

My muscles flexed, fighting the urge to bark and snarl at the wicked she-alpha.

Strayton laughed loud, the sound bouncing off the hollow walls and ceiling. "My brother did always attract simpletons."

Footsteps neared, and the tapestry fluttered. Tibbit appeared first, followed by a tall woman with long black hair. Her tattered blue dress and gray shawl were dusty and wrinkled. It looked as if she lived in a cupboard.

"You called for me?" the woman whispered. She looked

exhausted, with deep lines etched around her mouth and between her brows.

"Yes," Strayton flashed her eyes at me with an excited smile. "Yasha," she turned to the human witch. "Thank you for joining me."

Yasha's mouth pulled tight, and she crossed her arms, making her shawl slip off one shoulder. "How can I help?" she asked flatly.

"I need this rogue to shift back into his human," Strayton waved her red nails in my direction, acting as if I were vermin that needed disposing of.

Yasha's vibrant green eyes narrowed at me. They seemed so bright compared to her black hair and pale features. She was older, with fine lines at the corners of her eyes, but she looked as if she hadn't smiled in years.

"I'll need a few things," Yasha whispered, eyeing the blood on my paws and scruff.

"Fine," Strayton rolled her eyes, annoyed at not immediately getting her way. "I also need your council on this." She held up the box.

Yasha tilted her head, curious, but she didn't move, staying firmly at Tibbit's side.

"I need to know why the star finally glows red, but still can't be handled," Strayton stalked toward the witch—a predator approaching her prey. She stopped right in front of the weary human, then lifted the lid to the box. "I need you to confirm that my suspicions are true."

The whole room warmed with the bright red glow of the star. It made me restless, moving my hind legs beneath me, wanting to run.

"Goddess, help us," Yasha whispered, her eyes wide with fear.

Strayton snapped the lift shut, groaning loudly. "Your *Goddess*," she said the word in a mocking tone, "can't help you.

The *Moon*, on the other hand, has blessed me for my patience." She brushed her long nails over the lid, caressing it like a pet. "But I need to know why I can't possess the power? Why does it keep killing those that touch it?"

Yasha's mouth hung open for a moment, clearly unsure what to say. "The prophecy was clear," she whispered, shaking her head slightly. "Kill the marked wolves, kill the King, possess the power."

"*And?*" Strayton snipped as if waiting for the witch to reveal something more. "What have you left out? What more do I need to do?"

Yasha bowed her head, then mumbled, "Marked children of the blushing Moon, their end to start it all. The dawn of—"

"I know what the fucking prophecy says!" Strayton roared, making the poor woman flinch.

A heavy fist pounded on the main door, making Tibbit jerk and spin to the sound.

Strayton closed her eyes, then pushed out a long, pained sigh. "Don't fucking move," she growled at Yasha, her dominant tone making the poor woman shiver.

The witch held her breath, not moving until the main door shut behind Strayton. "I don't know why the star isn't working." Yasha grabbed Tibbit's arm, her green eyes pleading with the elder beta. "I can only guess, and if she...if she—"

"It's okay," Tibbit whispered in a soft, fatherly voice. "Can you remember the whole thing?" He caressed her upper arms, angling his head to look into her eyes. "What's the prophecy say, my dear?"

Yasha's eyes drifted over the floor, thinking. Then she whispered,

> *Marked children of the blushing moon, their*
> *end to start it all*

*The dawn of a new era, sparks the reason for
the fall
Trust the blue path paved in grief, to free the
fractured King
Eight marked wolves, cursed and dead, so the
star can be free
Walk the lands, control the Fae, none more
powerful than he
A chosen wolf, to restore the lands, and set the
people free*

Tibbit's wiry gray brows shot upward, and his eyes went wide. "None more powerful than...*he*?"

Yasha took a careful step away from the elder, then nodded. "I...didn't...I had to lie... she'd kill me and—"

"It's okay," Tibbit said quickly, cutting a quick look at the main door.

"But what do I tell her?" Yasha's voice rose, her fear prickling my skin and making my joints ache. The scent was just so *thick*. "She's going to *demand* I tell her why she can't touch it. What do I say?"

"Just tell her all the marked wolves haven't been found," Tibbit whispered.

Deep rage burned through me, and I forced my wolf back, determined to have my voice heard. My copper fur receded, and my fangs pushed back as my naked human-form took hold.

Panting hard, I pushed my fists into the floor, forcing myself to sit. The slight movement made the collar around my neck pull, and blood dripped down my chest.

"Don't," I gritted out, struggling to catch my breath. "Don't tell her that."

Tibbit jerked at my words. It seemed he forgot I was here. "Do you have a better plan, rogue?"

"No," I growled low in my chest, "but if you tell her there's another marked wolf out there, she'll start killing innocent wolves just like her father."

Yasha bowed her head, pushing her palms hard into her eyes. I could scent her tears from here.

"Then what would you suggest?" Tibbit asked me, his voice surprisingly kind. "Because based on the *real* prophecy," he glanced at Yasha, his expression not nearly as angry as mine, "the chosen wolf to handle the star is a man."

"I don't give a shit what you tell her, old man," I snarled, too exhausted to be kind or gentle, "but if she begins attacking her own people, I'll rip your head off and pike it in the main square."

Tibbit's expression hardened, and eyes narrowed, but before he could speak, the main door burst open, and Strayton marched back inside.

The anger that flowed off her was suffocating, her dominance pulsing all around me. "Byriel has escaped," she snarled at the elder, but then her expression shifted as her eyes fell on me. And just like that, her face brightened. "My, my witch. You work fast." She stepped up to me, the metal box still clutched in her hands. "Honestly, I wasn't sure she'd be able to get you to shift."

"I wanted to be able to tell you to fuck off at least once before I die." I forced a tight smile, glaring at the she-alpha.

The corners of her smile fell, and her back straightened. "Say whatever you like, rogue," she tried to look lazy, unaffected, but the muscles in her jaw were too tight, "but soon, I'll possess all the magic and power of the fae." Her fingers curled around the box. "And then I'll strike down everyone that ever questioned me."

Two of the elves shifted on their chains, nervous.

I let out a mocking laugh, filling the vast room. "Too bad

that will never happen," I smirked. "Because the witch told me why that star won't work for you yet."

Yasha's eyes went wide, fear draining her face of all color.

"And why's that?" Strayton cocked an eyebrow.

"My....my Queen!" Tibbit stuttered, walking briskly toward me.

I tipped my chin, giving her the most challenging task I could think of. "Kill Byriel."

Strayton glared at me for a moment, then she slowly turned, glaring at the witch. "Is that true?"

Yasha's dark eyes moved to me, then she bowed her head and whispered, "Yes."

The Witch's Office

Tzidal

"TIME TO GET UP!" Lonzie's voice jerked me awake. "The sun is up, and it's time for you both to go."

Lex's warm body pressed into my side, curling around me and sucking me deeper into the small cot. "What time is it?" I asked, my voice rough with sleep.

"Just after dawn," Lonzie pulled the blanket off me, urging me to sit.

Lex groaned as I pulled myself out from under him, then swung my legs over the side of the tiny bed. It was freezing, the floor like ice against my once warm toes.

"I have to open up shop soon," Lonzie picked up my cup from last night, emptying the now-dried leaves into a small wastebasket. "I don't want you two here."

"That's awfully kind of you," Lex cut in a flat tone.

Lonzie glared at the siren. "Strangers invite questions that I have no interest in answering. Things are tense in Ossory right now, and I have no intention of choosing sides in this war." He pursed his lips, giving Lex a firm look. "Now go."

"We're going," I whispered as I stood, arching my back to stretch my stiff muscles. "Thank you for your help."

"Don't thank him." Lex sat with a sour look on his face. His fluffy white hair stuck up in all different directions. "He didn't do it to be kind," Lex snipped at me, then he narrowed his eyes at the witch. "I had to part with more than one piece of myself just to get you a cup of tea."

Lonzie sucked in an angry breath, his lined face squished with anger. "Feeling a bit of regret this morning, siren? Do you wish you had let your friend suffer?"

Lex jerked to a stand, but I grabbed his shoulder, keeping him from lunging at the human. "We're going," I said pointedly to Lex. "*Now*."

For a moment, Lex didn't move, his black eyes squarely on Lonzie's face. The witch tried to stand his ground, glaring right back, but then Lex opened his mouth, baring razor-sharp teeth.

"Careful there, witch," Lex hissed in a dangerously low tone. "I'm not a morning person."

Lonzie's throat worked as he swallowed hard. "You offered your feathers, and I accepted your terms." His voice was soft, his fear taking hold. "I didn't have to let you sleep here, either," he quickly added.

"And we thank you." I pulled at Lex's shoulder, urging him to walk, but he stayed firm, pushing his dominance into the room. "Go, you ass." I popped Lex's butt, practically shoving him.

"Enjoy my feathers," Lex snarled as he passed Lonzie.

The witch ducked his head, hunching his shoulders and shying away from us. I tried giving him a sympathetic smile, but he just pulled a face and turned completely away from me, too angry for my kindness.

"That went well," I said to Lex as we stepped onto the small porch. My breath came out in little puffs.

The sky was gray, the sun just barely breaking over the horizon. For some reason, it made the already freezing weather feel that much more chilling.

The streets were still empty and quiet, most of the city still asleep. I took in all the shops, then looked at the witch's shop behind us. A small sign hung just next to the door with a bundle of worn twigs and wilted wolfsbane pinned to it, with the words "*The Gathering Witch: Herbs and Healing*" burned into the wood.

I was thankful for Lex's quick thinking. I would have never thought of going to a witch for help in a wolf-city. I probably would have wandered around, looking for a healer, until my body gave out and my heat took hold.

"We need to find Joon first," Lex said, looking me up and down. Lex's voice was flat, still annoyed, "I can't imagine that tea lasting more than a day or two before your heat comes back."

I shook my head, striking down the idea. "We'll find Blue first. If my heat hits, I'll just deal with it."

Lex gave me a pained look. "Tzidal." His voice was laced with fear. "If you go into heat, I don't think I'll be able to fight off—"

"It'll be fine," I said firmly. "Let's get Blue. What was that place they took him to last night?"

"I can't be sure," he pushed out a long sigh, "but I think it was a prison."

I jerked at his words, grabbing his arm tight. "They took an *omega* to a *prison*? Would they put him with ...." I trailed off, unable to finish my thought.

"It's okay," Lex said, his eyes going soft around the edges. "I doubt they threw Blue in the stocks with all the other criminals. I'm sure they kept him separate." But I could see the fear in his eyes. He didn't know either.

The door of the small shop across the street opened, and a small bell chimed. A male beta stepped outside, placing a signboard right in front of his store. The second I read the prices he had listed for his freshly baked bread, my nose twitched, filled with the salty, soft aroma.

"I'm hungry," I whispered, placing my hand over my middle. It was a shameful thing to admit, especially with Blue locked up and Byriel and Joon still missing. But I was tired, hungry, and scared. I simply needed something in my hollow belly before we stormed the prison walls.

"Come on," Lex wrapped his long fingers around my wrist, holding me gently. "I know where you can eat."

"YOU LOOK TERRIFIED," Lex teased me in his overly child-like voice. He wore the face of a literal child, no more than ten or eleven, with dark red hair and vibrant freckles all over his cheeks, nose, and chin. Watching the siren shrink into this form was weird, but I had to give him credit—hiding as a young pup was very smart.

"I've never been to an omega den before," I shivered as the cozy building grew closer. My black servant's uniform wasn't nearly warm enough for this weather.

"Do omegas in your village not live in them?" Lex asked, his golden brown eyes wide with interest. I wasn't sure if it was his innocent face, or simply an act, but he looked so fascinated by what I had to say.

"We have a den, but a lot of the omegas in my village live with their parents until they're mated."

"That sounds boring," Lex circled his plump fingers

around mine. "How do you have a wild love affair when you have to come home to Mom and Dad?"

I rolled my eyes, fighting the urge to scold him for talking about love affairs while looking like a youngling.

"Good morning, friends," a sweet older omega greeted us as I took the tiny steps up to the den's porch. She was maybe in her mid-fifties, and her pale dress was covered in flour. "It's always nice to see new faces." She bent, placing her hands on her knees as she talked to Lex. "Is this your mommy?"

I pulled a face, trying not to look too offended. While I wasn't exactly a spring chicken, I definitely wasn't old enough to have a ten-year-old child.

"This is my mommy!" Lex cooed, gripping my forearm with both hands. I forced a smile, trying to look happy with my *'son'*. "She promised me something yummy for breakfast."

The kind omega chuckled sweetly at Lex, ruffling his red hair. "Sweet boy. We're always happy to help our neighbors."

My smile softened, more genuine. "Thank you," I said as we stepped past her and into the den.

The air inside the lush house was sweet and soft, filled with the floral notes of the omegas that lived here. I walked slowly, admiring the lush couches and throws as we made our way deeper into the den.

"Here for some breakfast?" A young male omega walked around us, then stopped and bowed. "We're always happy to meet new friends." His short black hair was neatly combed, and his beard was trimmed, complementing his striking features well.

"You have gorgeous eyes," Lex complimented the omega, leaning in a bit to better examine them. "So blue." He giggled in a flirty way, making me pinch his side.

"Calm down, son," I gave the siren a pointed look. "I'm sure this nice man has lots to do today."

"Jassin," the omega smiled sweetly, flashing beautiful

straight white teeth. He smelled so lovely. Like lavender soap. "And you are?" He extended his hand.

Not wanting to be rude, I slowly slipped my hand into his, then squeezed. "Tzidal."

"Tzidal?" He leaned in as he repeated my name, making sure he heard me correctly.

"Yes," I cut a quick glance around him. The aromas drifting from the kitchen smelled lovely, teasing my very empty stomach.

"I actually have something you might like, little man." Jassin smiled at Lex. "Would you like to see? Assuming it's okay with your mom," he quickly added, waiting for me to answer.

Lex's wide brown eyes met mine, making me smile. It might have been this child-like form, but he looked almost excited at the prospect of a surprise.

"Lead the way," Lex said brightly, when I didn't protest.

"I have to tell you, we don't get many visitors here," Jassin sauntered through the house. His black slacks hugged his hips, and his thin white shirt gave a scandalous view of his abs. This omega was built like none I had ever seen before.

Lex pushed onto his tiptoes and whispered in my ear, "If your heat hits before we find Joon. We should come here. Jassin seems *very* hospitable."

I cut him a glare, not amused.

"Right through here, little man," Jassin unlocked the door at the back of the den, holding it open for us.

I stepped through, then looked up and down the empty alleyway. There was nothing here but a few trash bins and some empty crates.

I shook my head, then turned back to the male omega. "I don't get it."

"Food is scarce enough as it is." Jassin crossed his arms, giving me an angry look. "If you want to leave your alpha, then return to your family. Don't take the food from the mouths of the elderly who don't have anyone left to care for them."

"*Leave my alpha?*" I narrowed my eyes at his words, confused as to why he would assume such a thing. "I'm not leaving anyone."

"There you are, *mate.*" Kenji's deep voice made my wolf tense, then snarl. *I hated him calling me that.*

"Well, fuck," Lex shot, glaring at the damn alpha. "I forgot he might be a problem."

"Thank you," Kenji bowed to the male omega. "I'm so glad you found my *mate* before she could hurt herself."

I turned to yell at Jassin for betraying his own kind, but the door slammed shut, leaving me with only a wreath of wolfsbane and wicker to glare at. "Asshole," I muttered under my breath.

"Lex?" Kenji's dark eyes drilled into the siren's boyish face, but Lex didn't answer. He just glared right back at the alpha. "And where is Blue?" Kenji craned his neck as if the young omega might be hiding in my back pocket.

"Prison," I said simply.

Kenji blinked repeatedly, trying to process what I just said. "*Prison?*"

"We were hoping to get a bit to eat before trying to break him out." I crossed my arms, giving the alpha a firm look.

"Treason is so much easier to commit with a full tummy," Lex smirked, his round cheeks looking extra squishy.

Kenji's big body stiffened, and anger flashed in his dark eyes. "*This* is why omegas can't be left alone." He jabbed a finger at the ground. "You run off, get in trouble, then an alpha has to save your ass."

"First of all," I straightened my back, ready to rip into the alpha, "I don't need you to save my ass. Second, I don't care for you calling me your mate," I snapped. "I'm not *your* mate, and it's disgusting to hear you call me that. I would never—"

"Calm the fuck down," he barked, acting as if my anger was ridiculous. "The only reason I keep calling you my mate, is because unaccompanied omegas get obducted and fucked. Pretending you're mine, keeps you safe. But trust me," he let out a tight, bitter laugh, "I'd *never* mate an omega like you."

"What the fuck does that mean?" My voice rose, not sure if I was relieved or offended.

Kenji's eyes flashed red. "You are stubborn, disobedient, and fucking reckless!" He took a step back, assessing me. "All I want in life is a meek male omega," he mumbled as if talking to himself. "Not some head-strong wench that doesn't know when to quit. You should be at home in your village, sending you mate loving thoughts through your bond. Not racing all over a dangerous city with the monarchy on the verge of falling apart."

I inhaled deeply, ready to tell Kenji to fuck right off, but before I could utter a single word, Lex's little foot swung forward, landing hard, right in Kenji's balls.

"Run!" Lex yelled, pumping his short legs with all his might, but I didn't even have to make it three steps before I knew we'd never outrun an alpha.

Kenji flew past me, slamming into Lex's tiny body and forcing both of them onto the ground. "Shift!" Kenji roared, pinning Lex's arms over his head.

"Get off me, you fucking animal!" Lex screamed.

"What in the name of all that is holy!" someone gasped just behind me.

I spun, taking in an elderly omega's horrified expression. His crooked fingers curled around the back door to the den as he took in the sight before him: *A massive alpha, pinning down a screaming child.*

"It's okay!" I held up my hands, praying the elder didn't scream for help. "He's just in trouble with...." I cut a quick look at Kenji over my shoulder, then forced out, "...his father."

Lex snorted somewhere behind me, but I ignored him.

"My apologies," I bowed low, praying the omega would leave us be.

"You and your mate need to get out of here." He put his hands on his hips, holding his elbows out wide. "They take strangers around this den *very* seriously."

"My apologies, omega." Kenji dragged Lex over to me. The siren continued to grunt and groan, trying to pull free. "We're leaving." He grabbed my wrist, then moved, not waiting for the elder to respond.

My stomach growled as we moved away from the aroma of spiced meats and fresh fruit. It seemed we'd have to fight off an army of guards on an empty stomach.

"I can't believe she thought I was your kid," Lex snorted, taking in Kenji's dark complexion, then his own pale, freckled skin.

"Shift." Kenji pulled the siren to a stop, blocking our view of the main street. "I don't like this..." he waved a hand just in front of Lex's face, "form."

I smiled, thinking about how Joon preferred Lex's usual form as well. Taking a moment, I searched out my mate in our bond, but he was quiet. His consciousness was there, but he was calm. Maybe sleeping?

Lex let out an annoyed huff, then rolled his eyes as his image melted away, the young man taking shape once again. "What is it about wolves and their need for the familiar?"

"Familiar is nice," I shrugged. "It's comforting."

"It's boring," Lex pursed his lips. "Once our little adventure is over, I'm going to wear a thousand different faces in just one afternoon."

Kenji shook his head, motioning us forward. The streets were busy now that the sun was fully up. Wolves of all status mingled and shopped, making their way to their work or to the market.

"I'm *not* going to Madra," I said firmly to Kenji's back as he walked ahead of us. "I'm saving my friends and my mate, and I have no interest in arguing with you on this."

Kenji spun on me. His fists curled tight. Nothing set an alpha off like a lower status challenging them, except maybe being interrupted. "I will help you find Blue." Kenji's fangs flashed as his voice dropped to a dangerous whisper, "Then I will take you to Madra. If I have to tie you up and carry you over my shoulder the entire fucking way, then so be it."

"Why do you care?" I yelled, making a few passersby slow, watching us with weary expressions, but I was too tired and hungry to care. "You don't know me. You don't know Blue. And you didn't know Joon. What does it matter?"

"I made a promise," Kenji lowered his head, looking hard into my eyes. "I might not have any great purpose within the..." he paused, glancing from one side to the next, making sure no one was listening, "....within the allied forces, but I was given an order to protect you and your friends. To take you to Madra so that your mate could continue to fight without worrying about his loved ones. You might find that pathetic or a pointless task, but I gave my word, and that fucking means something to me."

A bit of my fire dimmed, and my shoulders fell. "You're right," I sighed hard, feeling guilty, "But you're also wrong."

Kenji shifted on his feet and tilted his head, silently asking me what I meant.

"You gave your word to my terrified mate to take me home," I said softly, keeping my tone respectful. "And I gave my word to my mate to save him if anything happened. If you make me leave, you'll be forcing me to break *my* promise."

Kenji snarled as he straightened his back. "It's not the same, omega." Then he turned and walked off, not giving me a chance to respond.

"Why?" I yelled, running up next to him. Lex moved just

behind us, quietly watching us bicker. "Is it because I'm an omega? I can't make a promise because I'm too weak?"

"Omegas are too emotional," Kenji said as if stating a fact.

I grabbed his arm, forcing him to a stop. He could have easily pulled from my hold, but he paused, waiting for me to speak.

"We're all in this situation because an *alpha* woke up one morning and decided to track and kill *his own people* for having a *birthmark*." I glared hard at Kenji, refusing to back down. "Don't tell me *omegas* are too emotional."

Kenji took a step back, letting my fingers fall from his arm. "I will get Blue back, and then we will go to Madra." Then he stalked off once again.

I wanted to throw something at the back of his head.

"Don't worry, puppy," Lex walked up next to me and wrapped his arm around my shoulders. "If nothing else, I'll eat him."

The Treehouse

Byriel

A SOFT SNORE left Blue's parted lips, and he shifted in my arms, curling tight against my chest. He was so warm and soft compared to the cold, rough wall of the treehouse against my back. I wished I had a better place for him to sleep or even a simple pair of pants, but I was happy to have him in my arms.

He had to be exhausted after last night. The poor omega struggled to remain conscious as I carried him through the underbelly of the palace, then snuck through the garden. After using his explosive power, he was simply drained.

The sun peeked over the tips of the palace towers, catching my eye. The whole city was hidden just on the other side of the mighty structure, but sitting in my childhood sanctuary, it was easy to pretend we were far away from here, deep in the forest.

"Look at that," Blue whispered in awe.

I looked down at my omega, surprised to see him awake.

His beautiful blue-green eyes were fixed at the top of the elm just next to us. A mighty snow owl was perched high in the tree, feasting on a dead rabbit.

"Aren't owls night creatures?" Blue asked, rubbing his cheek against my bare chest.

"Not always." I admired the bird's fluffy white plumage and black-tipped wings. "The snow owls in this part of Havre have always seemed to enjoy the sun."

I caressed his back, trying to warm him. While my hands were still raw with several deep cuts, I was finally healing. If I weren't so weak from lack of food and rest, the marks would already be gone, but at least I wasn't bleeding anymore.

Blue moved to sit up, but I tightened my hold, not ready to let him go.

"Am I not allowed to sit?" he teased, snuggling back against me. "Am I your prisoner?"

"Yes." I dropped my nose to the top of his head, inhaling deeply. Blue's delicate scent didn't have the vibrant sweetness that omegas normally held, but he was softer. Cleaner. So lovely.

"What is this place?" Blue asked, shifting so his back was pressed to my chest. He stretched his long legs out, wiggling his toes. Omegas needed boots this time of year. They couldn't handle the cold like an alpha could. I'd have to find him a pair before leaving the city.

"It's the treehouse my father had built for me and my sister when we were pups," I looked around, admiring the poorly cut window, worn roof, and uneven floorboards. I had many wonderful memories here, despite the poor craftsmanship. "We're actually in the royal family's private garden."

Blue tensed, then sat up, looking out the tiny door. I leaned forward, not wanting him to fall. We were a good four stories up. Maybe higher.

"Will we be found?" he asked, fear making his voice pitch higher.

"No," I said softly, pulling him back to me. He snuggled between my legs, pushing his knees to his chest.

"Did you come out here often?" he asked, looking up at me. "When you were little?"

"All the time." I tucked his vibrant strand of purple hair behind his ear. "Especially after my mother died."

Blue nodded but didn't say anything else. It was as if he could sense the sadness tied to my memories.

The cold winter wind howled, making the tree groan and sway. Blue gripped the top of my exposed thighs, shivering hard.

"It's okay. This old tree is very steady." I placed my hand on his cheek, urging him to look up at me. His pale face was gaunt and still covered in ash. The deep lines under his eyes were so dark they almost looked bruised. My poor omega was downright worn with worry, and it was all because of me. "You are so beautiful," I whispered, brushing his cheek with my thumb.

Blue's white skin blushed pink, and he ducked his head.

"Oh, no, my sweet omega." I placed a finger under his chin, forcing his head back up. "I want to admire you."

Blue's little tongue peeked out as he licked his lips. "Byriel," he whispered, his tone nervous and sweet, "Will you kiss me?"

My beast pushed a little closer to the surface, eager for me to claim our mate. "Yes, my love," I bumped my nose against his, then hovered my mouth over his plump lips. "Nothing would make me happier."

Then I kissed him.

Slow at first.

Then I worked up, dragging my lips over his and holding him tight. He gasped in shock as my tongue forced entry into his hot sweet mouth. His bright flavor burst across my tongue; light, sweet, and all-consuming.

My fingers skimmed down Blue's cheek, teasing the sensitive skin along his neck. A soft moan drifted from his throat as I moved my hand around the back of his head, holding him to me.

"Blue," I growled against his mouth.

Cold, trembling fingers slipped over my chest, and Blue's lips trembled as he whispered, "Please, alpha. T-touch me."

I moved.

Pushing myself away from the wall, I forced Blue onto his back. The blanket across my lap fell away, letting my hard cock spring free. I couldn't remember ever being this hard. But this tiny omega owned me. His throaty sounds, taste, and mere presence did things to me I just couldn't understand. I would destroy the whole world for him.

"Alpha," Blue moaned, wrapping his arms around my shoulders as I moved down to kiss just beneath his ear. "Don't stop."

I lifted, determined to tell him we had to stop. It was too dangerous to do this here. I needed to get him out of the city first, but then the sweet scent of slick filled the cool air around me, warming my chest.

My eyes flashed red, and my claws slipped into points. The urge to fuck and mark this omega was like nothing I had ever felt before.

"Blue," I snarled down at him. His vibrant eyes went wide with fear, but his fingers curled tighter into my arms, keeping me in place. "Tell me to stop," I begged, struggling like hell to force my beastly urges back. "Tell me to stop."

Blue's slight body jerked as he shook his head. "No." His voice was the tiniest whisper, but the determination in his eyes was unmistakable. "Take..." his throat worked as he swallowed hard, "Take me."

A sharp gasp flew from his throat as I jerked at the front of his robes, popping off two buttons and forcing open the sash.

He was gorgeous. His pale, white skin was flushed and glistened with sweat despite the cold, and his dark little nipples rose into points, begging for my teeth.

"Fuck," I growled, then leaned down, slipping my tongue over one of his pert little buds.

Blue keened and moaned, lifting his hips, trying to tempt me closer. He was so responsive, thrilling my wolf to no end. My cock strained, and my beast growled, wanting to fuck my sweet mate wild. But I forced my wolf back, trying like hell to go slow.

Blue's thin stomach quivered as I kissed down his sweet body. I paused at the dip of his belly button, slipping my tongue over it. He giggled, and I did it again.

Then, moving slowly in case he demanded I stop, I brushed my hands down the waistband of his slacks and over his hips. He lifted, urging me to continue. Desire tore through me, and I jerked at his belt, unfastening it quickly and ripping his pants down his pale legs.

His straining, pretty little cock sprung free, already leaking a bead of precum. My mouth watered at the sight of it, and I wasted no time swallowing him down.

While Blue's kisses tasted soft and delicate, his cock tasted like heaven. A deep sweetness burst across my tongue as I bobbed, swallowing him all the way to the back of my throat. My nose pressed hard against his hips, and he whimpered loudly, gripping the roots of my hair.

"By!" His whole body jerked as I sucked. "I've never....please, don't....Gah!"

I sucked again, and his whole body shot up, his cock twitching in my mouth. I popped off, not wanting him to come yet. A soft whimper of disappointment pushed from his chest. I wanted to chuckle and tease him, but my omega was too sensitive for that. *At least not for his first time.*

"Don't pout, my love." I pushed my hand up his chest, smiling at the difference between his skin and mine. We looked like the two sides of the Moon, light and dark, meeting in the middle. "I'll make you feel good," I purred. "I promise."

His eyes were a little unfocused as his omega instincts took over, urging him to submit to his alpha. "I know you will, alpha," he smiled sweetly. "I trust you."

My heart burst with so much love and affection as I lowered my head again, drifting my tongue over his shaft and balls. He was so smooth and soft—like all omegas. Gripping his pale thighs, I pushed his legs up and out, then lifted, admiring his delicious body. Then I inhaled deeply, letting his natural scent consume me. Control me.

His tight hole fluttered and slick pushed out, his body readying itself to take his alpha.

Leaning down, I pushed my tongue through the mess, then moaned long and loud. I fell into him, feasting. He tasted so sweet, and I lapped and sucked, trying to pull as much flavor as I could from his slight body.

Blue keened and moaned, pulling his knees up higher to give me better access. Needing more, I pushed my tongue out, breaching his little entrance. Then without thinking, I pushed a finger inside him as well, and Blue stiffened.

I immediately pulled away, scared I had hurt him. "Are you okay?" I looked up at my omega. His face flushed a deep red as I stared into his bashful eyes.

"I'm okay," Blue whispered softly, but before I could taste him again, he murmured my name. "Byriel?"

I lifted, planting my fists on either side of his head. My wolf snarled, begging me to just fuck him already. "What's wrong, my love?"

"I've never...." His hands moved just next to his privates. It was clear he wanted to hide from me.

"Do you want me to stop?" I prayed he wouldn't say yes.

"No," he said quickly, making my wolf lick his sharp fangs, growling with deep satisfaction. "I just..." his gaze fell away from my face, and he bit his bottom lip, "I don't want you to be disappointed."

Soft affection bloomed in my chest, and I immediately moved onto my elbow, cradling his perfect face. "I've never been with anyone before either," I confessed.

Blue's eyes went wide, and his mouth fell open. His reaction didn't offend me. After all, alphas were commonly known to be the kind of beasts that would fuck anything that moved. There was a reason Lex was such a successful hunter.

"But....why?" Blue whispered, then he grimaced, clearly regretting his question. "I didn't mean—"

"It's okay," I cut him off with a soft kiss. "I've never laid with anyone because I was waiting for you." It wasn't a lie. I had never met anyone that lit a fire in me like Blue did.

"You're teasing me." Blue ducked his head, unable to hide his smile.

"No, my sweet omega," I kissed his lips again, lingering this time. "I'm finally claiming you. Because you are mine, and I am yours. And I want you to have all of me. Even the parts no one else has ever seen."

His eyes brightened as a lovely smile consumed his face. "I want that, too. I want you to have me. All of me." He circled his arms around my neck, then whispered, "Kiss me. Please."

Gripping his hip, I leaned down and kissed him deeply, caressing and squeezing every inch of him I could reach. One of his hands fell away from my neck, then his tentative fingers wrapped around my cock, making a deep growl burst from my chest. His palm drifted up and down my length a few times before squeezing the tip.

"Fuck!" I snarled, pushing my hips up into his hand.

"Do you like that?" Blue whispered, his tone uneasy. Shy.

I nodded, squeezing my eyes shut tight so I could concentrate on his bashful movements.

"Am I doing it right?" His fingers teased the soft underside of my cock, slipping his hand up and down.

"Squeeze me hard, omega," I commanded in my alpha tone. I didn't mean to, but it just slipped out. "Faster. Harder."

Blue did as he was told, increasing both his speed and pressure. A deep tingle grew at the base of my spine, creeping up my back and down into my balls. I needed to be inside him now.

In one quick movement, I lifted, pulling my cock from Blue's hand.

He whimpered, then gasped loudly as I gripped the underside of both his knees. Then I pushed them up to his ears. "Stay still." My deep tones slipped over him, and he shivered, a dreamy smile lifting his pretty lips. I should have been more gentle and loving in my command, but I couldn't. I was too lost to my beast.

Moving as slowly as my beast would allow, I pressed my finger to Blue's wet hole. He was tight. So tight I had to *push* just to breach him.

"Byriel!" Blue called my name on a gasp. "What—"

"Relax, my love," I pushed on his chest, keeping him still. "Let me open you up." I slipped my finger in and out of him, picking up the pace. The second a soft moan drifted from his throat, I added another finger. Then another. I fucked his tight body, knuckle deep, stretching him, preparing him for my alpha cock.

Once I was happy with the mess of slick and sweat that coated Blue's lovely skin, I gripped the base of my cock and lined the crown up. Taking a deep, calming breath, I pushed forward, entering his virgin body. For a split second, fear pulsed in my omega's eyes, but then he snapped them shut, hiding his pain.

I kept going, watching his expression twist from lust to a pained grimace. A strangled grunt of pain jerked from Blue's lips, and I stilled, letting him adjust.

It was hell.

My beast roared and clawed at the inside of my chest, begging me to rut forward and fill my omega in one possessive thrust. But I stayed completely frozen in place, not moving an inch.

"It's okay," I purred, leaving gentle kisses on Blue's lips and cheeks. His chin quivered, and I cupped his cheeks. "You're doing so good." I kissed his nose, lingering on his bottom lip. "So good for me. Such a good omega."

Blue sniffled, and a few tears slipped out of the corners of his eyes. "Are you in?" he whimpered. "Is it done?"

I glanced down at where we were connected. Only half my cock was stuffed inside him, and I panicked, worried he might not be able to take all of me. "Not quite," I said honestly. "But almost."

Slowly, Blue opened his eyes and looked down. What looked like anger flashed in his eyes, but I quickly realized it was determination. But before I could ask him what he was thinking, he circled his ankles under my ass, then jerked me to him, forcing my cock deep into his body.

Blue clamped his mouth shut, stifling a pained scream.

I tried to focus on his pain, but my beast took hold, and I started to thrust. It was as if my body didn't belong to me anymore. I snarled, hating myself. And my hips faulted as I struggled to gain control.

"Don't..." Blue panted, circling his arms around my neck. "Don't stop." He lifted his hips, urging me closer, but he was so tense. Clearly in pain.

"I don't want you hurt you," I snarled against his neck,

continuing to fuck him. "Fuck," I gasped. "You feel so good. So tight."

I snapped my hips forward, and Blue's eyes flew open. Shock and lust twisted together as I pounded into him, setting a steady rhythm.

"Oh, my," he gasped as his legs fell open, more relaxed, and his head fell back. The pain in his eyes was gone, replaced with something softer. I prayed it was love.

"Bite me," Blue whispered, dragging his nails over the back of my neck. "Make me yours."

I knew it was a bad idea. He wasn't in heat, and it would hurt beyond belief, but the disconnect between my brain and cock was too great. *Blue was mine, and he was going to wear my fucking mark for all to see.*

Leaning up, I placed my hands on the backs of his thighs, forcing his body to bend slightly, then I rutted forward, hitting something soft and wet deep inside him.

Blue's mouth fell open, and his eyes rolled into the back of his head as I slammed into that little bundle of nerves over and over again. His cock twitched, then ropes of thick white cum burst across his stomach and chest.

My own end barrelled through me, and my cock seemed to double in size. Letting instinct take over, I released my consciousness over to my beast. My fangs punched forward, and I gripped Blue's hair, then jerked his head to one side. I struck, pushing my fangs deep into my omega's soft skin.

Sharp blood flooded my mouth.

Then it softened, dripping with Blue's delicious flavor.

My knot expanded, the pressure intense. Almost painful. I rutted forward, popping it into place. Blue jerked as another burst of cum spurted from his cock. My head swam with his scent, taste, and feel, but just before I could remove my fangs, something sharp and electrifying ripped from Blue's small body straight into mine.

Every muscle in my body locked up, and I grunted hard, struggling to keep from ripping his throat out. The tight, straining sensation burning through me was like nothing I had ever felt. It was as if I had been struck by lightning.

Then in one fierce moment, Blue's skin flashed white hot, and the sky seemed to burn with a vibrant electric light.

My fangs locked into place, and my fingers curled tight into his sensitive skin. Fear and panic flooded my veins, and I struggled to keep from killing him. Then all at once, the pain drifted away, and Blue went limp in my hold.

I immediately pulled my fangs from his throat, looking over his flushed face to ensure he was okay. He looked so happy. A gentle smile played on his lips with a healthy glow in his cheeks.

"Byriel," he whispered, holding me close to him.

A quick laugh jumped from my throat, unable to figure out whether I was scared, worried, or just blissfully happy.

Blue was finally mine. *My mate.* Bound to me forever.

This was what love felt like. And I prayed it would never end.

Strung Up

Joon

"WHO SENT YOU?" Arian yelled as Dynel's fist landed once again in my gut.

I doubled over as far as my chains would allow, choking hard. The muscles in my shoulders strained from having my wrists secured above my head, and blood and snot dripped down my face and chest. I wanted to scream at Arian to do his fucking job as an ally and stop this nonsense—put his blade in Dynel's side—but it seemed this was the game we were going to play: Arian pretended to question me, I pretended to fight the urge to talk, and Dynel beat the ever living fuck out of me. It was a shit game.

"Who are you with?" Arian snarled, flashing his flat teeth. "Are you in alliance with Byriel? The King? End this and talk!"

I slowly lifted my head, glaring hard at the beta. My wolf growled, trying to keep his strength, but the pungent scent of wolfsbane mixed with the mercury shackles had him weak. Too weak.

"The King is dead," Arian seethed. "You'd do well to answer me. There's no sense remaining loyal to a dead man."

Dynel shifted just next to me, his knuckles busted and bleeding from their unrelenting use. I flashed my fangs at the pale, bald alpha. He met my challenge, his dark eyes pulsing red.

"Who sent you?" Arian's voice rose, and Dynel's meaty fist connected hard with my ribs.

Bone crunched under the force, and pain ripped up my side. The urge to bow my head was strong, but I kept it up, letting out a forceful cough right into Dynel's ugly face. The fucker flinched hard as blood splattered all over him.

Dynel's whole body jerked, and Arian flung out his hand, stopping him.

"No!" the beta snarled before Dynel could hit me again.

Dynel growled low in his chest but stayed where he was, obeying Arian like a good dog.

"I understand," Arian sighed hard, "that you feel a certain sense of loyalty to your cause." He paused, and I gathered all the blood and spit in my mouth. "But you will not—"

I spit right at Arian, covering the front of his pristine black uniform in blood. It dripped over his brightly colored patches and down to his shiny belt buckle. He looked absolutely *enraged*.

An amused chuckle slipped from my lips, but before I could enjoy the moment too much, Dynel's fucking fist landed hard right in my side. My vision burst white, and my stomach twisted as saliva flooded my mouth. But before I could calm my gut, Dynel hit me again—once in the nose and the other in my side.

My stomach tightened and churned, and I lurched forward, vomiting blood and spit all over the floor.

"*Fuck*," Arian gritted out, carefully stepping away from the mess.

Breathing hard, I glared up at the beta, watching with glee as he tried to wipe my blood off his once pristine dress shirt. His crisp white handkerchief smeared red, and his upper lip curled in disgust.

I opened my mouth to mock the beta, but movement just over his shoulder caught my eye. A young blonde beta was strung up on the opposite wall, her arms stretched tight over her head, like mine. Her fair skin was sweaty and flushed red from trying not to sob out loud. She looked absolutely terrified.

When did they bring her in here?

Dynel settled his feet once again, drawing back his fist. I closed my eyes, ready to absorb the blow, but before it landed, Arian called out.

"Stop!"

Dynel spun to the beta, confusion wrinkling his brow. "Why?" he snapped in his rough, deep voice.

Arian's throat worked as his eyes flickered from me to the bloody mess at my feet. He was clearly struggling to come up with an excuse to stop the beating. I appreciated it.

I needed a fucking break.

And a drink of water.

"Because the Queen wants answers," Arian finally said in a loud sure voice. "Killing this rogue won't tell us anything." He glared hard into Dynel's eyes. *How the alphas in this palace hadn't already gutted this beta, I didn't know.*

Dynel's fists curled, then his fingers flexed. He clearly wanted to keep hitting *something*. "Fine," the pale alpha took a careful step away from me, letting Arian take his place.

"Rogue." Arian placed his hand on the curved hilt of his dagger. "End this. Tell me who sent you. Tell me who you are with."

"I was with your sister last night," I smirked, struggling to keep my head up. "But if I'm honest, it wasn't much to brag about."

Arian's fierce expression shifted to absolute annoyance. "Really?" he said in a flat, angry tone.

I let out a bark of a laugh, but it quickly turned into a horrible wheeze, making me cough. "I'm sorry the jokes aren't more to your liking, beta," I spit more blood onto the stone floor, smiling when it splattered against Arian's shiny black boots. "I'll work on it."

Arian pinched the bridge of his nose. "Dynel, you can return to your post," he groaned.

The alpha's dark eyes flickered from Arian to me, then back again, clearly confused.

Arian turned to the alpha when he didn't move, commanding him with a fierce bark this time. "Return to your post."

The bald alpha snarled, "I've only just started."

"And yet you're done," Arian's voice rose. "This rogue clearly doesn't respond to a beating." He turned his hard eyes to me, assessing my bruised torso and busted up face. "But a few days without food or water might loosen his tongue."

Dynel let out a vicious growl but obeyed, marching right past Arian and straight to the main door. It pushed open, wafting in the soft scent of burning cedar and smoked meats. My empty gut twisted, torn between hunger and nausea.

The moment the door latched shut, Arian closed the space between us, pulling a small water canister from his belt. He cupped the back of my neck as he brought it to my lips, helping me steady my head. I gulped, drinking as much as I could. It was cool but tinged with the coppery taste of my own blood. *I just prayed I didn't throw it all up.*

"Let me go," I panted hard, ignoring the twist in my stomach. The cold water sat like a fucking bolder, threatening to come right back up.

Arian shook his head. "I can't risk it."

Rage tore through me, and I jerked at my chains. The raw skin around my wrists pulled and pinched, and my shoulders ached. "Why?" I snarled as quietly as I could. "Let me fucking go. I need to get back to my mate."

I had been purposely blocking her out of our bond. The last thing I needed was for her to feel my pain or fear, but that also meant I couldn't feel her either. *It was killing me.*

"I'm sorry," Arian secured the empty canister to his belt. "But we all have mates to get back to. This is war, and—"

"Let me go!" I roared.

Arian took a careful step back, sympathy clear in his eyes. "I'm sorry, Joon. But this is so much more than just one alpha and his mate. I can't risk letting you go and compromising my post. Too much is at stake."

Pure hatred filled my weak chest, and I tried to growl as the beta backed up, then turned, disappearing out the same fucking door as Dynel had.

Defeated and desperate, I jerked at my chains again, trying to pull them from the ceiling, but the metal stayed firm, not giving an inch.

A deep chuckle cut the silence, and I paused, glaring at the older of the two elves. The elf's weathered face was gaunt and bruised, with dried blood covering his lips and down his pale pink robes. His clothes were filthy and wrinkled, clearly stuck here for at least a few weeks, if not longer.

"What's so fucking funny?" I snarled at the green-skinned fucker.

The elf rolled his head in my direction, then smirked. "You honestly think you're going to get out of here?" His pointed ears stuck out from his greasy black hair.

"Fuck you," I spat, not interested in anything this fucker had to say.

"We're all fucked, wolf." His voice was strained, sounding like he had screamed for hours on end. "Better to accept it now."

My eyes drifted from him to his friend chained on the other side of him. My anger dimmed as I realized the other elf was dead. His withered hands were curled inward, and his wrists were just bone. The dead elf's once white robes were covered in blood and hanging loose on his fragile shoulders. I wondered how long it would be before the body would start to rot.

I looked away from the dead elf, refusing to admit defeat.

"Just because you've given up doesn't mean I will." Tzidal's beautiful face filled my mind, giving me renewed purpose. *Did Kenji get her to Madra? Was she safe?*

I shook my head, knowing that wasn't likely. My fierce mate would gut that alpha like a fish before willingly leaving me in Ossory alone.

"Tell me," the old elf narrowed his eyes at me. They were pale blue and bloodshot. "What did you do to incur her majesty's wrath?"

Exhausted, I snarled at him. "I insulted her hospitality," I snapped. "My posh bedding wasn't nearly soft enough."

The elf let out a manic laugh, tipping his head back as if stretching.

My eyes drifted to another body chained next to me on the far side of the room. The small elderly omega was also dead, her lifeless body gently hanging from her chains.

"Whatever you've done to offend Strayton," the elf's voice rose, more confident, "As long as you can scream, Strayton will extract every ounce of pain she can from you. Your death will be brutal." He looked up at his dead friend, fear and sorrow flooding his eyes.

I tried twisting my wrists in my shackles, desperate to get free, but my arms suddenly felt very heavy. It seemed my exhaustion was quickly taking over. "And what did you do to deserve this punishment?" I asked the elf, trying to distract myself.

"I refused Strayton sanctuary," he said flatly.

I paused at that, confused. "What the fuck does that mean?" I narrowed my eyes at him, not believing that he was telling the truth. "Why would an *alpha* ever seek sanctuary from a fucking elf? And a royal member of the royal family at that?"

The elf stared at the steepled ceiling, seeming to look at nothing in particular. He was so quiet and still for so long, I thought he had fallen asleep, but then he cleared his throat and spoke, "Strayton wanted to marry—" He stopped, letting out a quick breathy laugh. "I apologize, wolf. She wanted to *mate*," he said the word as if it was stupid, "one of *my* people. The Emperor rightfully refused, not eager to have the Wolf King attack us for harboring his foolish daughter," he said firmly as if I might argue. "So, as the enforcer of our lands, I delivered the message and let her know that we would not be providing her sanctuary."

The dark-haired female across from me shifted, leaning far forward to see the elf. "What happened to the man she wanted to mate?"

The elf shook his head slowly. "Last I heard, the two of them tried to run away, and the Wolf King killed the poor boy. Rumor had it that he was gutted and left in the courtyard to rot."

The beta shook her head, clearly not believing it. "That's a lie."

I didn't have the heart to tell her that it was likely. The King was brutal enough to kill and torment his own people. Killing one elf was probably a very easy choice for him.

"What did you do?" I asked her, fighting the urge to close my eyes. *I was so sleepy.*

The beta's chin dropped, and her lashes lowered. "Nothing," she mumbled. "I did nothing."

"Bullshit!" The elf yelled, making the poor girl flinch. "Tell the truth, or anger your...*Moon*." He snorted like it was a wonderful joke.

The beta glared at him, and her cheeks flushed bright red with shame or anger. I couldn't tell which.

"What did you do?" I asked again, hoping she was an ally. I needed to know that others were working hard within the palace to overthrow Strayton. I needed to believe that someone would come and save us.

"I accidentally dropped her tea," the young beta said. "It splattered across the bottom of her majesty's robes. I didn't mean to." Her voice dropped, so small and scared. "It was an accident."

Rage boiled in my gut, followed quickly by deep fear.

I had to survive this.

I had to live so I could find Tzidal, then help put an end to all this suffering. I had to....

But before I could finish my thought, darkness overtook me.

Outside The Prison

Tzidal

"WHAT THE HELL HAPPENED?" Lex whispered, narrowing his gray eyes at the prison.

The large, imposing structure looked as if it had been attacked. There was a sizable hole at the back of the building, with brick and stone crumbling all around it. I narrowed my eyes, seeing what looked like a chain hanging from the ceiling. There were cuffs at the end to allow someone to be strung up. The very sight of it sent chills up my spine.

The main door to the prison opened, and two guards stepped out, followed by several alphas, all shackled and chained together. They marched in a single file line, the alphas glaring hard at the villagers that gathered to watch.

Kenji let out a heavy sigh. "They're moving the prisoners."

Panic rippled throughout my whole body, and I tensed. Where was Blue? Did they already move him? To where? Was he okay?

I tapped Kenji's shoulder. "Go ask where the omega prisoners are being moved to."

He snorted and crossed his arms across his thick chest. "I'm not a prison guard, omega. I can't just stroll up there and demand to know what's going on."

"You can't even say that—"

"No," Kenji barked at me, making my wolf snarl and my hackles rise. "I have no authority. I'm a grunt when it comes to the ranks."

I eyed the alpha, taking in his young age and plain uniform. He didn't have any patches or pins, nothing that might indicate he had any real power.

"And what's happening over there?" Lex stared just past me.

Across the bridge, the main road was brimming with countless wolves ambling toward the palace. Alpha's kept a protective arm around their omegas, and children ran around their legs, giggling wildly within the crowd.

"Move along!" A gruff alpha ushered a few onlookers away from the prison and toward the road. "The Queen is addressing the people. Make your way to the palace."

Kenji's dark eyes met mine, then Lex's. He let out a heavy sigh, then nodded toward the main road. "Let's go."

"But what about Blue?" I cut a quick glare at the prison, then leaned in, dropping my voice to a whisper, "This is the perfect time to search for him. Everyone will be busy."

Kenji's mouth pulled tight, clearly about to order me to get to the palace.

"How about this," Lex spoke up, "I'll shift into one of these guards and find out where they're taking the omega prisoners. You two go see what Strayton's got to say. Then we'll meet back here." He glanced all around, his eyes falling to the bridge separating the prison grounds from the rest of the city. "I'll wait for you right over there."

I shook my head, not liking that idea in the least. "I don't want to separate. I—"

"Make your way to the palace." The gruff alpha moved toward us with his hands out, trying to usher us along. "The Queen is going to address the people."

I forced a tight smile, then reached for Lex's hand, but he wasn't there. I spun, looking everywhere for the siren. But everything was quiet. Just blue skies, an empty prison, and a mighty snow owl lazily circling the bell tower.

"Come on," Kenji gripped my wrist, pulling me toward the main road.

"No! We can't just leave him," I hissed, still looking for Lex's fluffy white hair or intricate blue robes.

"He's already shifted," Kenji said, tightening his hold on my arm. I tried to jerk away from him, but the alpha had an immobile grip on me. "We need to hear what the Queen has to say."

"I don't give a shit what she has to say!" I slammed my fist into Kenji's chest, desperate to find Lex. Or Blue. Or Joon. *I needed my alpha.* I needed him to beat the ever-living shit out of this asshole.

Kenji jerked me across the bridge and into the city proper. I dug my heels in, determined to make this as difficult as I could on the alpha.

Blue was out there somewhere, and he needed our help.

"Careful there, youngin!" An elderly beta cackled, wagging his finger at me. "You piss off your alpha too much, and he'll correct you in front of the whole damn city."

I snarled at the elder, not interested in his *advice*, but before I could tell him so, Kenji snatched me up, flinging me over his shoulder. A rough grunt burst from my chest as his unforgiving shoulder pushed into my stomach.

"Calm down," Kenji ordered, popping me once on the ass.

My wolf roared within, wanting to destroy the asshole for

touching me in such an intimate way. Only Joon was allowed such an honor.

"Touch me like that again, and I'm going to bite your ear off!" I yelled as I moved my hands over my bottom, preventing him from touching me again.

"Maybe if you'd act like a proper omega, I wouldn't have to correct you," Kenji gritted out, moving amongst the throng of people. He was clearly sick of my behavior, his anger growing sharper by the second.

But I didn't give a shit.

I didn't ask for this alpha's help, and I wasn't about to feel bad for not bowing at his feet.

"I was simply to carry your stubborn ass to Madra," he whispered as if speaking to himself. "That's all I was asked to do. But no. I get stuck with a headstrong beast of an omega that wants to storm the fucking castle like she's a damn dragon slayer."

He continued to mumble under his breath, cursing Blue and me for not respecting the order of things. "This is dangerous, and you just don't give a shit," he snarled as he shook his head. "Ungrateful. The whole lot of you."

"Ungrateful!" I roared, and a hand landed hard on my upper thighs. I kicked and screamed, pulling at Kenji's hair and smacking him in the back. Most chuckled at my display, but a few complained about immature omegas and keeping your brat at home. I wanted to run each one with my blade.

My blade.

My dagger was pressed tight between my stomach and Kenji's shoulder. If I could reach it, I could get this ass to release me and find Lex and Blue. I could go and save my mate.

I immediately went limp, letting him carry me without complaint.

"Wear yourself out?" Kenji asked, his tone almost lazy.

I grunted, refusing to answer.

The movement around us slowed as people filed through the iron gate that separated the palace entrance from the rest of Ossory. Dozens of guards scanned each face that passed, puffing out scarred chests and flashing pointed fangs. Their presence was very telling. Whatever the Queen had to say, it might be enough to incite a few fights.

Once through the gate, Kenji edged near the front, then stopped. I tried looking over my shoulder, but I couldn't see anything other than the people around us and the looming shadow of the mighty palace.

"Quiet!" Someone with a loud, clear voice called out.

"I can't see." I squirmed, trying to get Kenji to let me down.

"Are you done being a brat?" He tipped his chin up and narrowed his eyes. He was clearly looking at someone.

"I'll behave," I stifled a growl. This was humiliating. "Please, let me see what's happening." My wolf snarled, not wanting me to be polite to this alpha at all, but if I was going to get away from the bastard, I'd need him to put me down first.

Slowly, Kenji bent, setting me on my feet. I turned my back to him, then looked up at the shining black palace. A middle-aged beta with flowing blonde hair and dark sunken eyes looked down at the crowd.

"Please, hold your tongues!" The beta's voice was deep, surprising me. He looked very feminine. "Quiet down!" he yelled, holding his hands up as if trying to command the crowd.

The guards all around us moved about, ordering the people to "shut up" or "be still."

I held my tongue, placing my hand inside my robes. The hilt of my dagger was warm and ready to be used the second this damn speech was over. I didn't want to stab Kenji, but I'd do whatever I had to.

"Make way!" The ugly alpha that stole Blue forced his way through the crowd. Marx and his sister Mary moved closely behind them.

"Bow for her majesty, Queen Strayton, daughter of the late King Ares!"

Murmurs swept through the crowd, followed by horrified gasps as the last of the city learned of the King's death. How anyone could not already know, I had no idea. I was there when the bastard died, and it felt like all of Havre knew before we even left the camp.

"My fellow shifters and wolves!" Strayton stepped into view at the edge of the balcony. The golden crown perched in her tight black curls glistened in the sunlight, making the large rubies shimmer and flash as if they were on fire. Her gown was modest and bright white—-a color traditionally worn when in mourning—but her relaxed posture and pompous expression didn't exactly portray grief.

"I am both saddened and honored to be standing here today as your Queen," Strayton continued in a loud, commanding tone. Her dominance over the land and people swept over the whole crowd, making some go completely still as they listened to her, but others just growled even louder. "As I'm sure many of you already know, my father, Ares The King of Wolves, has passed."

Someone gasped yet again, and a few muffled sobs could be heard near the back gate. I rolled my eyes. *None of these people actually knew the King, so why should they mourn him?*

"Now," Strayton's dark eyes flashed a vibrant red, mimicking the shimmering rubies on her crown, "What I'm about to share with you is not to scare you, but to warn you. My brother was once an honorable alpha with a determined heart and lovely soul." She paused, looking over the crowd for dramatic effect.

A restless energy moved through the wolves around me,

and I held my breath. I already knew what she was about to say, but I still prayed she wouldn't.

"In the years that my brother had been away from home," Strayton continued, "his heart has strayed, and his bloodlust has grown. He has become so feral, I'm not even sure if he's a true decedent of my father. The late King was mighty, powerful, and strong. But Byriel..." she let out a heavy sigh. "Byriel attacked my father. He killed the King."

Fear, confusion, and intense panic spread through the masses like a wave. A dark-skinned alpha just next to me growled low in his chest, curling his fists tight as he glared up at the Queen. One wrong word, and every alpha here was sure to lash out.

"Liar!" Someone yelled above the hushed murmurs, followed by the unmistakable sound of a scuffle.

My fingers tightened on my blade as the crowd shifted, and more people grew uneasy. Kenji grabbed my upper arm, pulling me flush with his chest. In any other circumstance, I would have shoved away from him, but there were far too many people here, and I was tiny in comparison.

"Now!" Strayton's voice grew louder, more commanding. "I want to remind everyone here of the sanctity of royal blood. The Moon chose my family to lead you, love you, protect you. We are chosen and blessed. So," her voice rose, more commanding, "if you see my brother, capture him, but do *not* kill him!" she ordered, her alpha command pushing down on each and every one of us.

I shivered at the force of it, moving a little closer to Kenji. His fingers trembled as they tightened around my arm, her dominance affecting him as well. It only made sense. After all, she was our Queen.

"I know you want to avenge your beloved King and protect me from Byriel's feral bloodlust, but do not put yourself in any danger, my people. Only a true and mighty alpha could take down someone as powerful as Byriel. Keep yourself safe. Keep your families safe. Stay away from him."

Rage boiled in my veins and I squeezed the hilt of my dagger hard. She was taunting these alphas, goading them into killing her brother for her.

"Come," Strayton spoke over her shoulder, motioning for someone to step forward.

The beta guard, Arian, came into view holding a small, ornate box. I narrowed my eyes at him, not sure if I should be relieved or worried to see an ally right now.

Strayton moved at a lazy pace, grabbing a pair of gloves that were draped over Arian's arm. She took her time, slipping the thick leather material over one hand, then the other. Once she was ready, she turned back to the crowd and smiled smugly. She looked as if she was lording a secret over all of us.

"I want you all to know that I will be a fair, but firm Queen." Strayton tipped her chin up, and I prayed Arian would just reach over and pop her in the nose. "Havre has never seen a ruler like me, and I will—"

"And what about those ready to challenge you for the crown?" An alpha right next to me roared up at the balcony. His freckled face was bright red with rage and the corded muscles in his arms pulled tight as he circled his fists. "We have a right to challenge you," he growled.

Kenji grabbed my arm, pulling me as far away from the alpha as he could. But it was packed, and the crowd was growing restless.

"Challenge me?" Strayton placed one gloved hand over her chest, pointing to herself.

"Yes!" the alpha roared, and murmurs swept through the air, excited at the prospect of a fight. "It's the right of the people to challenge you for the crown!"

Strayton tipped her head back, letting out a loud, bitter laugh. "Oh, you simple alpha," she glared down at him as if the alpha were a spec of dirt. "That stupid tradition holds no place in my kingdom, but," she turned to Arian, placing one finger on the box in his hands, "If you need some convincing of my power, I'd be happy to show you."

A few alphas yelled out along the edges of the crowd, snarling at the Queen for not accepting the challenge, but then Strayton lifted the lid of the box, and everyone went dead silent.

A vibrant red light poured from the tiny box, making Arian squeeze his eyes shut tight. Strayton reached into the box, then slowly picked up the most vibrant red crystal I had ever seen. She steadied the crystal in both gloved hands, touching it as if it were made of dust and might blow away at any second.

"You would be a fool to challenge me, wolf," Strayton glared over the railing of the balcony.

I glanced at the freckled alpha, not surprised to see three guards standing right in front of him. Even if he didn't get a chance to challenge Strayton, I had a feeling this alpha would still get his fight—just not a very fair one.

"If anyone here wants to challenge me for either my crown or their own foolish honor, just know what awaits you." Strayton held up the glowing crystal. "I alone wield the power of the stars!" Then she turned and pushed the red rock right into Arian's face.

The second the crystal touched Arian's cheek, his eyes went wide with shock, then his mouth popped open as if letting out a silent scream. Black lines crawled across his face, then red light burst from the beta's eyes and nose. Arian seemed locked in place, every muscle in his body going tight as bright blood streamed from his eyes and nose.

I slapped my hand over my mouth to keep from screaming, and backed up. But Kenji's warm presence behind me gave me no comfort. The alpha reeked of fear and rage, just like everyone else in the damn courtyard.

My wolf begged me to cut and run, but I had nowhere to go.

Strayton pulled the crystal away from Arian's face and his rigid body instantly collapsed, disappearing from view and landing on the balcony floor with a hard thwack.

Silence thrummed all around me.

No one spoke or moved.

Hell, I don't think anyone even dared to breathe.

"For any of you thinking you might overthrow me," Strayton cradled the crystal in her hands, caressing the top as if it were a cherished pet, "Just know that you are already dead."

Strayton's dark eyes looked down at a big bald alpha with milky white skin. He nodded up at her, then marched straight to Mary and Marx. He gripped Marx's upper arm, as another guard snatched up Mary. She screamed and clawed at the guard's arms, kicking out with everything she had.

"Treason will not be tolerated," Strayton then turned her attention to the freckled alpha. "Anyone that dares to defy me, will pay with their blood." Then she turned, and disappeared into the palace.

The stunned crowd didn't move at first, but then a few bowed, followed by a few more. I stayed rooted in my spot, glaring up at the balcony. The last time I saw my mate, he was leaving the camp with Strayton—that unhinged, bloodthirsty woman.

Joon was in danger.

Even though he was blocking our bond, *I could feel it.*

"Settle!" A fierce guard snarled. His face was deeply scarred and his fangs bared.

I half expected some of the crowd to disperse, but it seemed as if every wolf here held firm, glaring down at the palace doors.

"Byriel would *never* kill the King!" The soft voice of a female omega lifted above the crowd. People shifted, turning to the voice, but I couldn't see her. "I've known that boy since he was a pup! He'd ne—" A pained grunted cut the air, followed by several angry growls.

"Did they hit her?" A panicked beta yelled. "They hit her! The guards hit her!"

The change in the alphas around me was almost instant.

Several shifted into their wolves, making the guards rush them, beating them back with mighty fists, while others began rushing at the palace doors. Kenji's hand tightened on my arm, but before I could pull away, someone shoved him, pushing him deeper into the crowd.

My wolf yipped, urging me to run. Not sure where to go, I cut left, ducking under an alpha's swinging fist and around a beta brandishing a broom as a weapon. A shifted wolf roared and a woman screamed, but I didn't stop, running as fast as I could toward the courtyard wall. I stared at the smooth bricks in the distance, letting them pull me through the crowd.

A vicious gray wolf cut me off, blocking my path. I stopped, struggling to figure out how to get around him, but then he turned his glowing red eyes at me. He looked deranged, not the usual way an alpha would react to an omega, but vicious and bloodthirsty.

I pushed my hand into my robes and pulled out my dagger, ready to fight with everything I had. But before I could move, a twist of pain rippled from deep inside my stomach, making me grunt.

The gray wolf arched his back, ready to pounce, but before I could move, hard hands gripped the back of my robes, lifting me clear off the ground. I inhaled deeply, ready to tell Kenji to fuck off, but the alpha's scent was off. Unfamiliar.

It wasn't Kenji.

Still In The Treehouse

Byriel

"ALPHA!" Blue gasped as I fell forward over his back, my knot buried deep inside him.

"*Fuck*," I panted, rubbing my face between his shoulder blades. "You are so fucking perfect." I smoothed my hands down his sides, then under his belly, circling his limp cock. A string of cum dripped from it onto the treehouse floor. I teased it, swiping my fingers through the mess and teasing the head.

"Stop it," Blue giggled, wiggling his bottom. The motion pulled at my knot, and he hissed.

"I'm sorry." I wrapped my arm around his middle, then rolled both of us so he could lay comfortably against me. "Better, my love?"

"Much." He sagged against me, his legs splayed open, and his eyes closed.

I admired his soft beauty: the fresh mating bite, the blush

in his cheeks, the soft curve of his lips, even his purple strand of silky hair. I twisted it around my finger, then lifted it to my nose, inhaling him. *How could one person smell so good?*

"I love it when you touch my hair," Blue hummed, then his expression dimmed, and he opened his eyes. "But you probably shouldn't."

I jerked at that, making my knot twitch inside him. Blue grunted, and I immediately caressed his chest and stomach. "Why can't I touch my mate?" I asked, trying not to sound annoyed, but I was. Blue was mine. Every inch of him. And the thought of not being allowed to love everything about him made me possessive and restless.

"Tzidal said not to bring any attention to my hair," Blue's voice dipped, almost sad. "She said it could get me killed."

Confusion wrinkled my brow, and I gripped his chin, forcing him to look at me over his shoulder. "Why on earth would your hair get you killed?"

He bit his bottom lip and curled his fingers into the tops of my legs. He was scared. Our bond wasn't fully formed yet, but I didn't need to feel his emotions to know it.

"It's because of my birthmark," Blue whispered.

Fear coiled in my gut, crawling up my chest and into my throat. "What birthmark?"

He raised his hand, slipping it through his dark blue hair. He scratched, then parted his locks, and my heart plummeted. At the base of the purple strand of hair was a small crescent-shaped, red birthmark. *Just like the blushing moon.*

Guilt and shame wracked my entire body, and I squeezed my eyes shut tight, trying not to fall apart.

"Byriel?" Concern filled Blue's soft voice as he turned a little more in my lap. My knot pulled slightly; then it slipped free. Cum and slick pushed out of Blue, but he ignored it, moving to straddle my lap. "Alpha?" he whispered, cupping my cheeks. "Please, open your eyes. You're scaring me."

I slowly opened them, letting him see the tears that threatened to fall. "I'm so sorry," I whispered, not sure what else to say.

Blue cupped my cheek, caressing the edge of my beard. "What for?" He let out a nervous laugh. "I'll be okay. No one knows about my mark."

I shook my head, knowing I couldn't keep this from him any longer. "Did Tzidal tell you who killed her mate? Who killed Joon's mate?"

He shook his head, his brows drawn together. "I mean, I know the King order them to be killed, but they didn't say who held the blade."

I nodded at my lap, struggling to look him in the eyes. "I did."

The silence that thrummed between us filled my ears, ringing loudly. Finally, unable to take it any longer, I looked up at my mate, meeting his wide scared eyes.

"That's not funny," he whispered.

My fingers were like ice, sweat covering my palms. "It's the truth." I concentrated on breathing, forcing myself to take slow, steady breaths. "My father ordered me to hunt and kill the marked wolves. So I did." Disgust ripped through me as the voice in the back of my mind whispered, *'And you finally found them all.'*

Blue sat up, away from me, his hands slipping from my face. He held them out in front of him as if not sure what to do with himself. "You killed them?" His soft voice was filled with disbelief. "You *actually* killed them? You landed the blow that took their lives?"

I knew what he was doing. My sweet mate was trying to justify in his mind that I wasn't a monster. *But I was.*

"I lead the party that killed them. I carried out my father's orders." I pushed my hands over his thighs, terrified he'd try to run from me. "It was my fault and no one else's."

His eyes narrowed, and his jaw clenched. "You aren't answering my question."

I took a slow breath, trying like hell not to relieve every awful moment of pain I helped inflict. "I did not deliver the ending blow to Omega Tzidal or Joon's mates. But I did kill some of the others."

Blue held my gaze, not breaking eye contact. It was clear he was working something out. "I can feel how scared you are in my head," he whispered, his words clipped. I bowed my head, submitting to his anger. It made my wolf bristle, but I owed my mate this much. He needed to see my shame. "Did you destroy whole villages like those guards did to my home?"

"Never!" I snapped my head back up and gripped his upper arms. "There were only three of us. We slipped into the villages softly, tracked who we needed, then ended them as quickly as possible. I didn't want anyone to suffer."

Blue jerked from my hold, slapping my hands away. "You left whole families to suffer," he gritted out, flashing his small omega fangs.

"I'm so sorry, Blue," I said, my voice deep with emotion. "I have no excuses, and I deserve your hatred. But I promise you, I am trying to be a better man."

"Is that why you helped Tzidal?" His eyes went wide, and a soft trace of his shock moved through our bond. His voice slipped into a whisper as he leaned in. "Is that why you killed your father?"

"No," I shook my head. "I killed my father because he threatened you. He touched you. But my shame did urge me to help Tzidal."

"You told me you helped her because she saved your life." He crossed his arms. I was just thankful he was still sitting on my lap—I would die if he crawled away from me. "Was that a lie?" he asked. "Has anything you told me been true?"

"When Tzidal found me, I was injured and on the verge of

death," I said, hoping to calm his rising anger. "She spared my life. She knew who I was and what I did to her, but she spared me because she is good and kind."

Blue's chin jutted out, and his eyes narrowed. "You're lucky she didn't kill you."

"Joon wanted to," I said firmly. "And I begged both of them to end my suffering, but Tzidal forced me to live." I let out a heavy sigh, brushing my thumbs over the bruises on Blue's legs. The small dots were from my fingers, and a small part of me wondered if I'd ever get to make love to him again. "I am a disgusting alpha. I hurt the people I was meant to protect."

"I want to forgive you." His face was tight with his conflicting emotions. "I've killed people with this awful power inside me, and their loved ones will forever hate me." He looked down at his hands as if disgusted with them. "But even though I destroy everything I touch, it's still an accident. You killed people *on purpose*."

"You're right," I said, eager for him to say whatever he needed to forgive me.

"I can't talk about this anymore." He shook his head. "I hate you too much right now."

I nodded, accepting how he felt. At least he wasn't running away from me in absolute fear.

A hard breath pushed from Blue's chest, then he stood. "We need to find Tzidal and Lex." He grabbed his pants, refusing to look at me. Ignoring the streaks of slick and cum coating his thighs, he pulled them on. "Joon is missing and—"

"Missing?" I sat up, leaning toward my mate. The last time I saw Joon was at the allied camp. "What happened to him?"

Blue tugged his robes on, jerking at the green fabric with harsh movements. He was pissed. "He infiltrated Strayton's inner circle. He's with your sister."

Fear ripped through me, and I jumped to a stand. The

quick movement made Blue flinch, but he stood firm, still glaring at me. "We have to get him out of there."

"I know!" Blue snapped, securing the sash along his middle. His robes were filthy. Covered in ash and dirt and wrinkled to the point that the intricate pattern on the fabric was hardly recognizable.

"We need to get you something else to wear."

Blue balked at my words. "For me to wear?" His eyes went wide at the ridiculousness of my words. "You're naked." He jabbed a finger at me.

I glanced down at my body. My eyes immediately moved to the red scratches Blue left on my chest and shoulders. Fear that he'd never touch me like that again gripped me, and I rushed him, closing the space between us. I just needed to touch him. To know that he was mine and I was his. I couldn't let him leave me.

Grabbing his upper arms tight, I pulled him to me, ignoring the quick flash of fear in his eyes. "I promise you, mate," I looked deep into his eyes, trying to push my sincerity through our bond, "I will find Joon and Tzidal, and even Lex. I will find them even if it kills me."

"No," Blue tipped his chin up, meeting my energy head-on. "You don't get to die. You have to live with what you did and find a way to make it right. You have to." His chin quivered. "You have to make this better for the families that have suffered."

"I give you my word," I pledged to him. "I will live the rest of my life being the kind of alpha you can be proud of."

"Good," he snipped. But then, slowly, the hard lines between his eyes faded, and his shoulder fell. "Because I'll be by your side. Watching you. Making sure you do." The gentle look in his eyes crushed me, and I wrapped my arms around his thin body, hugging him.

"You won't leave me?" I whispered against his mating bite.

A shiver worked through him, and he crossed his arms over his chest. "You're my mate." His voice was so soft as he stared at his feet. "I don't really have a choice."

What was left of my honor drifted away as I realized he was right. *He didn't have a choice.* A good alpha would have told him it was his right to leave me, but I couldn't let him go.

I'd never let him go.

And I'd kill anyone that tried to take him from me.

In The Courtyard

Tzidal

I KICKED OUT MY FEET, trying to break free from the unknown alpha's hold, but it was no use. He simply lifted me higher, moving me out of the path of the enraged wolf. Another alpha slammed into the wolf, and I jerked to see who it was, but all I saw was a tuft of dark hair and a flash of white fangs.

Tightening my grip on my blade, I swung, trying to make contact with the stranger, but I couldn't reach behind me. I kicked my feet again, trying to spin myself around to face the bastard, but all it did was twist the collar of my robes tight, making it hard to breathe.

The alpha holding me grunted as if punched, then jerked. I prayed he'd be hit again so that I could get away, but then he started running.

'Let me go!" I screamed as he weaved through the crowd, making his way toward the side of the palace.

"Quiet down, puppy," he gritted out in a deep, hard voice.

I bared my teeth, ready to swing my blade again, when his words hit me. *Puppy*.

"Lex?" I whispered, praying it was him, but he didn't answer.

The alpha reached the stone wall along the side of the palace, then wedged both of us into a tight alley. The alpha dropped me, and I spun, relieved to see the face of a monotonous unknown alpha melt away, replaced by Lex's soft boyish features.

"I'm so happy to see you," I flung my arms around his middle, but he pried my arms off him, urging me to keep going.

"Go!" He pushed me away. "There's a shed in the trees we can hide in. Go!"

My brows drew together, not understanding how he knew that, but before I could ask, an ear-splitting roar ripped through the air. I flinched, then ran. The narrow path was barely wide enough to fit more than an omega or two.

"Keep going," Lex urged me when I slowed down.

But my stomach was cramping again, crawling around to my back and down the back of my thighs. The deep ache settled in my knees, making me unsteady.

"How much further?" I panted, terrified my legs were going to give out.

"Turn right up there," Lex pointed just past me. He was right at my back, breathing hard against the back of my neck.

I pumped my arms and legs, determined to make it, and just when it felt like I couldn't go any further, the alleyway came to an abrupt end. I turned, then slowed as we ran into a wild garden.

It was overgrown, with thick vines and dead clusters of grass and bushes everywhere. There was a small well with a faded red roof falling in on itself, and a tiny treehouse was perched high up in a tree. The baseboards were visibly cracked, even from here.

It looked as if it had been years since anyone had maintained the land.

"This way." Lex jerked my arm, pulling me into the thick trees near the back. I moved over the overgrown pathway, carefully moving around the thickets of prickled thorn bushes and broken rock.

"How do you know where to go?" I asked Lex, ducking my head as we entered the tree line. The branches hung low, making the tiny forest feel private. I just needed to focus on something other than the horrifying look on Arian's face and the thick blood that poured from his eyes. *What the hell was that glowing rock?*

"Dane told me where to go." Lex scanned the dense trees as if looking for something.

Hope bloomed in my chest and I gripped his arm. "Did he know where they moved Blue? Or where Joon might be?" But I knew the answer before the siren could even open his mouth.

Sadness pulled at the corners of his eyes, and he tilted his head before whispering, "No, puppy."

I nodded, determined not to panic.

"Come on." He walked deeper into the trees, going slow so I could keep up.

A small shed came into view, but I didn't ask what it was for. *My wolf was a mess.* I couldn't feel my mate, I couldn't find Blue, Byriel was probably dead, and now my heat was starting back up.

Lex pulled open the rickety door to the shed, then stood to one side, letting me in. The tight space was practically empty, holding nothing but a few logs of crumbling wood and an old rusted lantern near a tiny window. I peered through it, looking directly at a small servant's door on the side of a tower. A few cobwebs stretched from the hinges to a nearby bush. It looked like it hadn't been used in quite some time.

"It's okay," Lex whispered, picking up the lantern. The metal handle squeaked as he tipped it, listening for the sound of oil. He pulled a face, telling me it was empty. "Dane should be here soon."

"What was that crystal? Have you ever seen anything like that before?"

Lex shook his head. "Never." Fear made his voice breathy and soft. "Wherever it came from, it wasn't a good place."

The door creaked open, and I spun to it, my dagger at the ready.

Dane's dark eyes zeroed in on my blade, then my face. He slowly raised his hands, glaring hard. "Easy, omega," he said in a flat, annoyed voice. The dim light made the long scar on his cheek look especially sunken and sharp. "I'm on your side."

"Be careful, brother." Kenji stepped around Dane. "This one will definitely stab you. There's no keeping her calm. I've tried."

"Don't touch me," I pointed my dagger at Kenji, ready to fight tooth and nail if he even tried to force me to leave for Madra. I was done pretending I was going anywhere without Joon. "Did anyone follow you?" I took half a step back, looking out the tiny window. The overgrown garden was quiet and empty, just the wind rustling the dead grass.

"No one comes out here, omega. This garden hasn't been tended to in years." Dane huffed as he stood one piece of chopped wood on its end, then sat. "Now, how about instead of threatening to stab me, you thank me for saving your ass from that gray wolf back there."

I snarled, baring my teeth. "I was fine on my own. I didn't need you to save me."

Dane cut me a sharp look, eyeing the point of my dagger. It was aimed right at his exposed chest. He was sweaty, with a few bruises blooming beneath his ribs. I didn't feel sorry for him. He was an alpha. He'd be healed by morning.

"What kind of magic was that?" I sucked in a deep breath, praying for the strength to steady my arm, but the point of my dagger jerked slightly, showing my fear. "Where did Strayton get that crystal?"

"I'd like to know that as well," Dane scrubbed his face, scratching behind each ear. He was restless. We all were. "Did she call it a star?" he mumbled as if speaking to himself.

"Why did she kill Arian?" Lex asked. "Did she know he was an ally?"

Kenji's eyes widened and his mouth fell open. "The leader of her guards was an ally?"

I jerked at his words. "How did you not know that?"

Kenji squared his shoulders, glaring down at me with clear offense.

"We don't send out a list of our members, omega," Dane snipped, making my wolf bristle at his tone. "We only share identities when we have to, otherwise we'd all be fucking dead."

"There's no need to be hostile." Lex moved just next to me, his presence both protective and comforting. "We're just trying to figure out what's happening here. What that crystal was." Lex shook his head. "I've never seen anything like it in all my years."

"I'm hoping that Joon can give a little insight." Dane narrowed his eyes out the small window at the palace. "I pray he's learned *something* helpful."

"Is he in the palace?" I asked, my voice edging higher with both excitement and fear. "We have to go and get him! We have to go *now*!" I jerked to move, but Kenji blocked my way, holding out his hands like a big barrier. "Move!" I snarled, pointing my blade at the damn alpha.

Kenji's eyes narrowed, annoyed. "Calm down," he said flatly. "You can't just burst in there. We need a plan."

Dane snorted, eyeing me as if I were a trivial nuisance. "Omegas have no business in war," he huffed. "They're too fucking sensitive."

Rage burned through my veins, making my wolf growl and my hands shake. "I don't give a shit about your opinion on omegas and war." Another fierce cramp rolled in my belly, but I held my breath, trying like hell not to react. My heat wasn't coming on slow this time, but barreling through me like a fucking forest fire. Fear rose, but I tightened my glare, focusing on the two alphas in front of me. "I just want to find my mate and get the hell out of here."

"Yeah?" Dane growled, leaning forward and flashing his teeth. "Do you have any idea what you're doing to your mate?"

The tip of my blade lowered, pointing at Dane's knees. "What the hell does that mean?"

"Your mate is somewhere inside that palace." Dane pointed out the tiny window. "I don't know where he is or if he's in trouble, but he's in there somewhere, and *I* put him there." He beat his fist against his chest. "And *you*," he pointed a long finger at me, "are so wound up, pushing nothing but panic and fear through your bond." He shook his head as if disgusted with my behavior. "It has to be driving him crazy with that in his head." His eyes glowed red, and his voice dropped to a horrible whisper, "You're going to get him killed."

Tears stung the back of my eyes, and my throat tightened to the point I struggled to breathe. The truth was, I couldn't feel Joon. He was blocking me out, keeping me from knowing anything about what was happening to him.

"Don't talk about my mate," I whispered, terrified I'd start crying if I spoke any louder. "You don't get to say such awful things to me." I tightened my grip on the dagger, wanting to run the horrible alpha through.

"Put the fucking knife down." Dane crossed his arms, eyeing my full form, assessing just how weak I was. I didn't budge. "Omega," he leaned forward, placing his hands on his knees, "Put the dagger away, or I will rip it from your hands and beat your ass senseless for your disobedience."

Lex stiffened next to me, his anger warming the air. "How dare you—"

"No need," I cut in, placing a hand on Lex's shoulder. "I'll put it up." I looked Dane right in the eyes as I sheathed my weapon. His frown grew, making the scar along the side of his face more pronounced, and the dark circles under his eyes appear even more sunken.

"Be careful, omega," Dane warned in a deep rumble. "I don't take kindly to being challenged."

I tipped my head up and squared my shoulders, sick of these damn alphas seeing me as beneath them. "There's a beta in my old village named Dane."

His eyes narrowed, and his head tilted, clearly wondering where I was going with this.

"He wasn't a terrible man," I continued. "He was nosey. Talked far too much. I guess being insufferable is just a trait all men with your name share."

Dane jerked to a stand, rushing to close the space between us, but before he could strike me, Kenji stepped between us with his hand raised.

"If you want to get killed, that's fine by me!" Dane roared. "But you are being reckless. Wandering around the prison, asking questions, getting caught. I will not jeopardize everything we've worked for for one fucking omega!"

My fist curled tight, and I straightened my back, trying to look as mighty as possible. "If everything you've worked for can be destroyed by one fucking omega, then clearly, you haven't worked very hard."

Dane roared, then jerked. Lex shoved me behind him while Kenji struggled to control Dane.

"No!" Kenji gritted out, finally shoving the alpha hard away from him. "I agree that this omega is an insufferable beast, but I promised her mate I'd keep her safe."

Dane growled low in his chest, panting hard.

"You can't attack her," Kenji said before cutting me a stern look. "No matter how bad either one of us want to, you can't attack her."

I pushed away from Lex, shoving open the shed door, then marching straight toward the palace.

Lex's voice drifted through the tiny window. "She's already lost one mate, and she's terrified of losing another. You assholes could be a little more understanding."

I picked up my pace, not interested in hearing anything else they had to say. Was it possible that Joon had died, but I didn't feel it? Maybe we weren't mated long enough for our bond to truly seal. Or maybe he was knocked out and on death's door?

Either way, I wasn't going to stop until I found him. *I had to find him.*

"Tzidal!" Lex's voice called out, but I kept walking, not sure what to say to the siren. "Please, stop." His long fingers curled around my wrist, forcing me to slow down.

"Joon is in there," I said, looking up at the mighty tower. "I can't feel him, but I know he's in there somewhere."

Lex raised an eyebrow, eyeing the massive tower. "You can't feel him?"

"No," I tried to step over a large tangle of vines, but they took up the whole path, crunching under my bare feet. "I think he's blocking me out, but he's there." I stopped, taking in the sight of the enormous black palace. It was so big it would take weeks to search the whole place...and that was assuming I didn't get lost.

"Then let's go get him," Lex said simply.

I rolled my eyes, feeling so small and weak. "How? We can't exactly stroll in and ask where they keep the alphas that infiltrate the palace. We'd be captured in a heartbeat."

"Oh really?" Lex crossed his arms, popping out a hip. "You're a member of the prim-staff." He slipped a finger under the collar of my robes. "A dirty one," he eyed my wrinkled black uniform, "but still a royal servant. No one could stop us." His robes shifted, replicating mine perfectly—except his were exceptionally clean. "How about it?" His brows shot up, excited. "Want to go for a stroll through the common rooms?"

I glanced back at the small shed, not surprised to see Kenji watching me carefully. "What about them?" I jerked my head at the shed.

"Do you really care?" Lex pulled my arm, forcing me to turn my back to the alpha. "It's not like they can tell us what to do. They aren't your mate, and they sure as shit don't control me." He cut a glare over his shoulder. "How about it? Want to go on our own little mission?"

I opened my mouth, ready to race off with the siren, but a sharp pain cut through my gut, and my knees wobbled.

"Woah, there," Lex moved me to sit on a large rock. "Are you okay? Is it," he leaned down, whispering in my ear, "Is it your heat?"

I nodded, grimacing from the rolling pain. "I think so. I'm all achy again." It was horrible, rippling through my gut and stabbing inside my sex. I shivered just thinking about the horrible things I was going to beg for once it took hold and the strangers that would happily defile me.

"What about that gem?" Lex dropped to his knees in front of me. "The citrine? It helps with pain." He reached into my pockets, not stopping until he found the shimmering dark yellow object. "Open," he ordered, popping it inside my mouth.

It was smooth against my tongue, slipping carefully from one cheek to the other. I let out a soft breath as the tight pain in my lower back eased.

But I couldn't relax too much. I was running out of time.

"Lex," I whispered, feeling my wolf grow restless. "If we can't find Joon...." My chest tightened, and I licked my lips, trying to hold myself together. "If my heat hits, I might need help." Shame warmed my face. "Would you—"

"Tzidal," Lex cupped my face, forcing me to look up at him. "I will do whatever you want to get you through this. I can shift into Joon if it makes you feel better, or—"

"I'm asking if you'll kiss me!" I yelled, quickly spitting the gem into my hand. "Knock me out!"

Lex's eyes widened, then he snorted loudly, laughing with his whole chest. "That's a much better idea!"

Inside The Passageways

Byriel

"BYRIEL?" Blue's voice drifted from behind me, making me stop. "Alpha, where...where are you?" His wide eyes scanned the tunnel, not focusing on anything. It was so dark he probably couldn't see with his omega eyes. These passageways were always lit in the past, but they were cast in complete darkness, making them useless for everyone but an alpha.

"I'm right here, mate," I reached for his hand, pulling him closer. His fingers drifted up my arm, holding me tight. I moved to pick him up, then thought better of it. He was still angry with me...as he should be. "Can I carry you?" I asked softly.

He pressed his lips into a tight line, then he closed his eyes and nodded.

My wolf preened at the small victory, growling happily as I picked the omega up. Blue's arms circled my neck, but he didn't caress my skin or nuzzle my chest. He simply rested the point of his chin on my shoulder, his body stiff in my arms.

"Are you sure no one will find us here?" he whispered.

"I'm sure," I said as confidently as I could. "No one uses these passageways in the palace except the royal family and very trusted advisors."

"But you haven't been home in two years." Blue pointed out. "How do you know that hasn't changed?"

I thought on that, realizing I didn't really know, but I didn't want to scare my mate. "These passages are—"

"Don't lie," he cut me off, making my wolf bristle. "I can feel it when you're about to lie."

Pushing out a long sigh, I kept my mouth shut, deciding that saying nothing was probably best.

"Are we at least almost there?" he turned, trying to look over his shoulder.

"We're almost there," I cut down a tight corridor, noting the scent of death in the air. The pungent aroma was quickly followed by the overly sharp scent of an elf.

My father hated the elves. In all my life, not a single one had ever set foot in these halls, but now that my sister was in power, who knew what she was up to? But after what happened with her elvish lover, I was sure it wasn't good.

"The family quarters are just up here. We can get some fresh clothes before we head out."

Blue didn't say anything, but he did rest his cheek against my shoulder. It wasn't the affectionate cuddle that an omega normally gave their mate, but I'd take any love I could get from the angry omega. I'd wait a thousand years for him to forgive me if I had to.

"Okay," I whispered as we came to the right section of the wall. "Don't make a sound. We have to cut down two corridors to get to my room."

Blue nodded, staying quiet.

Moving slowly, I pulled the small handle on the hinged wall, then readied myself as it cracked open. The air outside the tunnel was warm, the smell of burning wood filling my chest.

Not scenting anyone around us, I took a tentative step into the corridor, letting the panel shut softly behind us. The palace was dead silent: no murmur of voices or the movement of feet. If Strayton wasn't in her room, there was a good chance there weren't even any guards in this wing.

I slipped my hand over Blue's back, holding him tight as I moved, creeping as quickly as possible. The first corridor was empty, but the second one held the soft voice of an elder. It drifted from Tibbit's room. It sounded as if the beta was speaking to a woman, and she smelled....*human*? Maybe a priestess or a witch.

Creeping silently across the long red carpet, I paused at the end of the hall. Strayton's room was first, then mine, and lastly, at the very end was my father's. In the past, he always had a guard posted at his door, but it seemed my sister wasn't following that practice. The hall was completely empty.

Tibbit's voice grew louder, and a doorknob rattled. I moved.

Not knowing who he was with, I couldn't risk an enemy seeing me. They might hurt Blue.

Halfway to Strayton's room, I realized her bedroom door was open. Sunlight poured out into the hallway, casting long streaks over the carpet. For half a second, I thought of returning the way we came, but it sounded as if Tibbit and his guest were now standing in the hallway, talking softly amongst themselves.

Fuck.

My bedroom door was just within sight, the brass door-knob calling to me like a beacon.

Tightening my hold on my mate, I inched forward,

peering into Strayton's room. A large guard stood in a casual stance with his back to the door. He was clearly watching someone move about.

"Hurry up!" a female spoke in a loud commanding tone. It was a beta, probably one of the older maidens changing the sheets or setting out my sister's afternoon tea. "Those hoodlums could break in here at any moment! They're practically beating down the fucking door!"

Worry slipped down my spine, and I rushed past Strayton's door to my room.

Were the allies attacking?

Could they be inside the palace even as we spoke?

I listened hard, not hearing anything other than Tibbit's soft tones and the sound of someone rustling around in Strayton's room.

Being extremely careful not to drop Blue, I turned the brass knob to my door, grimacing as the metal jerked and then squeaked. It felt as if it hadn't been used or oiled since I left. I placed Blue on his feet, then shut the door as quietly as I could behind us.

"This is your bedroom?" Blue whispered, his voice filled with awe. "This is huge."

I turned and scanned the room, a little shocked to see everything *exactly* as I left it. A small part of me always assumed my father had gutted the whole space and burned all my belongings, but it seemed that no one had set foot in here since the day I left home. My bed had the same dark blue bedding, but now it held the musky scent of dust. My diary was open on my desk, and even my carafe was still next to my bed, but instead of water, it was coated in a thin layer of grime.

Moving toward the bed, I reached for the blade still resting on my favorite quilt. The day I had left, I struggled to decide which dagger I'd bring.

"What did that beta mean by hoodlums?" Blue pulled me

from my thoughts. Flurries of dust floated in the air just around his face, dancing in the thin cuts of sunlight that broke through the dark green curtains.

I shook my head, then whispered, "I'm not sure, but it can't be good. We need to hurry."

Blue nodded in agreement, clasping his hands in front of him. He looked so small and lost. *Scared*. He was scared. I could feel a trace of it in our still-forming bond, but it was there.

I was just so impressed at how composed he was.

"I'm sure I have something you can wear," I whispered, moving quickly across the room and into the closet. I immediately pulled on a pair of sturdy black leather pants and a worn cream-colored shirt. It was wise to pick simple clothing to blend into a crowd.

Crouching down, I pulled out a few old boxes from the bottom of my closet. I was sure I had a few outfits from my younger years within at least one of them, but all I found were some old toys, notebooks filled with long-forgotten lessons and every card my mother ever gave me. I was ready to give up when a heavy bundle caught my eye. I reached for it, quickly undoing the knot. The clothes inside were all formal—from when I presented as an alpha. The celebratory events seemed never to end that year, and I found myself with more clothes than I'd ever wear.

Searching quickly, I finally settled on a pair of gray slacks and a well-tailored white button-up with pearl buttons. They were the plainest items I could find.

"These should fit you." I held the garments up as I stepped back into my bedroom.

Blue's sniffles hit my ears, and I jerked my head up, finding him at my desk, my diary in his hands.

Fear and shame beat hard in my chest. I dropped the

clothes, rushed to him, and ripped the book from his hands. "Don't—"

Blue flung his arms around my neck, pulling me down to hug him. I was frozen in place, terrified of what he had read. My most horrible moments were written in that damn book, but I never felt the need to hide it. If my father or sister wandered in here, they'd simply read the truth.

"I'm so sorry," my mate whimpered against my neck. His warm tears dripped over his cheeks, soaking the front of my shirt.

Curious about what had upset him, I turned the book over in my hand and read over Blue's shoulder.

> *Found a young pup stealing fruit in the kitchens today. The starving pup ate the entirety of my father's favorite strawberries., then he kicked me in the shins before running off.*
>
> *I hated the idea of my father hunting the savage child, so I confessed, and took my beating well. But at least that pup will sleep well tonight with a full belly.*

The entry was from four years ago. I was an adult—in my mid-twenties at the time—and I allowed my father to beat me over a few pieces of fucking fruit.

I flung the book onto the bed as shame burned my face and chest. While I didn't want to hide my past from my mate, I didn't want his pity.

"I'm just so sorry," Blue repeated, pressing his nose between my pecs. He was scenting me. Loving me. It felt like heaven. "I didn't know it was that bad. You said your father wasn't a good man, but I didn't know he...he..." His voice dropped to a tiny squeak, "...beat you."

"Don't feel sorry for me, my love." I caressed his back, cherishing his touch. "He made his choices, and I made mine. In the end, we all pay for what we've done."

Blue nuzzled his cheek against me. "Still." He paused, and I heard him audibly swallow before saying, "I don't forgive you for what you've done, but I know you didn't *want* to do it. You couldn't have." He looked up at me, resting his chin on my chest. "You're too good, my mate. You have too much honor to want something so evil. To want to k-kill people."

My throat tightened, and the back of my eyes burned hot with the threat of tears. There were many things I wanted to tell my sweet omega, but I couldn't. Not without losing myself to my more shameful emotions, and right now wasn't the time.

"We need to go," I whispered, sucking in a quick breath through my nose. "If Strayton were to return to her room, a whole battalion of guards would join her. We need to leave while we can."

Blue released me, then immediately started stripping down. Tiny bruises from my rough handling littered his pale skin. *Proof of our mating.* It warmed my heart to see him so thoroughly loved. He was mine.

"They fit," Blue said in an excited whisper as he turned to me. The pants were loose on his hips, and the shirt was too long to tuck in, but it still looked presentable. No one would stop him or suspect him of being out of place.

"Are you ready?" I whispered, grabbing my old dagger off the foot of my bed. I immediately checked the steel blade, noting the rust along the hilt and the dull tip. It was why I didn't take it with me. I didn't have time to sharpen it, but for now, it would do. "Come here, my love." I turned to Blue, securing the blade to his belt.

He pulled a face and balked, "I don't know how to use that."

"Tzidal didn't know how to use hers at first either, but I taught her. I'll teach you too." I tested the double-knot in the fastening, jerking on it once to make sure it would hold.

"Do you think I'll need it?" He pressed his small fists to his chest, trying to hide a noticeable tremor.

"There's no need to be scared," I smooth my hands up and down his arms. "I'll be right by your side, protecting you. This is just in case."

A quick smile lifted the corners of his mouth, and he nodded quickly, but the motion was tight. Jerky. "I know. I just get anxious sometimes."

I placed a quick kiss on his temple before escorting him back to the bedroom door. "I know you do, my love. And it's okay. I'm right here." I circled my hand around his wrist, then paused. "Want me to carry you?" I asked, my fingers perched on the doorknob.

"No. I'm okay." He shook his head, but I could see the fear in his eyes.

I let it go, not wanting to steal his chance to be brave. "Stay very quiet," I whispered, looking deep into his hypnotic eyes.

He nodded, and I opened the door.

Strayton's bedroom door was shut, but there were no guards in the hallway or stationed at her door. Either my sister felt she didn't need them, or she wasn't in her room.

Keeping my steps light and quick, I tugged Blue along, rushing past Stray's door, around the corner, and straight to the hidden passageway. A swift wash of relief moved through me as we slipped behind the hinged wall, but I tempered it, knowing we weren't safe yet.

I wrapped an arm around Blue's middle, and he jerked, startled. "It's just me," I whispered to him in the dark. Then I lifted him, carrying him back down the way we came.

The scent of elves and death grew stronger as we walked. Curious, I paused at the hinged door to the Judgement Room and inhaled deeply. At least two elves were just on the other side, along with the muted scent of death. Someone had died, and recently. But there was someone else. Someone familiar, but there were too many other odors in the air to be sure of who it was.

"What's wrong?" Blue whispered as I stared at the door.

"I'm just thinking." My eyes drifted over the rough wall as I realized who the woodsy scent belonged to. It was Joon. "I think..." Fear and dread pulsed in my veins as I tried to figure out what to do first. Help Joon or get Blue out of here?

I'd have to leave Blue in the treehouse while I returned to get Joon, but the thought of leaving my mate was unacceptable.

"What is this room for?" Blue turned in my arms, his wide omega eyes not focusing on anything in the dark.

"It's the Judgement Room," I said in a tight voice.

Blue's brows pulled together, confused as to its purpose.

"It was where noblemen were confronted for their crimes. They'd be judged by their peers and sentenced by the King, but it hasn't been used for that in years. My father preferred handling high-standing wolves that broke his laws in private."

But it seemed Strayton was using it once again.

Blue shivered, understanding my meaning. "He k-killed them?"

I didn't answer, just narrowing my eyes once again at the wall.

"Wait!" Blue whispered harshly, and I froze. His nose twitched as he turned his head one way and then another, scenting the air. Then he jerked, pushing himself out of my arms. I reluctantly let him go, waiting nervously for whatever it was he could smell. *Blue's speed and nose were almost as good as an alpha's.*

"Joon!" He slapped his hands to the hinged wall. It pushed, cracking open, but I jerked the omega back, hugging him tight against my chest.

"We don't know who else is in there," I whispered, refusing to let him go.

"Joon is in there," Blue's voice rose, pushing hard at my chest to get away. "We have to help him!"

"Calm down," I ordered him, knowing he wouldn't be able to disobey me.

And just as I expected, Blue went still, not uttering a word, but his eyes glared hard in my direction, not quite able to see me in the dark. He looked like he wanted to rip me to pieces, but it was my job as his alpha to protect him.

"Come." I pushed gently at Blue's back, but he didn't budge. "Let me get you to safety, and then I'll return for Joon."

My mate's soft scent edged sharp, flooded with his intense displeasure. My wolf snarled and growled low, hating that I was upsetting the tender omega.

"No," he whispered through clenched teeth. "I'm not going anywhere."

Frustrated and desperate to hurry this along, I let out a long sigh, then leaned down to whisper in Blue's ear, "Stay at my side, and if I say run," I spoke slowly, letting my alpha tones wash over him, "Then run. Do you understand?"

Blue nodded once, crossing his arms.

Once I was sure he'd obey my command, I placed my hand flat against the hinged wall, then pushed. The scent of death grew, but it wasn't the wet scent of a rotting corpse. It was still fresh.

Moving slowly, I brushed the tapestry out of my way, then I stood, scanning the whole room.

Two elves were strung up against the wall, one clearly dead. Across from the living elf was one of my father's advisors, Omega Janie. She was loyal to the King and had been very open about her disgust with Strayton's union with an elf.

"Oh my goodness!" Blue gasped loudly, then ran toward the opposite end of the room. I swiped out to stop the omega, but he was too fast.

"Blue!" I whispered harshly, cursing the fact that he was already disobeying me. I opened my mouth to scold him, but then shock slammed into me as I finally saw Joon.

He was strung up, like everyone else in this damn room. His shaggy brown hair hung in his face, sticking to the blood that covered his nose and mouth, and his exposed chest was covered with deep, ugly bruises.

"Joon?" Blue whispered, peering up into the alpha's face. "Alpha?" His voice edged higher, filling with sharp emotion. "Byriel," he turned to me, his eyes glassy and wide with fear. "Is he..." he trailed off, unable to finish his thought.

"He's not dead," I assured my mate. "He's still breathing." I ignored the sharp wheezing sound pushing from Joon's chest and lifted his head, looking over the alpha's face. His lip was busted, one eye was swollen shut, and his nose was definitely broken.

"We have to get him out of here," Blue whispered.

I turned, looking for a key.

"*Byriel*?" A beta strung up across from Joon whispered my name as if she couldn't believe I was here. "My Lord. Is that really you?"

I moved to the young blonde beta, looking her over for obvious wounds. She looked unharmed for the most part, just exhausted and scared.

"Why are you in here?" I asked, narrowing my eyes at her common uniform. "Are you..." I lowered my voice, whispering, "Are you an ally?"

Confusion twisted her brow, and she shook her head. "I'm just a maid, My Lord. No one important."

Blue rushed past me to a small table, pulling open the tiny drawer along the front. "Found it!" He held a small brass object up with a triumphant look on his beautiful face. *It was a key.*

I narrowed my eyes, not believing my sister would be so reckless as to leave the key in such an obvious place. "Let's see if it works." I held out my hand, moving to examine the young beta's shackles.

Blue placed the brass key in my palm, watching me carefully as I pushed into the lock. The beta's face scrunched up as I turned the key, briefly tightening the cuffs before they sprang free. She remained frozen in place for a moment before pulling her hands free.

Her face brightened, and she let out a deep breath of relief. "Thank you. I—"

The chains that dangled from the ceiling jerked, rattling loudly. I took a step back, pulling Blue with me.

Then they did it again, jerking a full foot upward.

Then again.

And again.

Heavy feet pounded the stone floor on the other side of the door.

"It's an alarm!" I yelled, dropping the keys and racing to grip the doorknob. It rattled hard, someone trying to open it from the other side. "Run!" I commanded both the young girl and my mate.

The beta bolted, going straight for the doorway hidden on the other side of the tapestry, but Blue stayed put, trembling hard as he disobeyed me. His eyes flickered between me and Joon's unconscious form.

"Run!" I roared, and the door jerked, but I pulled it closed again. The person on the other side didn't have the strength of an alpha. Maybe a beta. But it wouldn't be long before a whole drove of guards broke down this entire fucking wall. "Blue! Fucking run!"

My mate's feet finally moved, but instead of following the beta, he grabbed the keys off the floor, then raced to Joon. "I have to help him!" Blue pushed up on his tiptoes, fumbling to get the key into Joon's cuffs.

The door jerked again, followed by the angry yell of an alpha. I instantly recognized Dynel's deep tones—my sister's favorite guard.

"Blue!" I looked over my shoulder at the omega, still struggling with the key. "I'm not telling you again," I snarled, making a shiver work through my mate's slight body. "Get your ass—"

Joon's cuffs sprang free, and he pitched forward, smacking hard into the stone floor. His chains jerked up, rattling and clunking loud enough for the whole damn palace to hear.

Desperate, I did the only thing I could think of: I opened the door and immediately kicked my foot out at the first person I saw. Shocked, Dynel stumbled backward, taking two alpha guards down with him. I spun, heaved Joon's heavy body over my shoulder, then moved as fast as I could to the hidden door. Blue's soft feet padded against the floor, right at my back.

"Stay with me!" I panted, running hard down the corridor and toward the back of the castle.

Hurried feet filled the dark passageway as Dynel and at least two others picked up their pace, chasing us.

Blue's fist pushed at my back, urging me to go faster.

I just needed to get out in the open to fight these fuckers off properly without worrying about hurting Blue.

I just needed to get to the gardens.

In The Garden

Tzidal

"OMEGA!" Dane's annoying voice cut through the cold winter air, forcing my attention away from Lex. "Come." He snapped, beckoning me to return to the tiny shed.

I stayed rooted in place, crossing my legs and getting comfortable on the large rock. If he wanted something, he could come to me.

Dane's expression went hard, narrowing his eyes as he marched toward me. "Come back here now," he ordered, making my wolf snarl and growl. But his alpha tones had no affect on me. I was too focused on getting Joon back...at least until my heat started. "You're going to get yourself killed walking around where you don't belong." He motioned at the pathetic garden all around us.

"I'm wearing a servant's uniform," I held out my arms to show him my prim-staff frock. "I don't look out of place." I eyed the alpha's bare chest and informal linen pants. "Besides, you said no one comes out here."

Dane let out an angry snort, but I turned my back to him, not interested in anything the alpha had to say. Instead, I choose to admire the tiny servant's door at the base of the tower. Its hinges were black, and a long spider web connected from the cold lantern on the step to a nearby bush.

"Omega," Dane growled, coming up hard and fast behind me. "I am sick and fu—"

The servant's door burst open, and I jerked to stand, ripping my dagger from its sheath. It took a moment for my eyes to focus on the fight before me, simply not believing it.

Byriel.

And he was carrying Joon!

I opened my mouth, ready to scream with joy, but then Blue raced out of the palace, followed by three massive alphas. Without pausing to think, I immediately drew back my hand, then threw my blade at the nearest alpha. It spun, flying through the air, then the tip of the blade slipped into a dark-skinned alpha's breast bone, not stopping until it hit the hilt.

Dane stared at me, shock keeping him in place.

"Help!" I snapped at the alpha before racing to retrieve my weapon.

The wounded alpha struggled to breathe, his chest jerking with each painful breath. I ripped my dagger from his body, then turned, looking to attack my next target.

But the other two alphas were already down.

Kenji stood over an unconscious bald alpha with ashen skin and deep, ugly scars all over his body. Lex was hunched over the last guard, ripping the poor alpha's neck out and slowly chewing. Kenji narrowed his eyes at the siren, then abruptly spun, gagging into the grass.

"Tzidal!" Blue crashed into me, hugging me with all his might.

I squeezed him with everything I had, thankful he was alive. But he smelled....*off*. The omega's usually fresh, bright scent was laced with the aroma of weathered leather and something smokey. I sniffed Blue's shoulder, realizing what it was. *Cedar*.

His scent was mixed with Byriel's.

And only one thing did that to an omega.

Leaning back, I pushed Blue's hair away from his neck, finding a fresh mating bite right beneath his ear.

Blue's cheeks warmed, the flush traveling down his neck as he grinned wildly. "It just kind of happened," he whispered, tracing the edge of the mark with his finger. Then he leaned into my ear and whispered, "Byriel was a good alpha, just like you said. He didn't let it hurt long."

I wanted to be angry that the alpha claimed the youngling, but I could only feel joy for my sweet friend. This was what Blue wanted, and he looked so damn happy and proud.

"It looks good," I cupped the omega's cheek. My eyes flickered to Joon's unconscious form still draped over Byriel's shoulder. I wanted to race over and check on my mate, but I knew the second I examined him, I'd fall into deep despair. The scent of Joon's blood already had my wolf spiraling.

"We need to go," Byriel's breathless voice pulled my attention. He groaned, adjusting Joon over his shoulder. "Now." His green eyes met mine, and I grabbed Blue's hand, ready to run.

"I know a place, My Lord," Dane bowed quickly. "It's safe, and we can stay there while we figure out our next steps."

Byriel eyed the servant's door, nervous energy flowing off him. I half expected more guards to burst out of the dark at any second.

IT FELT as if we walked forever.

Through the forest behind the palace.

Far along the border wall.

Around the poorest houses near the gully and into the alleyways where sketchy alphas roamed.

I stared at Joon draped over Byriel's back. His ribs were a concerning black and blue, and blood dripped from an ugly cut on the back of his head. Familiar memories of tending to him after the fight in Vaesen lingered in my mind, but I kept trying to force them back. Joon needed good thoughts from me. Sweet affirmations that would help him heal faster.

"What is this place?" Byriel asked, looking up at the tiny building. It was well after nightfall, and the alleyway was tight, with no signs on this side of the street telling us where we were.

"It's the caretaker's office for the greenhouses," Dane said, pulling open the rickety back door. "Alpha CariAnn works here. She's a friend."

I raised my brows, a little surprised to know an alpha was responsible for tending to *flowers*. Alphas were fighters, hunters, or warriors. They weren't exactly known for having green thumbs.

Blue grabbed my hand as we stepped inside, and I turned, searching for Lex. He had kept up the rear of our little party, making sure we weren't followed. I couldn't help but notice he didn't try to project any kind of scent. He smelled muted. Not a wolf, but a predator, warning anyone to stay away.

"This is very small," Blue whispered, looking around the dimly lit office.

The walls were a pale white wood, with smooth wooden floors and matching wooden desks. I had expected the space to smell strongly of flowers, but all I could scent was oak and fresh dirt.

"Can I help you?" A tall woman with a deep, tan

complexion and long, beautiful braids stepped out from a back room. She wore faded blue coveralls and had a pair of gardening shears in her hand. "This office isn't open to the public."

Dane stepped forward, making his presence known.

"Dane," the statuesque woman smiled, seemingly happy to see him. "To what do I owe the honor?"

"CariAnn." Dane returned her smile. "I brought some friends that would love to see the gardenias." An entire conversation seemed to pass between the two alphas as they stared at each other.

CariAnn finally nodded, glancing at each one of our faces. Her eyes drifted from me to Blue, Kenji, Byriel, then Lex. But they shot back to Byriel going wide. "My Lord?" she whispered as if not believing he was here.

"Please." Byriel attempted to bow, but Joon's weight on his shoulder made the movement jerky and shallow. "My friend needs help, and the omegas need food."

CariAnn seemed to struggle to think for a moment, her mouth hanging open. "Of course, My Lord." She gave a quick jerk of her head. I assumed it was meant to be a bow, but the she-alpha was too nervous to do it properly. "Right this way." She turned, disappearing into the main part of the store.

The walls in this part of the office were lined with tall shelves, each holding little pots of plants. None of them had bloomed, as flowers rarely flourished in the winter, but their lush green leaves all looked healthy and strong—probably grown in the greenhouses somewhere within the city. A long table in the center of the room held pruning shears, clippings, and a water canister.

"You can place him here," CariAnn opened a door beneath a set of narrow stairs, ushering us inside.

The storage room was tight, filled with boxes and empty planters stacked on top of one another. A few spades leaned against one corner of the room, along with trowels, pickaxes, and even one very long sword.

"I'll send a message to the healer," CariAnn bowed once again to Byriel. "There's also a room upstairs you can sleep in, but there's no bed or cot. Just some burlap tarps."

"Thank you." Byriel slowly lowered Joon. Kenji moved to help, cradling Joon's head so it wouldn't smack against the floor.

Once my mate was settled, I moved to him, kneeling at his side. The lantern overhead cast a hard light over Joon's face, giving me a clear view of his busted lip and swollen eye.

Desperate to know how deep his injuries ran, I leaned down and licked his lips. He tasted muted, but his heartbeat was strong. I licked him again, cleaning the cut on his upper lip, before moving up and over the side of his face.

Omegas couldn't heal a wound like an alpha, but I could still help soothe Joon's injuries so his wolf could grow stronger and fix him faster.

"Let me help." Blue settled on the other side of Joon, grabbing my mate's hands. He lapped at Joon's wrists, pulling out all the dried blood and what looked like rust. I assumed it was from some kind of shackles or chains.

Lex sat at Joon's head as we worked, and Byriel moved protectively to Blue's side. I half expected the dark alpha to protest that his mate was helping me. Even though there was nothing inappropriate or odd about what Blue was doing, many alphas would consider it grossly unacceptable for their mate to tend to a non-family member like this.

We spent the next hour cleaning every scratch we could find while a few unknown alphas and betas arrived, pushing into the already tight space. I ignored everyone, letting Byriel and Dane focus on greeting each new stranger.

"What do we have here?" A soft-spoken beta settled next to me. I turned, eyeing her tan complexion and long red hair.

"This is Susi. She's a healer," Dane said, introducing us. "The alpha was found within the palace. We don't know how long he's been out or the extent of his injuries."

Susi nodded, lifting one of Joon's eyelids. She leaned down and looked through a circular glass, examining one eye, then the other. Fear beat in my chest, followed by a slow-rolling cramp deep in my stomach. I was sure I didn't have much more time before my heat started, but I'd die before leaving Joon's side. *Maybe it would even wake him up...*

"Jonelle," Byriel's deep sigh of relief made me look up. "How are you?" He reached for her hand, shaking it.

I scanned the tiny room, recognizing a few familiar faces—Kenji, Jonelle, and Dane, but then there was also Yari, a service beta I had met at the allied camp.

"I'm so happy to see you alive, My Lord." Jonelle settled onto a stack of bags filled with seed, patting Dane on the back. "I don't know how you managed to blow the whole side of the prison out like that, but it was impressive," she snorted.

My eyes immediately shot to Blue, but he ducked his head, ignoring my gaze. I immediately knew it was his doing.

"A friend helped me escape," Byriel said simply. He was right not to share Blue's power with these people. After all, at this point, I had no idea who we could really trust.

"This is everyone," CariAnn said as she shut the door.

Dane's eyes narrowed, taking in all the faces around us.

"Where's Arain?" Yari asked, tucking a long strand of her black hair behind her ear. Everyone shifted, not quite able to meet the young beta's eyes. "Dane?" She turned to the alpha. "Where is Arian?"

Dane swallowed hard, deep sorrow pulling his brows together. "I'm so sorry, Yari. But Strayton killed him with some kind of crystal."

"She said it held the power of the stars," Kenji whispered.

A sharp squeak jumped from Yari's throat. She slapped her

hand over her mouth to muffle the sound, then she curled inward, crying into her lap.

"It's okay, beta," Jonelle pulled at Yari's arm, forcing the beta to her side. "Arian died an honorable death."

Deep sadness filled the small room, making me wish I could sob with the poor girl, but if I fell apart right now, there'd be no putting me back together.

"Arian was a strong and honorable beta," Byriel said. He looked so stoic and strong, keeping his head up. It was odd, but I clung to his calm presence, letting it settle my wolf. "When this is all over, our people will remember his name as a true warrior."

Yari nodded, wiping her nose with the back of her hand. "He was a good friend," she whispered, pressing tighter to Jonelle's side.

"It's okay," Susi said in a rush of words, holding up her hands just in front of Joon's face. "I'm a friend. I'm not hurting you."

My wolf sprang to life, yipping loudly. Joon's dark eyes were wide open, darting all around the room, but they were glassy and unfocused. Dazed.

"Where am I?" Joon snarled, but his fangs weren't distended. His teeth were flat and white, his human-form firmly in place. That wasn't good.

"You're safe," I reached for my mate's hand, kissing the back of it. The raw skin around his wrists made my chest squeeze hard. "I've got you."

Joon lifted his head off the floor, squinting as if struggling to see me. "This is a dream," he said firmly, squeezing his eyes shut tight. "This has to be a dream."

"Is he okay?" Byriel leaned forward, glancing down at my mate over Blue's back.

Susi forced one of Joon's eyes open wide, looking through the circular glass again. "It looks like he's been drugged."

"That's likely," Dane said simply. "Arian has been knocking out allied prisoners when he can. Give them a chance to heal before being questioned again."

Yari let out a muffled sob, and Jonelle rested her cheek on the beta's head, shushing her.

"Where is my mate?" Joon glared at me, then his head wobbled, falling limp once again.

"Don't move," I urged him, pushing at his chest. "You need to rest."

"I need to get the star before it gets Tzidal!" Joon grunted hard, raising his hands as if to snatch something out of the air.

"The star?" Byriel knelt next to my side.

Joon pressed one hand to his temple. He looked as if he was thinking, but then Joon lunged, grabbing either side of Byriel's face and glaring hard into his eyes. Jonelle jerked, but Byriel held out a hand, stopping her. "Tell me about the star, Joon." His voice was soft and even, patiently waiting for Joon to collect his thoughts.

Joon's dark eyes moved over his lap and then off into the distance. I jerked as our bond burst with his crazed emotions. Letting out a pained hiss, I curled inward, trying to push back all soft, loving feelings, but it was a losing battle.

"It's okay, Joon," Lex whispered, placing his hands on either side of my alpha's head. "Relax your mind, and soften your heart, sweet wolf." The siren's tone was so gentle. It felt as if each word warmed the room, urging me to curl up and fall asleep.

Yari let out a loud yawn as she slumped against Jonelle, and Blue's head rolled forward, then jerked back up, struggling to stay awake. Even Susi sat back on her feet, rubbing the back of her neck.

Realizing what Lex was doing, I touched his forearm. "Too much," I whispered. "Pull your spell back."

"I tend to be too much." Lex gave me a playful smile as he

scratched softly at Joon's scalp. The room cooled, and my fingers tingled. "Better?" Lex asked.

I immediately nodded, then arched my back to stretch it out.

"I had no idea you could do that," Byriel whispered as if in awe. "Do you...*play*...with our emotions often?"

"Fucking sirens," Dane snarled, abruptly standing up. His quick movements made Kenji back up, hitting the door. "He shouldn't be here!" Dane pointed at Lex. "He's too fucking dangerous."

Byriel held up his hand as if to stop Dane's spiraling anger.

"I don't *play* with your emotions," Lex whispered, smoothing his fingertips over Joon's brow and down the length of his crooked nose. "I simply find a desire or an emotion that you're already feeling, and I bring it forward."

Blue tilted his head, clearly not understanding, but neither did I. "Are we all...*sleepy*?" Blue asked.

"Oh, yes," Lex kept his a deep whisper. Soothing. It reminded me of how Byriel frequently spoke. "This room is bursting with exhaustion and fear and far too much uncertainty. It makes the air horrifically bitter."

Dane growled low in his chest, and Joon quickly followed suit, snarling up at Lex. It made my wolf restless, and my stomach began to ache once again. I pressed my thighs together, praying I had time before my heat started.

"It's okay," the siren repeated to my mate. "Tzidal is safe. And you're safe. Everyone you love is safe and sound." He glanced up, winking at me. I couldn't help but smile in return.

"Tell me, friend," Byriel leaned over Joon, looking hard into his face. "What do you know about the star?"

Joon's eyes flickered to me, then back to Byriel. "We took a gate," he whispered, speaking as if in a dream. "It was light but made of water. We went through the ruins and found the red star. She killed the pixie with it, then threatened the witch,"

Joon grabbed Byriel's shoulder, pulling him closer. "But once Strayton has all the wolves in the ground, she'll really have all the power. And then we'll all be fucked."

My bond with Joon eased, clearly happy with the story he just told.

"What the fuck does that mean?" Kenji shot.

Joon closed his eyes, letting out a long breath. "I don't want to blame the witches for what they've seen," he said to no one in particular, "but I can't help but wonder what life would be like without their fucking prophecies. Stars and birthmarks and blue fucking paths. It's all bullshit."

Byriel immediately stood, turning to Dane. "I need to speak with Tibbit."

"The advisor?" Dane's voice edged higher, clearly thinking Byriel's request was impossible. "I'm a perimeter guard, and Jonelle is a tracker. Neither one of us have any business within the palace. There's no way to get him a message."

"I can do it," Lex spoke up. Joon's head rested in his lap as soft snores left his throat. I wished like hell there was some way to capture a picture of the moment to tease my mate with later. "Just tell me where to go."

Dane crossed his arms and rocked back and forth on his heels, clearly not liking the idea.

"I'll draw you a map," Byriel said. "But please know, Tibbit is very old and fragile. He's not used to seeing predators like yourself. It would be best to hide your true form from him."

Lex clasped his hands just under his chin, smiling wide. "Maybe I can even try some posh cuisine. Something from the Queen's kitchen."

"Only if Strayton is on the menu," Joon mumbled.

Blue giggled, but the pain in my gut was growing.

Restless, I tried to stand, but my knees gave out, and my sex ached. Slick was starting to gather, making my panties damp and uncomfortable. Deep panic set in, followed by absolute horror. Joon didn't have the strength to tend to me. I'd have to do this alone.

"Byriel!" Blue's hands flew to my shoulders. "Get Tzidal out of here."

I tipped my head back, trying to protest, but it was no use. My whole body curled inward as a horrible cramp ripped through me, and slick poured from my trembling body.

Where Am I?

Joon

SOMEONE MOVED NEXT TO ME. A familiar presence. Someone that settled my wolf and eased the tension in my bones. "Tzidal?" I mumbled, my words slurred.

"Joon?" My mate's gentle voice made my heart quicken, and I wiggled my fingers, not sure if I was alive or dead. "Joon?" she repeated, but this time I could hear the panic in her voice.

I forced my eyes open, then quickly sat, ignoring the deep pain stabbing in my ribs.

Tzidal moved around me, pushing some rough fabric right up against my side. I admired her for a moment—her wild chestnut brown hair and flushed cheeks. She looked like a dream.

But then fear ripped through me, destroying the tender moment.

Pushing out a vicious growl, I grabbed Tzidal's arm, then

jerked her behind me. I was ready to defend my mate from any danger, but I wasn't in the long stone room anymore. No dead bodies were hanging on the walls, or hardened elves glaring at me from across the room. Even the soft-spoken beta was gone.

"Where are we?" I asked, struggling to focus on all the clutter around us, but the pain in my ribs was so intense I had to lay back down. "Is that potting soil?" I pointed to a burlap bag with a green leaf stamped in the center.

"We're above the greenhouse offices in the main part of Ossory." Tzidal pushed her wild hair from her face. But several strands stuck to the sweat in her brow. My gorgeous mate looked so tired. Her pale face was thin, and her bright eyes were sunken with too much worry.

"You're gorgeous," I purred, tugging her closer. "I was so worried about you." I tried to place a kiss on her lips, but she jerked back.

"You were worried?" she snarled, her fierce energy catching me off guard. She seemed so *on edge*? No. She was angry. "I wasn't the one blocking our bond, you asshole." She smacked my shoulder, and I hissed. "Oh!" Tzidal let out a panicked gasp. "I'm sorry." She cupped my shoulder, placing several sweet kisses all over my deep bruises.

I reached up and held the back of her head. "I'll live." I pulled her to me, kissing her softly. She slanted her lips over mine, and I drifted my hand around, cupping her cheek. She was burning up. "Are you okay?" I looked up at her, noticing the way she seemed to tremble.

Tzidal nodded, but her expression was too tight.

My wolf moved within me, and I scanned the room, making sure there was nothing in here that could have upset or scared her. It was then that I noticed the makeshift nest beneath me. Tzidal was one hell of an omega, fierce and brave. Not the kind of omega that needed a nest to settle her wolf.

"What's going on, omega?" I narrowed my eyes at my

mate, watching her reaction to make sure she was being honest. It was then I realized that our bond was still closed, but it wasn't my doing. "Tzidal." I gave her a firm look, and she dropped her gaze.

"My heat..." she trailed off, rubbing up one side of her arm.

I inhaled deeply, trying to catch any scent of slick or her wild pheromones, but my nose was too busted and swollen. "Open—" My voice caught in my throat as I tried to sit again, but a painful stabbing sensation in my ribs forced me to lay back down. "Open our bond," I gritted out. "Now."

Tzidal narrowed her eyes, not happy with my command. "You think you can just disappear, get the shit beat out of you, then order me around the second you come back?"

The corner of my lips twitched. She was a force to be reckoned with, *and I loved it*.

"*Now*, omega," I repeated. My entire body jerked, and I stifled a groan as wave after wave of Tzidal's unrelenting pain burst inside my head. "Fuck," I hissed, instinctively curling inward. Pain shot up my side, and I coughed, unable to focus properly.

"It's okay," Tzidal whispered. "I'm okay." But her hands trembled as she caressed my chest and shoulders.

She was in so much pain.

"Omega," I grunted, trying to sit, but my mate's pain was pounding in my head, mixing with the ache in my chest. It was too much, and I fell back against the floor. If my wolf would just wake up and help me, I could push through the pain, but my beast was too weak.

"Don't move," Tzidal urged me, pressing gently at my shoulders. "You've been drugged and beaten. You have to rest." Her voice was tight, and her thighs noticeably shook even though she was sitting on her feet.

I inhaled deeply, barely catching the softest trace of slick.

My cock jerked to life, pushing hard at the front of my pants. "I need to tend to you."

Tzidal's expression hardened, and she shook her head. "No." She cleared her throat as another rip of her pain pushed through our bond. She paled, lowering her head. "You need to rest," she whispered.

"Straddle me," I gripped her hip, trying to force her on top of me. "Strip down and take what you need."

She shook her head again, but I fisted a handful of her wild hair, jerking her head down to me. Speaking slowly, I flashed my fangs, letting my stubborn omega see my rage, "You will get naked and ride me hard and fast, or I will spank your ass raw the second I'm able to move."

The corner of Tzidal's lips twitched, and she leaned down, hovering her lips right over mine. "You're shit at making threats." Her beautiful brown eyes narrowed. "I like being spanked. Remember?"

A burst of determination tore through me, and I spun us, pinning Tzidal beneath me. Her eyes widened as I forced her hands above her head, making her feel my power and strength. In all fairness, I was on the verge of collapsing, but she didn't need to know that.

"Do you want me to rip off your clothes for you?" I asked, eyeing her worn black uniform. It was the very frock she had been wearing when we left the allied camp. It seemed my omega had yet to truly rest, either.

"I just want you to get better," Tzidal whimpered, and her chin quivered as tears gathered in her pretty eyes. My poor mate was worn, forced to stay strong for me. She needed me to hold her and care for her. Make her feel protected and loved.

"I'm so sorry," I leaned down, kissing her plump lips with a sweet, lingering kiss. "I'm sorry I left you."

Tzidal opened her mouth—probably to argue—but her face scrunched up, and she grimaced as her heat burned through her, making her body shake once again. "It hurts," she whined, arching her back and sniffling hard.

The base of my cock pulsed, stuffed tight in my pants, and my wolf paced, eager to claim our mate. "It's okay," I whispered, bumping my nose against hers. "I've got you now. Your alpha is here. Let me care for you."

Tzidal bit her bottom lip, thinking. I wanted to laugh at her impressive determination. Her whole body was trembling beneath mine, and so much slick was pushing from her sweet body I could actually smell it through my useless nose.

"Okay," Tzidal finally whispered. "But at least," she pulled one wrist free, pushing at my chest, "lay down. Let me control it."

I nodded, then fell back onto my side, away from her. My heart pounded, and sweat coated my brow. The simple movement was too much. Tzidal was right in that sleep and food would probably help me heal the fastest, but there was no way I'd be able to live with myself if I let my mate suffer.

"Let me know if it hurts too much," Tzidal whispered as she tugged at my belt, pulling my pants down my legs. She paused and closed her eyes, inhaling deeply as my cock sprang free. When she opened them, all the color was gone, swallowed up by her blown-out pupils.

My wolf snarled and growled, excited to taste my pretty omega's slick, but I stayed firmly on my back, letting Tzidal take whatever she needed from me.

Once, Tzidal had my pants off, she moved back up my legs, stopping just at my cock. Her little tongue pushed out, brushing over the tip. Once. Twice. Then she opened wide and swallowed me down, sucking with all her might. I grunted and moaned, fighting the need to push her head down further.

"Fuck," I snarled, lifting my hips to meet her wild movements. "I missed you so much." I laid my head back and closed my eyes, reveling in the feel of her warm mouth and soft tongue.

If this was a dream, I prayed I'd never wake.

"Alpha," Tzidal's soft voice made me look down. Her top was gone, exposing her beautiful tits, and she moved quickly, removing her pants as well.

"Come on." I gripped the base of my cock, then moved it up and down, taunting her with it. "Grind down on me, omega. Take all of it."

Tzidal's eyes zeroed in on my cock, and she licked her lips. For a moment, I thought she was going to suck me again, but then she quickly scrambled up my body, straddling my waist.

Swatting my hand away, Tzidal gripped my cock, then positioned it at her soaking-wet entrance before slowly lowering herself inch by mind-blowing inch. A flash of hormones filled the air, and I grunted from the force of it.

Tzidal let out a shuddering breath as she settled all the way down on my cock. "Oh, that feels good," she moaned, tipping her head back. She looked so relaxed and flushed, rocking gently against my hips.

I reached for her tits, palming and squeezing them. I wanted to grip her hips and force her to ride me like a wild beast, but this wasn't about me. This was about my mate and taming her pain. She could do whatever she wanted to me.

Slowly, Tzidal rolled her head forward, making her hair fall all around her face. "I missed you," she whispered, bouncing a little faster as she smoothed her hands up my chest. Her touch shifted feather-light as she moved over my bruises.

"I missed you more." I lifted my hips, meeting her quickening movements. "I'll never leave you again."

A slow smile filled her flushed face, and her tits began to bounce with each jerk of her hips. "Promise?" Her voice was breathy and soft.

"Promise." I gripped a handful of her hair and jerked her

down, capturing her mouth in a searing kiss. Her tongue struggled to keep up, unable to focus on her growing pleasure and our kiss at the same time.

Tzidal gasped and trembled, coming softly on my cock.

Slick poured from her fluttering pussy, covering my hips and balls. My knot started to expand, but I couldn't stop it. I'd normally beat back the urge to come, and fuck my mate a little longer, make her come a few more times before I took my pleasure as well, but exhaustion had its grip on me. My end slammed into me, and my knot popped into place as I pumped Tzidal's eager body full of my release.

"My mate." I caressed her back as she fell limp over my chest. "Rest, my sweet omega. Rest, and I'll tend to you again."

She nodded, mumbling something soft against my chest. I closed my eyes, sleeping while I had the chance. While I had never been with an omega in heat, I had heard it could last several days. I just prayed I didn't disappoint her.

The Greenhouse Offices

Byriel

"WHAT DO you think of the gate that Joon mentioned?" Dane asked, setting a wrapped bit of rasher bacon on the table before me.

I passed it down, placing it right in front of Blue. He smiled sweetly at me before tucking in. A freshly marked omega needed food and rest. And while I couldn't give him the rest he needed right now, I was damn well going to make sure he ate.

"The gates have always existed," I said simply, watching as Dane sat down across from me at the small table. His fresh guard's uniform was pressed and clean, ready for a good day's work. "But the gates are powered by fae magic," I continued, "so my father had always forbidden them from being used. Most were boarded up or destroyed, but a few remained."

Blue held up a piece of bacon, waiting for me to eat it. I

happily obliged, loving the way he ducked his head when the tip of his finger grazed my lips.

Dane cleared his throat roughly, his intense gaze flickering between me and my mate. "Sir," he paused, clearly trying to choose his words carefully. "This omega—"

"Omega Blue is my mate," I said with a firm look. I knew Dane wasn't aware, but I wanted Blue's position to be clear should the alpha try to force him from the room.

"Your mate?" Dane's brows lifted and his dark eyes zeroed in on Blue's neck. My bashful omega, hunched his shoulders, hiding behind my arm from the scarred alpha. "My apologies, My Lord. I didn't know."

"That's okay," I waved my hand, then stopped. It was a gesture my father and sister did when dismissing someone they didn't care for. It always felt nasty when they did it, and I crossed my arms, preventing myself from doing it again.

"Why do you think Strayton is using the gates now?" Dane asked, leaning across the table. "Do you think she's working with the fae? There have always been rumors about her love of their kind, especially the elves."

I picked up Blue's cup of water, taking a quick sip. It was ice cold and fresh, no doubt from a local spring. "Strayton isn't working with the fae," I said firmly. "She's just wild enough to run through a shimmering gate without knowing what's on the other side."

A swift knock rapped on the back door, and Blue jerked, then pressed hard against my side. "It's okay," I whispered as Dane moved quickly, disappearing into the back offices. "It's probably someone looking for bulbs."

Blue pressed his cheek to my arm. His swirling blue and green eyes were so stunning. Unable to help myself, I cupped his cheek and placed a quick kiss on his pretty lips.

"Alpha," Blue giggled, pressing his nose to my arm. "Someone might see."

"Let them see," I growled, loving the way it made his eyes dilate and his breath hitch.

Dane's deep voice drifted from the other room, making my wolf restless. He was taking his time. I stood, needing to know if something had happened.

"Stay here," I kissed the top of Blue's head. He hummed in response, continuing to eat his breakfast.

Dane stood in the doorway, speaking to a young beta. He had a very round, pale face with wild curly black hair that stuck up in the back. "Everything okay?" I asked, staring at a small letter in the beta's hand.

"*Byriel*?" the beta's eyes widened, and his mouth hung open.

Dane stared at him for a moment, then snatched the letter from his hand. "Show your respect, Marx," he barked, making the wild-haired beta flinch.

"Sorry," Marx bowed quickly.

"Good morning, My Lord," Kenji appeared behind the alpha, carrying a small basket covered in a tea towel. "I've brought strawberries for your omega." He held them up, puffing his chest out with pride. "My uncle grows them year-round, but they're best in the winter."

"Thank you," I lifted the towel admiring the fat, ripe fruit. "Blue will love them."

Kenji smiled wide, and I stepped to one side, letting him in.

Marx's big hazel eyes drifted from Dane to me. Then he rose on his tiptoes, looking into the office. Curious as to what he was looking at, I turned, noticing I had left the kitchen door open, allowing the beta to see my mate. Blue was oblivious, admiring the basket of fruit Kenji had brought. But it felt dangerous to have this beta see him. So much so that my wolf snarled, and worry tightened my fists.

"Thank you, Marx," I gave the beta a curt nod, clearly

dismissing him. Dane's brow furrowed, but he still shooed the younging off the back step, closing the door in his face.

"Everything okay?" Dane whispered, cutting a cautious look at the door.

I paused, not sure how to describe my worry. "Do we know Marx well?"

Dane pursed his lips, thinking, and it immediately set off an alarm inside my head. "He and his sister have been friends of the cause."

"But?" I asked, sensing that wasn't the full story.

Dane looked around me, ensuring Blue and Kenji weren't listening. "Marx was very vocal against the king," he whispered, "but it seems his fire has died since Strayton took the throne. He's done nothing outright questionable, but his behavior lately has been...lazy."

My eyes rolled upward, thinking of Joon upstairs tending to Tzidal's heat. "We need to move," I said firmly. "I don't want to stay in one spot for too long."

"Agreed." Dane held up the letter Marx had delivered. I eyed the yellow seal stamped with a daisy, relieved to see it still intact. At least Marx didn't try to read it. "Hopefully, Jonelle will have reinforcements here tonight," Dane continued, "and we can plan our attack."

"Alpha!" Blue called out, waving me over. "Come have some strawberries!"

The wicker basket was bursting with ripe strawberries and winter melon, filling the room with their lovely sweet flavors. "I'll make sure to save some for Tzidal and Joon." Blue lifted a large berry, then took a big bite, humming at the taste.

"Any word from Lex?" Kenji asked as he spun a chair around, straddling it backward. Dane settled in the seat next to him.

"Not yet." I didn't bother to hide my disappointment. "He left late last night to hunt before heading to the palace and has yet to return." I leaned back to glance out the only window. The clear blue sky was just visible through the slit in the curtains. "It's what? Midday?"

Kenji quickly responded, "Yes, My Lord."

I wanted to ask them to stop calling me that, but there was no point. I was next in line for the throne, and we all knew how this would end. Either Strayton or I was going to end up six feet under, and someone was going to have to carry the crown when it was all over.

"Everything okay?" Blue slipped his hand over my forearm, squeezing gently. I covered his hand with mine and smiled at the gentle omega.

"Wonderful," I lied. I knew he could feel that I wasn't telling the truth, but that didn't matter. He'd let me lie, and we'd both pretend I was, in fact, wonderful and not counting down the minutes until we finally attacked the palace. "Do you think Jonelle will be able to get the reinforcements here in time?" I glanced up at Dane, catching an odd look on his face before he could fix it. "What's wrong?"

He shook his head, dismissing my question. "She won't be able to get everyone," he stared out the window, "but we have a few smaller camps near the black river. Given how late she left last night, they should arrive within the next few hours."

"Dane." I waited for the alpha to look me in the eye. Finally, he turned back to me, but his eyes flickered to Blue first. "What's going on? Why do you keep looking at my mate like that?" My wolf bristled, ready to put this alpha in his place if I had to. Dane would treat my mate with the respect he deserved.

"It's just that," Dane licked his lips, then shifted in his seat. "Can I speak informally, My Lord?"

I narrowed my eyes but figured there was no reason to refuse him. After all, before this was all over, we might all be dying together. "Please."

"I've known you for years." Dane rested his arms on the table and squeezed his hands together. He was fidgety. "We have fought side by side and have broken bread together. Hell, you were even my direct commanding officer for a few years."

I nodded, waiting for him to get to his point.

"In all those years," his gaze moved to Blue once again, "I've never seen you smile. Like, *really* smile. Until now."

Blue's happy emotions burst through our bond, but he didn't move to lavish me with attention. Instead, he stared at the half-eaten strawberry in his hand, trying to hide his bursting smile behind his long dark hair.

"It's odd seeing you happy," Dane said plainly.

It took everything in me not to laugh out loud, but I managed to keep my composure. "I *am* happy." I nodded, keeping it at that.

A loud gasp followed by a mighty roar echoed overhead, and we all glanced up at the ceiling.

"How can we not smell her heat?" Kenji asked.

Dane smacked his arm, giving the young alpha a firm glare. "Not an appropriate question." He jerked his head toward Blue.

"The room upstairs is insulated for brewing positions," I said, having already asked CariAnn the same question last night. "She said they create some dangerous concoctions in the spring to help ward off the orcs and nether-dragons."

Kenji nodded, glancing up once again.

"It could be another day or so until it's over," Dane said, breaking the seal on the letter. "I think we should wait to speak to Joon before making a move on the palace."

I scratched the scruff of my short beard, thinking about that. It was smart to have all the information before charging in, but at the same time, the longer we waited, the more time Strayton had to fulfill her plans with that damn star. Because my sister had a plan, she *always* had a plan.

"Knock, knock!" Lex's bright and bubbly voice rang out just before the sound of the back door opening.

Dane stood and raced into the office, probably to make sure it was really him. "Shit," he cursed. "I forgot to lock the damn door."

"Good morning to you, too." Lex stepped into the small storefront with his hands on his hips. "This is cozy." He glanced at the small table, then at the lush plants on the shelves around us.

"Were you able to get a message to Tibbit?" I asked.

"I've done one better," Lex winked at my mate, making him smile wide.

I opened my mouth to ask the siren what he meant when Tibbit slowly appeared in the doorway. The elder shuffled as he walked, pulling his long robes up so as not to step on them.

I immediately stood and bowed to the elder. Kenji followed suit, then stood back, offering his chair.

"Thank you so much for coming, Tibbit," I said, pleased when Tibbit took Kenji's seat across from me. He huffed as if exhausted. I sat back down, leaning toward the elder. "We have much to discuss, old friend."

"You know, it's been ages since I had a stroll through the city," Tibbit flashed a gummy smile. "It's changed a lot over the years."

"Strawberry?" Blue pushed the basket toward the elder, and Tibbit's eyes went wide. I was a bit annoyed, wanting to get to it, but Blue was right. We needed to be polite.

"Where on earth did you find these?" He held up a berry, admiring its vibrant red color.

"Kenji brought them." Blue pushed a bit of bacon toward the elder as well. "Try the bacon too. It's very yummy." My wolf snarled, wanting my omega to eat everything in front of him, but my heart was proud of how hospitable he was. *He'd make a good Luna.*

I jerked at the random thought, not sure why that entered my mind.

"Good morning," Tzidals soft voice drifted through the room as she appeared at the foot of the stairs. My shirt was draped over her slight shoulders, falling all the way to her knees.

"How do you feel?" Blue shot out of his seat and raced to her, taking her hand in his.

"I'm good," she laughed, letting Blue lead her back to his chair. Both omegas squished together, sharing the seat. "We're both good." Tzidal glanced up at the doorway, smiling sweetly as Joon came into view.

"Good morning." Joon gave me a quick nod, which I happily returned, but I was eager to get down to business.

"I know you're probably exhausted," I stood offering him my seat, but he shook his head, refusing. "But I'd like to talk to you about what you said yesterday. I'm hoping your head is a little clearer."

"What I said?" Joon's dark eyes narrowed before they moved to his mate. "What did I say?"

"You were a little out of it," Tzidal said around a big bite of bacon. "You rambled about a gate and ruins and a star."

Joon's gaze dropped to the floor, his eyes moving as if thinking. "I thought that was a dream."

"Please," I offered my seat again, and this time Joon relented, walking around the table.

He plopped in the chair, letting out a long sigh. "I don't have a lot of information. Most of the time, Strayton had me locked in a guest room or strung up on a wall."

Tzidal stiffened at his words, but she didn't say or do anything to otherwise show how upset she was at the fact.

"Anything you can remember," Dane encouraged him. "No matter how small."

Joon took a deep breath, then fell into the whole story. He

spoke of the shimmering gate beneath the palace, the ruins at Cristal Terre, and how my sister threatened Yasha. Tibbit nodded through the last part, adding a few details that told me he was there.

"Strayton is pissed she can't control the star's power," Joon rubbed the back of his neck. The bruises on his chest were already fading, but his ribs were still puffy. They'd probably take a few more days to heal properly. "She's convinced there was another marked wolf out there."

"Great," Dane snarled. "She's going to start killing us just like her father did."

"Well," Joon sighed, "I tried to force her attention away from the marked wolves."

"How?" Dane narrowed his eyes.

Joon snorted, giving me a wicked grin. "I told her the only way to gain the star's power was to kill Byriel." He snatched up a small strawberry, popping it in his mouth.

Blue flashed his little fangs at Joon, shocking me. "How could you do that?" His voice rose, and Tzidal immediately turned to my mate, trying to calm him.

"Don't worry," Tzidal whispered. "We'd never let that happen."

"That's actually pretty smart," I nodded in approval.

"*Smart*?" Blue snapped at me. "How is that smart? Strayton is going to come after you. She's going to—"

"It keeps *everyone else* safe, my love." I smoothed my hand through his hair, twisting the purple strand.

Blue ducked his head, and his anger quickly faded, clearly remembering that *he* was the last marked wolf. "I just don't want you to get hurt," he mumbled to his lap. My wolf whimpered, begging me to scoop our mate up and love on him, but now wasn't the time.

"I can't believe Yasha is alive," I said, forcing the focus away from Blue's tender emotions. "I assumed Strayton had killed her the second I left home to find the marked wolves, but I'm happy to be the target of Strayton's anger, if that means she'll leave the people be."

"Honestly," Joon sighed, "I'm not sure your sister believed me. Strayton grabbed Yasha and started questioning the poor woman about the last wolf like her life depended on it. It probably did," Joon said flatly.

"The witch is a rather lovely woman." Tibbit reached for another strawberry, gnawing the bright red fruit with his gums. "She's been through a lot but still very resilient. And *very* alive."

I narrowed my eyes at the elder, hopeful. "Have you spoken to her since then?"

"Oh, yes." Tibbit smiled. "I immensely enjoy talking to Yasha." He turned slightly in his chair to look at me properly. "We've talked at length about the ways of witches and the visions they see." He looked off into the distance, seeming to remember something fondly. "It's just so lovely how her kind can see things that affect every creature. Wolves, elves, fae, orcs. They see visions for all of us. And it's just fun to learn that our oldest legends are true."

"Legends?" Dane tilted his head.

"Oh, this is my favorite part," Lex jumped up on the counter, listening carefully. "Tell it again, Tibs."

The elder scrunched his nose at the siren, chuckling. "If you insist, my sweet boy."

Every alpha in the room balked, giving Lex a weary look. It just baffled me how the siren was able to charm lesser-statused wolves.

"Legend has it that hundreds of years ago," Tibbit began his story, "the red star, Huit, was a beloved child of the Moon and worshiped by the Fae. Well, one day, she fell in love with a mortal. An alpha." He added, holding up a finger as if to make a wonderful point. "Being a star, of course, meant Huit was forced to love him from afar—the alpha was something she'd simply never possess." Tibbit smiled as if he had lived the story himself, and not simply heard it passed down from previous elders over the centuries.

"After some time, Huit's broken heart weakened her, and she began to dim. The Moon, being loving and merciful, gave the sweet star mercy and allowed her to come to our lands to meet the alpha. But the journey was so far and dangerous when the star finally met the earth, she broke, scattering her power all over the land. Legend stated that one day she would find her way into the water and fill all the plants and animals, eventually making her way into the werewolves. Finally, letting her be a part of the people she loved."

"So," Tzidal sat forward, speaking softly with the elder. "You're saying the star fell from the skies and landed in Cristel Terre?"

"Yes," Tibbit nodded, clearly pleased the omega was listening.

"And the star's power seeped into the land?"

"Yes." Tibbit nodded again. "And based on what I've discussed with Yasha, we think the marked wolves hold the star's power. When those wolves die, the power returns to the Huit. Once all the power is restored, the star's power can be harnessed. Controlled. But until all the marked wolves are dead, it's just a deadly rock that kills anyone that tries to touch it. It's as if the star is desperate to reclaim its power, pulling the life out of everything it touches until it's whole again."

"But," Tzidal shifted in her seat, uncomfortable. "My first mate was one of the marked wolves, and he had no powers. He was a great alpha, but nothing magical or—"

"Oh, sweet omega," Tibbit reached across the table, taking Tzidal's hand. "Magic doesn't always burst out of us. Sometimes it simmers under the skin, warming us until it's needed."

Joon glared at the elder, clearly not liking his answer. "What's next?" he asked forcefully, turning his attention to me.

"We remove Strayton from the throne," Dane said in a cold, flat tone.

I resisted the urge to snarl, knowing damn well that my brotherly affection for my sister would need to die, and rather quickly. After all, Strayton brought this on herself.

"Thank you, Joon," I extended my arm, shaking his hand. "I can never thank you enough for your sacrifice."

Joon's brows pulled together, and he narrowed his eyes. "You sound as if you're dismissing me."

"Am I not?" I glanced at Tzidal, taking note of her determined expression. "You wanted the king dead," I said to the omega, trying not to let my guilt of the situation seep through, "That's been done. I assumed you'd want to return to your village."

"Oh, no," Joon stood, popping his knuckles. "Tzidal and I aren't going anywhere. Not until this is over."

Sitting At The Table

Tzidal

"I HOPE YOU DON'T MIND," Blue whispered as the alphas, and Tibbit talked—it seemed as if they had been talking forever, "but I snuck into your room last night and stole your robes." He pointed to my freshly washed garments draped over an empty chair. "They needed a good scrubbing."

"Thank you so much," I crossed my legs and winced. I was so sore. My legs, my arms, and especially my pussy. "Where did you sleep?" I glanced around.

"The storage room." A deep flush bloomed across Blue's cheeks as he whispered, "Byriel takes such good care of me. But I worry that I'm..." he glanced at the alphas, making sure they weren't listening, "I'm too inexperienced."

"Oh, Blue." Lex slipped into Joon's chair, waving the alphas away. "Let me tell you a few things I know to be the truth." Blue's big eyes focused on Lex, listening as if terrified he'd miss a single word. "When we met that alpha," Lex pointed at Byriel, "I searched his mind and found nothing but grief and deep regret. But since meeting you, his aura has shifted dramatically."

I nodded, quickly agreeing. "He's calmer. More focused."

"He's horny!" Lex shot, and the room went quiet. Dane and Kenji glared at the siren for his outburst, but Joon and Byriel were too used to Lex's loud presence to be bothered.

"And what about the courtyard gate?" Joon asked Byriel, slipping back into their conversation.

Lex waited to make sure the alphas were deep in their conversation again before whispering to Blue, "That alpha is obsessed with you." He poked Blue's nose, making him giggle. "I know for a fact that if I slipped on your form for even half a second, your Byriel would *beg* me to kill him."

Blue wrinkled his nose, pretending to gag. "That's so gross," he laughed.

"I can't help but to agree with the young omega," Tibbit's bright blue eyes sparkled as he gave us a gummy smile. "But I guess there are many things that we find rather off-putting until we try them."

Lex let out a mighty laugh, and I snorted, deciding I liked Tibbit.

"Siren," Dane snipped a little too forcefully. "Can you return Tibbit to the palace? I don't want his absence to be noticed."

"Of course," Lex stood, offering Tibbit his elbow. "You simply have to finish telling me about the priestess and her tempting lips."

Tibbit rolled his eyes upward, smiling as if savoring the most amazing dish. "All I know is, there are some things worth going to hell for."

Blue's mouth fell open, not closing until the two of them left out the back. "I'm not sure I like that beta."

I pumped my shoulder into his, raising my eyebrows in a suggestive manner.

"My Lord," Dane said to Byriel, but he was looking at me. "There's an omega den just north of here that can take in both omegas while we coordinate our attack."

Blue immediately stood, clenching his fists tight, and I snarled, "There's no way in hell I'm sitting in a damn den while my mate charges off to war!"

Joon smiled at my outburst, looking at me with far too much affection. "I don't think my mate is capable of sitting out of a fight." He smiled, pushing his absolute adoration for me through our bond. "She's one hell of a beast. Incapable of doing what she's told."

"You're telling me," Kenji grumbled.

Joon turned to the young alpha, his brows raised with interest. "Yeah? Has she given you a hard time?"

Kenji pressed his mouth into a tight line, his eyes flickering between me and Joon. It was clear he wasn't sure just how honest to be with my alpha, but after a moment of indecision, Kenji let out a loud groan, then snapped. "I have been ditched in the woods, drugged by a siren, kicked in the balls, and threatened to be stabbed." He cut me an angry glare. "I have tried like hell to get your mate to Madra, but if I'm honest," his voice rose as his anger built, "I have never in my life been happier to be rid of a responsibility. You deserve a medal for putting up with this woman!" Kenji growled, then his expression fell as he realized just how disrespectful he was being. "I'm sorry." He swallowed hard, looking at Joon as if he expected the alpha to attack him at any second. "

"No need to apologize," Joon's brown eyes moved to me, "Not just any alpha can handle my mate."

I crossed my arms, not amused in the least. "This is how you defend me?" I leaned back, assessing my smirking mate.

He looked way too cocky for his own good. "I'll remember this, Seonjoon."

"Kenji," Joon patted the young alpha on the shoulder. "Thank you so much for watching over what is mine." The young alpha let out an audible breath, and the tension in his shoulders eased. "But," Joon held up a single finger, "insult my mate again, and I'll rip your fucking throat out." He turned, giving me a quick wink.

I rolled my eyes at his lackluster attempt to appease me.

"Yes, sir," Kenji mumbled as he bowed his head.

Byriel pinched the bridge of his nose, trying to hide a smile. "My dagger is dull." He finally looked up at Dane. "Any chance we can have it sharpened?"

Dane nodded, looking very thankful for the change of subject. "I have one you can use."

"Come on," I tapped Blue's knee. "I'm done with these animals. Let's sit in the other room while they talk about knives and bitch about alpha things."

Blue happily snatched up the basket of strawberries, following me into the back office. The small window near the best had lovely yellow cotton curtains, making the whole space warm and inviting.

"It's nice being inside for a change," Blue peeked out the window, "but I do miss having the sun on my skin."

"Where did you bathe?" I asked, not remembering a bathroom or even a washbasin upstairs.

"I used a jug of water and a cloth." Blue pressed his nose against the windowpane, looking up and down the small alleyway. The sun illuminated the back step, making even the patchy bit of grass look especially inviting. "I left it outside your room upstairs." He turned to look at me. "Did you not see it?"

"No." I rubbed the back of my neck, trying to stretch my

still-stiff muscles. *It was hard tending to your own heat with an injured alpha.*

Blue's big eyes drifted back to the window. "I kind of want to sit outside."

"Don't you dare." I pointed at the young omega, giving him a firm look. "Byriel would spank your ass raw if you wandered off."

Blue pulled a face and grumbled, "Wasn't going to wander off."

"Stay here," I placed a playful smack on his bottom. "I'll be right back."

"Okay." He lifted the basket, sniffing what was left of the sweet strawberries.

The jug of water was right where Blue said it would be. I picked it up and carried it into the small room Joon, and I spent the night in, eager to wash the dried fluids off the inside of my thighs and stomach. I'd normally lay in my ruined nest, covered in my mate's seed for a few days after my heat, letting his scent soothe and comfort me, but there was no time for that.

It felt as if there was no time for anything that made me feel normal anymore.

But soon, this would all be over...*I hoped.*

Once every inch of my skin was freshly scrubbed, I pulled on my clean uniform, secured my dagger at my belt, then checked the two necklaces around my neck. One was a gift from Joon, and the other was Byriel's, with a clear image of the King's seal on one side. I needed to return the charm, but I just kept forgetting.

Moving around the small room, I brushed out my hair with my fingers, putting off going back downstairs for as long as I could. As much as I wanted to be a part of the plans, I also needed a break. Almost losing Joon was too much, and my wolf was still struggling.

"It is a lovely day," I whispered to myself as I looked out the only window. I looked down over the back alleyway, then up at the mountains in the distance. They were covered in thick layers of snow, shimmering in the sun. "Maybe Blue and I should sit outside." I wanted to sit with my friend and eat strawberries while pretending everything was right with the world.

I let out a contented sigh, then moved to turn, but froze. Something bright red in the alleyway caught my eye. I pulled at the windowsill to lift it, but it stayed firmly in place. "Stupid, fucking—" My fingers slipped, and I fell backward, landing hard on my ass. "Dammit," I snarled, then turned and rushed back down the stairs. I didn't want to panic, not yet. It could have been a flower or a discarded handkerchief. Hell, there were a thousand things the red objects could be.

The alphas continued talking in a tight huddle, not even pausing to glance my way as I passed. Then I stepped into the office, and every muscle in my worn body went tight.

Blue wasn't here.

He could have been in the storage room, but something told me it wasn't likely.

Panicked, I ripped the back door open, then dread slammed into me, making my wolf yowl loudly.

Strawberries littered the ground, covering the back step and the tiny patch of grass.

And Blue was nowhere in sight.

The Main Room

❧

Joon

"BLUE!" Tzidal ran into the main room, flying to a small door beneath the stairs and ripping it open. "Blue!"

Byriel stiffened beside me, every muscle in his big body going tight. "Did you lose him? Where did he go?" The alpha jerked, racing into the office, then returning almost immediately. This whole office was so small. There was nowhere to hide.

"Tzidal," I grabbed her arm before she could run up the stairs. "Where did you last see him?"

Byriel looked manic, his eyes darting all over the room. I could only imagine he was trying to find his mate through their bond, but if Blue were unconscious, there'd be nothing for the alpha to feel.

"I went upstairs to change," Tzidal pointed at the stairs, "and when I came down, he was gone. I think he was taken!"

Byriel moved, slamming into the back door and busting it

open. The bottom hinge barely hung on, making the door creak and groan as it swung lopsided.

"Blue!" Byriel yelled out loud.

A fussy beta at the end of the alley narrowed her eyes, mumbling to keep it down. I grabbed Byriel's arm, desperate to keep him calm. "Byriel, we need to—"

"BLUE!" He roared, then jerked as if to run, but Dane slammed into the alpha, tackling him to the ground. "Get the fuck off me!" Byriel snarled, and his eyes flashed red. Fangs and claws pushed into place, struggling to keep control.

I had only seen Byriel this unhinged once before...right before he killed his father.

"My Lord," Kenji said as he bent, picking something off the ground. It was a bit of folded parchment with an obviously rushed wax seal on the front. It was lopsided and slightly smudged—clearly having been touched while still hot.

"Get the fuck off me!" Byriel shoved hard at Dane, pushing the alpha off of him.

"My apologies, My Lord," Dane panted hard as Byriel stood. "But you can't—"

Byriel turned and swung, landing a heavy fist right against Dane's jaw. It was shocking. I had never seen Byriel lose his head for any reason. The fucker was steady and calm in every situation.

Dane rubbed the edge of his jaw, tipping his head up high. "I understand your anger," he said to Byriel. "But if Blue has been taken, we need to rally and attack now, but with a plan intact."

Byriel snarled at the scarred alpha before turning and holding his hand out to Kenji. "The letter, please."

Kenji quickly set the parchment in his hand, looking especially uneasy. The young alpha was a lower-ranked wolf within the guard, clearly not used to seeing higher-ranked officials slug it out.

"What's it say?" Tzidal's voice was jittery, filled with deep-set fear. I reached for her, hugging her tight and scenting her hair. Her usually sweet jasmine scent was flat and sharp with her worry.

"Come and get him," Byriel read the note, then looked up, glaring at the tips of the palace towers in the distance. "She fucking took Blue. How did Strayton know to take Blue?"

Rage burned through Tzidal as she pushed me away, glaring at Dane. "You have a traitor in your group."

"Not possible," Dane snarled. "Every wolf we invited here last night was a tried and true friend to the cause. Each and every one of them has sacrificed more than any—"

"What about that beta?" Byriel's eyes flashed red, his wolf pushing hard at the inside of his mind. "The one from this morning."

Dane's eyes widened, and his mouth fell open. "I just can't believe..." he shook his head. "Marx isn't that kind of—"

"Marx?" Tzidal said as if alarmed. "As in the beta from the brothel?" Her eyes met Kenji's, and I stiffened, wondering what the hell this damn alpha had been doing with my mate. "He's the one that kidnapped Blue and threw him in prison. He's *not* an ally."

"Fuck," Dane scrubbed his face. "I'm sorry, My Lord." He turned to Byriel. "I would never have thought—"

"There's no point in dwelling on it now," Byriel said, his tone a little calmer, more in control. "But we can't wait for all the extra forces to arrive. We have to move *now*."

"Sir," Dane held up his hands, speaking softly to not anger the alpha. "I honestly don't think Strayton will hurt him. She needs your mate as bait. If we can wait—"

"Blue *is* the last marked wolf!" Byriel snarled, flashing long, pointed fangs.

I blinked rapidly, trying like hell to process what the alpha just said. It was impossible. There was no way Blue was the last marked wolf, but then I saw the fear in Tzidal's big brown eyes. "It's true?" I whispered to her, and she slowly nodded.

"If Strayton finds out what Blue is," Byriel whispered, trying to control his spiraling fear, "she will fucking gut him on the front steps, then wait gleefully for me to seek my revenge."

Dane pushed out a heavy breath, then took a quick step back as if he had been physically punched. "Okay." He licked his lips, panic making his fair complexion ashen. "Kenji."

The young alpha stood a little taller, ready for his orders.

"I need you to gather as many of our friends as you can," Dane said. "I'll get you a list."

"There's no time for that," Byriel spun, marching off.

Tzidal ran, cutting him off. "There's at least enough time for you to trade out your dull blade for a new one." She pulled the dagger from its sheath, holding it out to Byriel. "This one once belonged to you anyway."

Byriel eyed it, then turned to me, seemingly at a loss for words. The poor alpha was clearly struggling with his mate gone, and I completely understood the feeling.

"Come sharpen your blade." I walked to him and placed a hand on his shoulder. "Then we'll go get Blue together."

Byriel dropped his voice to a whisper, speaking softly so no one else could hear him. "I can't feel him. Why can't I feel him?" His voice was filled with thick emotion.

"Please." Tzidal reached for Byriel's hand, squeezing gently. "I'll never forgive you if you run in there unprepared."

Slowly, Byriel bowed his head, then he nodded. "Maybe Lex will see Blue and be able to protect him."

Tzidal quickly latched onto the idea as she led the dark alpha back inside the small office. "We'll save him, alpha," Tzidal said in a firm tone. "I promise you. Nothing bad will happen to Blue."

But my wolf snarled, not convinced in the least.

To The Palace
❧

Tzidal

WE WERE able to get Byriel to wait an hour before he finally threatened to kill everyone in the whole damn city if we didn't leave immediately. Dane wanted to give Kenji a bit more time to round up any fighters he could find in Ossory—most of the allied wolves were outside the city and still a few hours away. We might truly be starting this war alone. Just me, Joon, Byriel, and Dane.

I hated that Lex wasn't here.

"It's okay," Joon whispered in my ear.

I nodded, not believing him at all. "I know."

"Are you sure about this?" Dane cut a weary look at Byriel.

The dark alpha's face was hidden beneath a cloak as he walked slowly to avoid attracting any attention. "She'll kill Blue just to spite me," Byriel whispered. "I can't wait any longer."

I pulled in a deep breath, filling my lungs with the crisp

mountain air. The sun was bright in the cloudless sky, and a few winter starlings chirped in the distance. The cheery day felt so wrong, contrasting wildly with the storm of emotion raging inside me.

"I'll meet you around back," Dane gave Joon a knowing look, then cut toward the empty prison. The hole in the side had a few boards wedged against the wall to keep it from crumbling any further.

"Tzidal." Joon wrapped his big hand around my upper arm, pulling me to a stop. Byriel paused, giving us a movement. "Keep in mind that the security in this place is shit. You're pretty likely to be overlooked."

"I know." I pushed up onto my tiptoes, placing a soft kiss on Joon's lips. "Be careful."

"You too, mate." He tucked a strand of my hair behind my ear, brushing his fingers along the edge of my jaw. "Remember to stay calm and walk with purpose. You belong in the palace." He smoothed his hand over the collar of my robes, running his finger along the chain around my neck. "You're a member of the prim-staff. No one should question you."

I straightened my back, holding my head high. "I'm ready."

Joon smiled, his pride pulsing in our bond. "I know you are, but try to remember that your job is to get Blue out of there and not to take on every alpha you see." He kissed the top of my head, then pushed me toward Byriel. "Leave a few guards for the rest of us."

I shook my head and walked away from my ridiculous mate, praying it wouldn't be the last time I saw him.

Keeping my shoulders squared, I kept pace behind Byriel, letting him take the lead. The large wrought-iron gate that separated the palace from the city quickly came into view. Byriel walked straight past the stationed guards, not stopping to show his face or announce who he was. It didn't really surprise me. It seemed most of the people within the city just didn't give a shit anymore.

I made my way to a small servant's door at the edge of the courtyard, then paused, pretending to fidget with the sash around my middle.

Byriel raised his fist and pounded against the enormous main door. It echoed, filling the courtyard with a deep, hollow sound. "Open!" Byriel demanded.

The door jerked, then creaked.

Trying to be discreet, I risked a quick glance sideways, watching Byriel speak to someone inside the palace.

"I believe the Queen is expecting me." Byriel lifted his hood, showing his face. For a moment, he just stood there, staring into the open door, then he stepped up and disappeared inside the palace.

I immediately pulled open the small door and rushed inside, slamming hard into the broad chest of a massive alpha.

"Who the fuck are you?" The angry guard snarled down at me.

Shocked, I blinked repeatedly, praying my eyes would quickly adjust to the dim light. *Why did they keep this palace so damn dark?*

"My apologies, alpha." I hunched my shoulders and held up my hands, trying to look small and frightened. "I'm just a lowly maid. Please, don't hurt me."

Footsteps echoed on the other side of the stone wall, followed by Byriel's deep voice. It sounded even but clipped, talking to another man.

"Why are you coming through this door?" The alpha crossed his arms over his thick chest, and I quickly glanced up, meeting his dark eyes for the briefest of moments. "The servant's entry is around back. This is only for the guard."

"Please, sir." I moved my hand to my belt and untied a small bag. "Her majesty wanted fresh fruit." I opened it, holding it up so the alpha could see the strawberries within. "It took me so long to find some that would please her. I know I should have come in the proper door, but...." I pretended to struggle to breathe for a moment, hoping this alpha's instinct to calm an omega would take over quickly. "I'm just trying so hard to be quick. Please," I sniffled, making my bottom lip quiver, "she'll punish me if I'm much longer."

The guard let out a heavy sigh, followed by a groan, then he slowly moved to one side. "Use the right damn door next time."

"Yes, sir," I clutched the bag of strawberries to my chest, giving the alpha my sweetest, most innocent smile. "The Moon will remember your kindness today."

He snorted, waving me in. "Hurry up."

I moved, not waiting for him to change his mind. The long stone hallway was cold with the distinct scent of mold, and a thick layer of grime clung to the soles of my feet. It seemed no one was cleaning the Queen's palace.

It made me wonder how many good wolves had abandoned her.

The hallway came to an end, and I stepped under an arched passage into the entryway of the palace. The massive main door looked exactly the same from inside the palace— tall, dark, and *very* heavy—but only one guard stood next to it. The uneasy alpha tipped his head back, resting his eyes. *He looked bored.*

Walking softly on the balls of my feet, I moved into the impressive room and looked up. The ceiling was taller than any temple I had ever seen, with a domed glass ceiling and two twisting sets of stairs on either side of the grand entrance. But these stairs didn't lead anywhere other than a landing where two beta guards stood with bows slung over their chests. One of them narrowed his eyes at me but then turned to his friend, chatting softly.

Smoothing one hand down my uniform, I straightened my back, trying to act like a proper maid. *Did maids walk a certain way?*

"Where the fuck are you taking me?" Byriel's voice was loud and clear, echoing from behind the furthest staircase.

I moved, walking as quickly as I could without drawing any attention to myself. Just behind the stairs, a set of double doors was open, allowing me to see into another long corridor, but this one was well-lit, with a plush red carpet and small tables covered with sweet winter flowers. I took note of the absence of wolfsbane.

The guards might be able to shift, which could make this much harder.

I paused at the first table, then pulled a tiny strawberry from the bag, placing it just behind the vase of vibrant yellow primrose. I said a quick prayer that Joon would be able to find the scent and follow it to us, but fear that someone would find the odd bit of fruit and throw it away was still very real.

Coming to the end of the hallway, I paused and scented the air for Byriel's smokey cedar scent. He had cut right. I pulled out another strawberry and then bit it. Hoping to be discreet, I glanced up and down the long hallway to make sure I was alone, then I let the fruit fall from my mouth. I ground it into the carpet with my foot, pleased when it disappeared into the equally red carpet.

"What are you doing?" A stern older beta yelled out behind me, making me jerk and spin around.

"I'm so sorry." I bowed, noting the beta's crisp, black uniform and shiny black shoes. He looked like a butler of some kind. "Her majesty asked me to retrieve her some fresh strawberries," I slowly palmed the bitten fruit, trying to hide it, then held up my other hand, showing him the bag. "She wants them urgently."

The beta let out an annoyed huff, as he marched right up

to me. "You silly girl." His tone was sharp. Annoyed. "You know you're supposed to—" He stopped, narrowing his eyes at my uniform, then the small bag in my hand. He assessed me head to foot, taking his horrible time.

My wolf snarled, urging me to run, but I stood still, with my head bowed respectfully, hoping he would just let me go.

"Is something wrong, sir?" I whispered in a tiny, meek voice.

"What's your name?" the beta asked, crossing his arms so they rested on his slightly rounded belly. He must have been nearing fifty with streaks of gray in his trim mousey-brown hair.

"Tzidal," I answered honestly—there was no point in lying.

"Tzidal," he repeated my name, staring at my chest. It made me uncomfortable, but I stayed completely still, refusing to let him see how much his gaze affected me. "Come with me, Tzidal." His mouth lifted into a tight smile. "Her Majesty is in the Judgement Room."

Not sure what else to do, I nodded, following the beta through the palace.

I just hoped I wasn't being led to my death.

The Palace Hallways

Byriel

"WHERE THE FUCK are you taking me?" I barked loudly, hoping Tzidal would be able to follow the sound of my voice.

"Her Majesty is expecting you." Bracken led me deeper into the palace. "She's been waiting for a bit, so I expect her to be very agitated," he warned me. I didn't say anything. Strayton was always agitated. It was a trait she inherited from our father.

"Did you get tired of working in the prison?" I asked the older beta as I glanced over my shoulder. I couldn't sense anyone's presence, but hopefully, Tzidal was close. This place could be very confusing to an outsider. "Or is palace duty a promotion?"

"There was some damage at the prison," Bracken turned slightly, giving me a pointed look. "But you're already aware of that. Aren't you, My Lord?"

I cocked a smile, and he laughed, shaking his head as we continued down the narrow hallways. I could already tell exactly where we were going, and it filled me with dread.

"I always liked you, Byriel," Bracken said with a doleful sigh. "I'm sad to see the way things are going."

"It's always hard when the crown passes to a new monarch," I said simply, downplaying the horrible situation.

"Well, I wouldn't know." He walked a little faster as we entered a narrow stone corridor. The carpet was gone, and the wilting wolfsbane covered tiny tables along the way. "King Ares came into power when I was just a pup," he continued. "I do remember the stories of him being challenged for the crown, though. I heard the fights were vicious."

"He kept his own," I said, recalling my father's most favorite stories to share from that time. "It's tradition. Even if a challenger doesn't really want the crown, there's honor in saying you were defeated by the King. Or Queen," I quickly added.

"I don't think the Queen is going to entertain that tradition," Bracken said as he came to a stop at a large wooden door.

Four guards were posted, two on either side, and each one was younger than the last, and they were massive. It was a little disheartening to see that all my old friends were gone from this place, replaced by young, inexperienced alphas.

"Her majesty is just inside." Bracken motioned to the door.

I extended my hand to the beta. "Thank you, Bracken." He eyed my hand for a moment before finally shaking it. "You were a good and loyal servant to my father, and I thank you for everything you've sacrificed for our people."

Something like sadness pulled at the corners of the beta's eyes. "I'm sorry for how things have turned out." He bowed his head. "But I look forward to seeing you on the other side, brother."

I squeezed his hand one more time, then turned to face the door to the Judgement Room. Two guards flanked me, ready to enter alongside me.

"Strayton!" I roared loud and clear as my wolf growled right along with me. He was ready for a fucking fight, and honestly, so was I. "Where the fuck is my mate?" I turned the brass doorknob to the heavy door, pushing hard and forcing it to swing fast.

The scent of rot hit my nose first. It was bitter and sharp, flowing off bodies that hung from the walls near the tapestry. I stared at them, shamefully relieved that none was Blue.

Omega Janie's dead body hung limp from her shackles, the flesh around her wrists slipping away, exposing thin bone. Not wanting to look at her face, I turned to the other prisoners. Two dead elves hung from the walls as well. One seemed freshly killed, but the other's waxy face was gaunt and hollow, clearly gone for at least a few days now.

Turning, I searched the rest of the room, seeing a few alphas and one footman chained up. Each one was bloody and beaten, and the footman was knocked out.

Then my eyes fell on Strayton.

My vicious sister stood next to a small table with a metal box on top of it. She wore a pair of thick leather gloves and a long black dress that drifted around her bare feet—our mother's gold jewels were draped around her neck and wrists.

"There you are." Strayton smiled, but her expression was more pleased than happy. She liked that she beckoned, and I ran—even though I was only here because she took Blue from me. "I was shocked to hear you had taken a mate, brother." Strayton moved to me, but I turned away from her, double-checking all her prisoners to ensure Blue wasn't among them.

"Where is he?" I searched through our bond, still not feeling Blue anywhere.

Did she drug him?

Hurt him?

Was he knocked out somewhere?

"He's here," she said simply before walking past me toward the center of the room. Her long black curls bounced as she moved, looking all around the mighty chamber. "This was always one of my favorite rooms. Regal. With a definite purpose." She looked up, admiring the massive steepled ceiling, before turning to me. Her voice remained light despite her cutting glare. "Very few things in this damn place have any real use." She scanned the length of my body as her upper lip curled in disgust. "Are you happy with how you've turned out? Abandoning your family and your people all for a fucking blue-haired harlot."

"Where is my mate?" I snarled, curling my fists tight. My wolf slammed hard within my body, begging to break free, but the softest hint of wolfsbane kept him in place, trapped. "Stop with this fucking game!"

"You want your mate?" Strayton barked, her emotions instantly hard and angry. "I'll give you your fucking mate!" She turned toward the tapestry and yelled, "Dynel!"

The embroidered fabric moved as the hinged door swung open. It made the image of the black wolf wrinkle and shift. Finally, Tibbit emerged, followed closely by Dynel, with Blue's limp form slung over his shoulder. Every muscle in my body tightened, and my wolf roared, desperate to rip my omega out of the bastard's hold.

"What did you do to him?" I asked as calmly as I could, but a deep growl still pushed from my chest.

"He's fine." Strayton waved her hand at me, brushing my concern away as if I was being ridiculous.

"What the fuck did you do to him!" I repeated in a loud, angry roar as I took a careful step toward Strayton. My sister's eyes widened, pretending to be shocked by my behavior.

Dynel edged a little closer to Strayton, his stance protective, despite my omega still in his hold.

"So uncivilized." Strayton eyed me. "Your mate hit his head while trying to run away, and you yell at me for his clumsy mistake. Doesn't really shock me that you'd fall for someone so uncoordinated." She slipped a gloved hand down her throat, grimacing at Blue. "He's too gangly, and his skin is blue." She turned her back to my mate as if refusing to look at him any longer.

I let out a deep growl, whispering, "Say one more fucking word, and I will cut your tongue from your mouth" I moved my hand to the hilt of my blade, my wolf so fucking desperate to attack.

"Don't be stupid," Strayton crossed her arms, pushing her chest up and out. "You touch me, and Dynel will kill your precious mate before you can even blink."

I took a calming breath.

She'd kill Blue just for fun.

"Please," Tibbit spoke up. The elder looked a little off. His bright blue eyes were not quite as vibrant as usual. "Let me check on the young pup," he offered in his kind, soothing voice. "It will be easier to talk with your brother if he's not worried about his mate."

Strayton rolled her eyes, then gave a quick wave of her hand. "Fine," she said in a clipped tone. "Dynel." She snapped her fingers at the floor, indicating the alpha could lay my mate down.

I held my breath as Dynel slowly lowered Blue to the floor, carefully resting his head so as not to hurt him. I was thankful for that bit of kindness from the alpha, and I was sure it was the only mercy he'd give me today.

I watched as Tibbit moved over Blue, cradling his face, but a swift knock on the main door jerked my attention away from them. The hard sound echoed throughout the room, bouncing off the stone walls and steepled ceiling.

"My Queen." The heavy door pushed open, and the house butler, Saron, poked his head inside. "There's a member of the prim-staff here to see you."

Dread threaded up my spine as Tzidal came into view. Her shoulders were hunched, and her head bowed. She looked so meek. It was odd for the usually bold omega.

Moving slowly, the omega padded in, following Saron. The two guards that had escorted me inside moved to Tzidal's back, watching the tiny omega as if she were a dangerous weapon. It made me want to laugh out loud. These inexperienced pups should have been at my side, watching my every movement, but they were poorly trained and completely useless. It seemed my father had destroyed everything proper about this place before he left this earth.

"Well?" Strayton glared at Tzidal's innocent expression, confusion pulling her brows together. "What is it?"

But it was Saron that answered, "She's pretending to bring you strawberries, My Queen. But I wouldn't recommend eating them." The beta leaned in and whispered loudly, "She's a supporter of your father. Probably a spy."

Tzidal kept her head down, clutching the small bag of fruit to her chest.

"How do you know that?" Strayton asked, taking a careful step toward Tzidal.

Saron tipped his chin up, then pointed right at Tzidal's chest. "She's wearing a medallion with the King's seal on it."

Strayton tilted her head, narrowing her dark eyes at the necklace. "And what is your plan, omega?" she asked in a deep, cautious tone. "Were you hoping to kill me out of some kind of allegiance to my father?" She let out an exaggerated sigh as if bored with the whole situation. "There's no point. He's dead, and so is your cause."

"No, My Q-queen," Tzidal stammered at her feet. "Please. I just wanted a word with you."

"About what?" Strayton barked, making Tzidal flinch. But I could see it in her steady hands and clenched jaw. The omega was pretending to be scared.

"My position in the palace." Tzidal slowly lifted her lashes, struggling to look Strayton in the eye. "Your father. The King. I loved..." Her throat worked as she swallowed hard. "I loved him so much, and I wanted to...." Her cheeks went bright red as she trailed off. I knew her well enough to know it was the result of anger, but to a stranger, she just looked flustered. Maybe embarrassed. "I wanted to bring you a gift and offer myself to you in any way you see fit." Tzidal held out the bag of strawberries, waiting for Strayton to speak.

"*Saron*," Strayton growled the beta's name. He took a careful step back, fear making his eyes wide. "You interrupted me because one of my father's whores was wandering around the palace?" She paused long enough for him to open his mouth, but then she spoke up, cutting him off. "I am speaking with my brother, but you felt *this*," she stabbed one long finger in Tzidal's direction, "was worth wasting my time with?"

"My Queen," Saron's voice pitched higher, his fear taking hold. "My Lady, I meant no harm. Only to bring you a trespasser. I wanted to help."

My sister's sweet cedar scent grew deeper. Sharper. "I don't need your help," she whispered as she inched closer to the beta, pushing into his space. "I don't need anyone's help."

Saron quickly nodded as he recoiled from her angry glare. "Yes, My Queen." Strayton held the silence, scanning every inch of the frightened beta's face.

Tzidal's eyes flickered from Blue to me. I could see it in her eyes: she was working out how to get him out of here, ready to fight if she had to. I trusted her to get Blue to safety.

Strayton let out a slow, rumbling growl, then flashed her elongated fangs at Saron. "Get. Out."

The beta turned and ran, not bothering to bow or excuse himself.

"Dynel!" Strayton barked as she turned back toward the room, making her black dress swish. "Chain this omega up. I'm sick of looking at her."

The Judgement Room

Tzidal

I TOOK SEVERAL STEPS BACKWARD, praying Dynel wouldn't tackle me. He was massive, with scars all along his face and arms, and his skin was white and waxy. He looked like the kind of creature you expected to live under your bed as a child.

"Please," I whispered to the terrifying alpha as real fear set in. "I'm just an omega."

The corded muscles in Byriel's arms flex as his claws grew into mighty points. A vase of wilted wolfsbane was on a side table, but I didn't know how fresh the flower had to be to keep an alpha's wolf trapped within them. Even though I wanted Byriel to be able to shift, I did not want to see what Dynel's wolf looked like.

"Now!" Strayton snarled, impatient.

Dynel marched straight at me, his fists tight and his face pinched. "Come!" he barked, using the full force of his alpha tone. My wolf roared within me, and I closed my eyes, trying like hell to run in the opposite direction, but between the horrible alpha's command and my stubborn beast, my feet tripped over themselves, and I pitched forward, smacking my hands, and knees hard on the stone floor.

A big hand grabbed me by the back of my robes and lifted me clear off the floor. I swung in Dynel's hold, turning away from his hard, black eyes.

"Please," I pleaded, trying to ignore my stinging palms. "Have mercy."

"Mercy?" Strayton balked. "If you want mercy, then live with the fairies. Our kind craves blood."

"My Queen," Tibbit spoke softly, pulling Strayton's attention away from me. "The young omega is waking up." Byriel stiffened, and I narrowed my eyes at Blue's back, hating that I couldn't see his face.

In one fierce movement, Dynel dropped me hard onto my stomach and pinned me in place. "Don't move," he snarled as he watched Blue.

The omega's legs straightened as he slowly lifted his head off the floor. Hope pounded in my chest as I silently pleaded for Blue to get up. There was no way I could carry him out of here. I needed him up and moving.

"Easy there," Tibbit whispered when Blue's upper body swayed. Byriel jerked as if struggling to stay put. "I've got you." Tibbit held Blue's upper arms, helping the omega steady himself.

"What happened?" Blue mumbled, pressing his palm to his temple. I wanted to scream at him to get up and run with all his might, but between Dynel, Strayton, and the two guards standing next to Byriel, we were grossly outnumbered. Blue would never make it.

"It looks like you smacked your head good." Tibbit examined Blue's face. "But I think you'll be alright. Can you stand?"

Moving carefully, Blue pushed his feet under his bottom, but then he froze. His chest expanded as he pulled in a deep breath. Byriel let out a soft rumble, telling me he could finally feel his mate through their bond. There was nothing more painful than a silent bond.

Slowly, Blue turned his head, and his vibrant eyes immediately landed on Byriel. "Alpha?" he whispered, his voice breathy and sad. The tender look that passed between them felt so personal. I closed my eyes, trying to give them some privacy.

"It's okay, mate," Byriel said softly.

"It's not okay." Strayton's hard voice made me flinch and glare at the horrible woman. "But it will be soon." She turned her fierce energy to her brother, snarling, "I'm going to cleanse these lands of every evil creature that has dared to cross me."

"Stray," Byriel said in a calm, even tone, but I could see the tremor in his hand as he gripped the hilt of his dagger. He was losing control. "Let the omegas go. Your fight is with me."

"My fight is with too many to count." Strayton gave him a pinched smile. "But if a few innocents die in the process, then so be it."

"What the hell do you want!" Byriel yelled, catching both myself and Strayton off guard. Her wide eyes and shocked expression mimicked my own. "Do you just want to torture me? Hurt me? Fine, but let the omegas go first."

"You don't get to tell me what to do!" Strayton pointed at her brother. The fingertips of her gloves pushed out as sharp claws cut through the material. "I have spent my entire life being told what to do by alphas that have looked down on me. Forced me into submission. Mocked me for who I fell in love with! They hated me for how I supported our father, then loathed me even more for getting rid of the old man." She sucked in a tight breath and shook her head. "I am sick and *fucking* tired of being controlled."

Hard voices and angry growls drifted through the floor, vibrating against my belly. Dynel moved above me, pressing more of his weight into the center of my back. I couldn't see his face, but the other two guards turned to look at the main door. *Something* was happening.

I pressed my lips into a tight line, praying Kenji was able to find *hundreds* of fighters. It wasn't likely, but I needed to believe Joon and Dane weren't out there fighting for their lives all by themselves.

"I was supposed to have great power," Strayton mused, seemingly unaware of anything else happening around her. She stared at Byriel like he was the only awful thing in this world. "I have worked so fucking hard and waited so long." She tipped her head back and inhaled deeply. "Yasha promised I would have power over the land and skies, even greater than the fae. But I can't find one fucking marked wolf." She held up a single finger as if to make her point. "It's all ruined because of one."

"Why on earth would you want that kind of power?" Byriel asked, clearly not understanding any better than I did. "You are the Queen of Wolves," he gritted out. "The most powerful of all our kind. The most dominant of any other creature in these lands. What more do you fucking want?"

"No," Strayton shook her head, her expression tight. Angry. "I don't have real power. I can't see visions or command magic like the sirens or fae. Hell, even a simple pixie has advanced charms to aid them in their hunting. Our kind," she pressed a gloved hand to her chest, "have no real power, and I need it, Byriel." Her voice broke, and her words slipped into a pained whisper, "I need to make all of them pay for stealing away the only man I ever loved."

Realization made Byriel go completely still, and his mouth hung open for a moment. "Is all of this really just about an old lover?" His neck bent forward as if struggling to see the she-alpha. "Is this just about revenge?"

The soft pain in Strayton's eyes disappeared, replaced by thick rage. "Lavant wasn't *just* an old lover," she seethed. "I loved him, and he was killed for simply not being a wolf."

Byriel shook his head. "Wolves and elves don't mix."

"Yeah?" Strayton's eyes went wide at his words. "Then what the fuck is he?" She pointed at Blue. "Because he definitely isn't pure, Byriel!"

Byriel's eyes flashed red, and the muscles in his jaw ticked. "Lavant is dead. There's nothing you can do to change that."

Strayton's face split into an evil grin. "I'll tell you what." Her eyes flickered to Blue. "Let's see how well you fare with your mate six feet under."

And then everything happened all at once.

Strayton marched straight to Blue. Dynel released me, hurrying to catch Byriel, who was already running at full speed toward his mate. Strayton gripped a handful of Blue's hair and jerked hard just as Dynel wrapped his massive arms around Byriel's chest. The two guards jumped into action. One raced to Dynel's side, helping to wrestle Byriel to the floor. The other grabbed Tibbit, forcing the elder away from Strayton, but the young alpha grunted as if really struggling to hold onto the elder.

"What do you think, omega," Stryaton mocked Blue as she dragged him across the room. "Will your alpha crave revenge, or will he simply let your death go, completely unaffected?"

I pushed myself up and unsheathed my dagger, but before I could move, Dynel reached out and snatched my wrist, trying like hell to hold both Byriel and me at the same time.

"I will fucking kill you!" Byriel let out a guttural roar, spinning and jerking as the two alphas struggled to hold him in place. It made me fall backward, slamming hard into Dynel's side.

Strayton turned and smiled at her brother while Blue clawed at her arms, trying to get the she-alpha to release his hair. "I think this is an important lesson for you, brother." She flicked one finger out, popping the lid of the box up. The vibrant red light burst from the tiny box, warming the otherwise cold room.

The ground shook, and dust pushed out from between the rock walls. It felt as if someone had blown something up.

"Terrince!" Dynel snapped at the alpha holding Tibbit. "Find out—" But before he could finish his thought, Byriel kicked out, making Dynel fall backward and release me.

I ran as fast as I could toward Strayton, watching in horror as she pulled the glowing star from the box. Her face lit up as she held it high, then she turned and looked down at Blue's tear-streaked face. Fear poured from the tiny omega, and his arms went slack.

"Are you ready, sweet omega?" she purred.

I pumped my arms and legs, angled my head down, then slammed right into the horrible woman. Strayton let out a pained grunt from the force of my shoulder as we both fell hard onto the stone ground.

Caught off guard, Strayton stumbled back, and the star tipped from her hand, rolling across the stone floor. She watched it in horror as it moved right toward Byriel. His green eyes widened as it neared, and he jerked once again, desperate to free himself from the two alphas still struggling to hold him.

The star rolled to a stop a few feet from Byriel, and the enraged alpha jerked, pushing all three of them toward the star. The young guard moved his leg back to regain his balance, and the heel came into contact with the star.

Dynel's eyes went wide as he realized what had happened. He released Byriel and jerked back as the young alpha started screaming and jerking, blood pouring from his eyes and ears.

Blue let out a tiny squeak as Stayton released him and ran to the star. Byriel moved to grab it.

"Don't!" I screamed at the alpha as I tried to get up, but sharp pain burst from my ankle, and I fell over once again. "Don't touch it!"

Strayton laughed as she slowed to a stroll, then bent over to pick it up. "Be careful," she teased Byriel.

Something heavy slammed into the door, and the ground shook again. "My Queen," Tibbit walked toward the door. His back was straight, and his feet fast for his age. I didn't remember him moving so well before. "I think we're under attack."

"I know," Strayton gritted out, flashing her red eyes at Byriel. "And after I kill you, I will walk through the city streets and kill anyone that has ever spoken to you, my dear brother."

Byriel squared his shoulders and tipped his head back, meeting his fate head-on. "Do what you must, but our people are done with evil Kings and crazed Queens. I'm sure we'll share a plot next to each other sooner rather than later."

A pinched smile filled Strayton's face as she raised the star high in the air, poised to hit her brother with it. "I'll be sure to leave flowers on your grave." She brought the star down, but just before it could touch Byriel's exposed chest, Blue pushed between them, catching the full force of the magical object.

Energy exploded from the omega, knocking both Strayton and Byriel clear back across the room.

The air crackled and burned, the heat making my eyes sting.

The ground shook again, and the door burst open, flying clean off its hinges. Joon and several others rushed into the room, but it was too late.

Blue was dead.

The Chosen Wolf

Joon

"HURRY UP!" I roared at CariAnn as she covered the door's hinges in the smoking green liquid.

"Back up," she grabbed my arm as it sizzled and smoked, turning the metal into a clumpy goop. The door groaned and then sagged as the hinges gave away. "Go!" CariAnn yelled as she backed up.

I steadied my feet, then kicked out as hard as I could, forcing the heavy door to buckle and then fall back onto the rough stone floor. I rushed in and scanned the room. Panic pounded hard in my veins as I scanned the massive room for my mate. I turned, then relief washed over me. Tzidal sat on the floor near the lone table, but her sad eyes were fixed just past me. She looked gutted.

"My Lord!" Dane yelled as he rushed past me.

Byriel ignored all of us, crawling slowly to the center of the room...toward Blue's lifeless body.

The sight of the tiny blue-haired omega made my hands go cold and my face numb. I just couldn't believe he was dead, but his chest didn't rise, and his eyes were cloudy and unfocused. Empty.

"No," Byriel whispered as he pushed his arms under Blue's limp body, then rolled the omega against his chest. Byriel's face was covered in soot and tears as he rocked his dead mate in his arms. "No, no, no," he softly repeated, burying his face in Blue's neck. "No, no, no, no, no."

I took a step back, remembering that horrible moment two years ago when I had lost my mate. Her eyes were vacant, and her skin was cold to the touch. Death would have been preferable.

"Joon?"

I turned to Tzidal's fragile voice, then rushed to her side. "Are you hurt?" I sat beside her, pulling her into my arms.

Dynel and another alpha moved cautiously to examine a dead guard. Tibbit sat in a crumpled heap on the other side of the room. He stared at Byriel and Blue, his face blank of all emotion, but it was Strayton that caught my eye. The vicious she-alpha looked as if she had been knocked on her ass and was struggling to get her feet back under her.

Slowly, Strayton finally stood, but her knees were noticeably unsteady.

For a moment, everything was quiet.

Just the muffled sound of Byriel's sobs and his sister's labored breathing.

It almost felt peaceful.

Almost.

"What the fuck?" Strayton snarled, ripping a leather glove off one hand and wiping the ash off her cheeks and forehead. "What the fuck was that?" She glared at her brother, but he wasn't paying her any attention. He was too busy staring lovingly at Blue's face.

"Tibbit," Tzidal whispered the elder's name, beckoning him closer, but the beta shook his head. Then he pointed to the vibrant red star just next to Blue's feet. It wasn't a steady glow of light anymore but flickered and crackled. It seemed unstable.

"What's happening to it?" Tzidal whispered to me as she pressed deeper against my chest. Her cold fingers wrapped around my back, holding me tight.

"I don't know." I shook my head.

Just then, the star started to shake, then vibrate. I squinted at the bright object, trying to figure out if it was actually lifting off the ground or if it was just a trick of the light. But the damn thing was so bright, I couldn't tell.

"Tibbit!" Strayton turned to the elder and barked, "What is happening?"

The beta shook his head as he slowly stood, staring with wide eyes. "I have no idea."

A deafening boom cracked the air, followed by a flood of red light that was so intense I couldn't see anything. I curled Tzidal tight against my chest, trying to shield her from the falling dust and splintered wood that fell from the ceiling. I prayed to the Moon the roof wouldn't collapse.

"Are you fucking kidding me?" Strayton roared, and I looked up, relieved and shocked to see all the red light was gone. The star was black and dull, like glass. "What..." She cut an angry glare at Blue. For a moment, I thought she was going to lash out at the dead omega or attack her brother, but instead, she reached down with her gloved hand and picked up the broken star.

Tzidal whimpered, and I smoothed a hand down the back of her head, trying to calm her. But my emotions were just as shot as hers.

Strayton inspected the black star, turning it over in her hand. Her eyes pulled in the corners, but her mouth was a tight, angry line. "Such a waste," she gritted out, then, without thinking, she pressed her other ungloved hand to the star, and her whole body instantly locked up.

The room warmed once again, but this time, the red light didn't burst outward. Instead, it crawled up Strayton's arm, making every vein under her skin glow an eerie red. Her eyes widened as they moved up her body and into her chest, but the she-alpha didn't scream or shake; she just watched with wide dark eyes as the light consumed her.

"Is it killing her?" Tzidal asked, hopeful.

But before I could answer, Strayton gave a pained grunt, squeezing her eyes shut tight. The star shook, then cracked. I thought it might explode or erupt, but it disintegrated like dust, falling softly onto the stone floor.

The quiet moment had my wolf on alert. Strayton was still standing, and her skin was still glowing.

"Stay close," I whispered to Tzidal, pushing her behind me. She willingly moved, poised to protect my back if I needed to attack.

Slowly, Strayton lowered her head. Then she finally opened her eyes. All white was gone, replaced with pure black irises that shone like vibrant lava glass.

Strayton hummed, running her hands over her hips and up to her stomach and chest. "So this is what it feels like to be immortal," she purred, moving her hands up into her wild hair. "It feels," she let out a sultry breath and licked her lips, "Good."

Tibbit moved, running at full speed straight at the she-alpha, but before he could make contact, Strayton spun and flung her arm out, hitting the elder with a shocking burst of light. Tibbit flung backward into the air. His aged body contorting and shifted, turning to Lex as he landed hard, skidding across the rough stone floor. Lex's robes were gone, replaced with his rough, gray skin and small wiry feathers. I had seen his true form once before. He was smaller than this, more birdlike. But I didn't know enough about the siren's biology to know if he was alive or not.

"Lex?" Tzidal jerked behind me as if to run, but I pushed a firm order through our bond, letting her know she wasn't to move.

"Now, that's real power," Strayton's excited voice filled the massive, dusty room. The support beams overhead were cracked, and the tiny windows along the ceiling were blown out. "This is too good, brother," she chuckled, examining her hands and arms. The red light pulsed just beneath her skin, flowing like the ripples in a stream. "I've never felt so alive."

Byriel ignored her, caressing Blue's cheeks and pushing the hair out of his face.

"I told you I'd find a way to hold the star's power," Strayton glanced at her uninterested brother. Her happiness dimmed as he continued to pet Blue, caressing his cheeks and tracing his lips. "Byriel!"

In a burst of movement, Dane sprinted straight for Strayton. He managed to wrap his clawed hands around her throat, and I held my breath, praying he'd be able to end her. But Strayton didn't seem affected by the alpha's strength in the least. Instead, she simply smiled.

"What..." Tzidal whispered behind me, but I couldn't take my eyes off Dane's hard expression. It shifted, his eyes going wide, and his mouth falling open in a painful scream. The horrible sound echoed into the air and off the walls, making me wince. Then his voice cut off with a sharp gurgle, and his lifeless body fell to the floor with a heavy thump.

"I am the chosen wolf!" Strayton glared down at the dead alpha, but her eyes didn't glow red. They stayed pitch black, almost as if her wolf had no power within her. "No one can challenge me ever again!" Strayton scanned the quiet room, clearly looking for her next victim. "Who's next?" She turned her vicious energy on Byriel. "How about that other omega?"

He didn't react or respond, still staring at Blue's face.

"Or how about your old friends in the guard?" Strayton continued. "I could end the whole battalion with only the flick of my wrist." She moved her fingers, making a red electric light dance between them.

Byriel stayed completely silent in his grief, acting as if he couldn't hear a sound.

"Byriel!" Strayton roared at her brother. "You will listen to me!" Her anger rose, and her skin glowed red. "Do you hear me?" She grabbed Blue's arm, then jerked the small omega's body away from her brother.

"No!" Byriel roared, wrapping his arms around Blue's middle and pulling the limp omega back to him. Strayton struggled but didn't let go. "Don't fucking touch him!" Byriel jerked on Blue again, but this time Strayton stumbled forward, almost falling over Byriel.

"Stop it!" Strayton snapped at her brother.

"Fucking leave him alone," Byriel snarled, flashing his long pointed teeth.

"I can't!" Strayton barked just as loudly. "I'm trying, but I can't!" She shook her arm, but her fingers stayed firmly around Blue's wrist. She did it again, and the poor omega's body flopped at the motion.

"My Queen," Dynel's deep voice was laced with panic as he rushed to help Strayton. He grabbed her arm, but before he could do anything else, his big body seized up just like all the others. And before I could blink, the alpha was dead at Strayton's feet—blood pouring from his eyes and mouth.

"What the—" Strayton's voice caught in her throat. It looked like she couldn't breathe, but then her body locked up.

Byriel pulled Blue against him, then rolled the omega's face so it was pressed against his chest. "I've got you, my love."

Byriel braced an arm over Blue's face as if to protect him. The poor bastard just couldn't accept that his omega was gone, and I feared he'd soon be dead too.

"Let him go!" Tzidal pleaded with Byriel as Strayton let out a vicious scream, but I knew it was no use. *Byriel would happily die with his mate in his arms.*

The red light from Strayton's body moved slowly, crawling down her arm and into Blue's. His skin glowed a crisp white then he began to shake right along with Strayton. The scent of blood filled the air, and red seeped from Strayton's flesh, pouring out of her nose and ears, but Blue wasn't bleeding, *not yet.*

Then all at once, all the light vanished, and Stayton fell onto the floor in a puddle of her own blood.

Tzidal pressed hard against my back, peering over my shoulder. I could feel her small body tremble with so much fear and adrenaline. "Is it over?" she whispered.

"I think so," I said, taking in all the carnage around us.

Bryeil was draped over his mate's lifeless body while Kenji and CariAnn were pressed against the furthest wall, both staring at Lex's withered form. Dane was dead in the center of the room, next to Dynel's corpse. And I didn't even want to think about the guards we had wounded or killed as we made our way through the palace.

"Is Lex..." Tzidal whispered behind me, and I glanced over my shoulder. Her eyes were glassy, and her cheeks flushed. "Is he dead?" she asked calmly.

I didn't know how to answer her, so instead, I turned and grabbed her arm, pulling her back into my lap. "It'll be okay, mate," I whispered against her temple.

Tzidal was quiet for a moment, her body stiff, then all at once, she sagged against me, crying softly against my chest.

Then a soft cough pushed from Blue's limp body.

At first, I wasn't sure I had heard it, but Byriel lifted his head off his omega, listening.

And then he coughed again.

"Blue?" Byriel's voice rose, and his hands trembled as he moved his mate so he could see his face. "Blue?"

"What happened?" Blue's words were slurred and weak as he drew a sharp breath.

"What—" he coughed hard, curling tight against Byriel's chest.

"Don't move," Byriel said in a rushed, urgent voice. His dark green eyes scanned the room as if looking for help. Then his gaze landed on Tzidal. She pushed from my arms in one powerful movement, racing to Byriel's side.

I stood and quickly followed her. I should have been checking on the injured and dead, but I couldn't leave my mate's side. Not even for a single second.

"It's okay." Tzidal reached for Blue's hand, but before I warned her not to touch the omega, she threaded their fingers together, squeezing gently. My wolf whimpered, terrified Blue would pulse or explode, but everything seemed okay. "It's all going to be okay," Tzidal whispered as she cupped Blue's cheek.

"Joon," CariAnn pulled my attention away from the pair. "Dane is gone." She knelt over the alpha's body, then brushed her fingers over his eyelids, closing them.

"A lot of good alphas lost their lives today," I stared at Dane's face. It wasn't exactly a touching or inspirational thing to say, but I was too numb to offer much more. Dane was a hard alpha who sacrificed a lot to end the suffering in these lands. He would surely be missed by many and celebrated often, but I just couldn't say any of that out loud. Not yet.

"You really shouldn't stand," Tzidal said, trying to get Blue to sit back down. But the determined omega ignored her, standing tall on his unsteady legs.

"I need to see," Blue whispered, giving the room a sweeping look. Byriel pressed his lips together, clearly not liking how much his mate was moving.

"Blue," I said, giving Byriel a sympathetic look. I knew how hard a stubborn omega was to handle, especially when they were injured. "You died. Maybe sit for a minute."

Blue's eyes went wide as he turned to Byriel. "I died?" he sounded genuinely shocked.

Byriel nodded, his tears still drying on his face. As if noticing them for the first time, Blue cupped his alpha's cheeks, brushing them with his thumbs. "Are you okay?" he whispered.

"I am now," Byriel pulled his mate to his chest and kissed the top of his head. "I am now."

Looking a little defeated, Tzidal stood, then walked through the dirty room. She moved near Dane, glancing at his face, before moving toward Lex.

A swift pulse of fear moved through our bond as Tzidal approached the siren. "Lex," she whispered his name, clearly terrified that her dear friend was dead. "Lex?" she repeated, settling on her knees just next to the withered siren.

"It's okay," I placed my hand on Tzidal's shoulder, feeling her deep sadness grow, but then Lex let out a muffled groan.

"Lex!" Tzidal gasped, forcing him onto his back.

Lex's features were unrefined, a blank slate of just wet black eyes and a slit for a mouth. "I'm not having fun anymore," he mumbled.

A nervous laugh pushed from Tzidal's throat as she draped her body over her friend. "Me either."

My eyes flooded with tears, relieved to hear Lex's voice, but I turned my back to the pair. I'd rather die than for the siren to know I cared that much.

The Dawn of a New Era

Tzidal

"Now what?" Blue whispered to his mate.

I lifted my head off Lex's chest and turned to Byriel, curious as to what the alpha would say.

I mean, what did we do now?

There were so many of Strayton's supporters left to fight. There were loved ones to bury and even more to comfort. The people of these lands had been terrorized for the last two years straight, and there was no simple way that we could all just go back to normal and pretend it didn't happen.

"Lex," Byriel asked, hugging his mate. "Where is Tibbit?"

"In his room," Lex whispered, his voice strained with pain. "He and Yasha were enjoying a cup of tea when I left them."

The tension in Byriel's shoulders eased, and he let out a soft sigh. "Thank you."

Lex mumbled a quick "you're welcome" before closing his eyes again. I had seen the siren in worse shape, but not much worse. This was probably going to take a few weeks and one very large meal for him to heal completely. I was just sad that Strayton wasn't alive to fill his belly.

"Can you bring them back?" Joon asked Blue. I turned to my mate as his eyes drifted over the dead around us, but they lingered on Dane. "It might be a long shot," he shrugged, "but you never know."

Worry twisted between Blue's brow as he glanced down at his hands. "I don't know how."

"What if you just touched them?" I motioned around the room at no one in particular.

Blue's big eyes widened at the possibility. "Okay." His voice was small and uncertain as he slowly walked over to Dane.

The lifeless alpha was sprawled out, his arms out wide, knees slightly bent, and his expression was soft. It was almost as if he was sleeping.

It was funny how death always looked that way to the living. Peaceful. And not the horrible destruction of a soul that someone loved.

"It's okay, mate," Byriel whispered as Blue knelt beside Dane. "Even if it doesn't work, it will be okay."

Blue nodded, then reached out and brushed his fingers over Dane's forehead.

But nothing happened.

A wash of deep grief moved through my bond with Joon, but he stayed quiet next to me, not reacting at all. But I still threaded my fingers through his, letting him know he wasn't alone.

An angry huff pushed from Blue's chest as he moved his hand, pressing his whole palm to Dane's cheek, then his arm, and then his chest.

"It's okay," Byreil took Blue's hand, forcing the omega to stand. "It was a lot to ask of you."

Blue sniffled, tucking his arms against his chest as Byriel

hugged him. "I'm sorry," the omega whimpered. I could smell his tears even from here. "I can't save anything."

Anger flashed in Byriel's eyes as he gripped Blue's arms and forced him away from his body. "You just saved *all* of us," Byriel said forcefully. "And not just the people in this room. Everyone, Blue." Bryeil swallowed hard, trying to reign in his anger. "All of Havre was in danger because of Strayton....and...." His fangs flashed, struggling to keep his emotions in control. "That fucking star was going to kill everyone and everything, and *you* saved us."

A slow smile slipped across Blue's face as he hung his head. "Thank you for saying that."

"Byriel?" Kenji slowly stepped away from the wall, bowing to the dark alpha. "There is still fighting in the streets, My Lord." He tucked his hands behind his back, standing at attention. "It would probably calm the people to show your face. Let them know they aren't alone."

"What do you mean?" Blue looked between the two alphas. I could scent the omega's fear from here.

"He means," Byriel released his mate, then walked slowly to his sister's dead body, "That the people of Ossory need to hear some words of comfort from their new King."

Being more gentle than she deserved, Byriel lifted Strayton in his arms, then carried her quietly out of the stone room and into the palace.

Joon immediately reached for Lex, carrying him, while Blue and I walked closely at his back.

I felt so numb like it wasn't real, and danger was waiting around the next corner, ready to destroy us at any second.

"It's okay, Tzidal." Blue pushed into me. "We're all going to be okay." I squeezed him back, feeling his slight body shiver next to me. His feet were still unsteady, and his scent was too sharp. He needed to rest, but then again, we all did.

The walk through the palace was odd.

We stepped over dead bodies and passed a few bleeding alphas that were still slowly dying, but what stuck with me was those continuing to fight. The moment we passed, each and every one of them stopped, staring at Byriel carrying his sister's lifeless form. It was as if their energy and bloodlust was stripped away, carried off with Byriel as he walked.

"So many are following us." Blue looked nervously over his shoulder as we moved through the entryway.

Several armed villagers and even more guards fell in line as we walked, showing their support and loyalty for Byriel. It warmed me to know that if anyone within the city wanted to fight him, he'd have an army at his back.

The cold air outside was cutting, and the sun touched the tips of the mountains, casting deep orange and pink across the evening sky. The fighting outside the palace had stopped. Alphas were picking up their dead and checking on the wounded, but for the most part, it was quiet.

Blue's feet stumbled across the uneven ground, making Kenji move closer to us. He stood protectively at our backs as we stepped into the marketplace near the town square.

A few betas moved around their little shops, locking their doors. Rising whispers and a few shocked gasps made them stop, stepping out into the streets as Byriel passed.

"The Queen is no more!" Byriel yelled, stepping into the center of the open road. "Strayton, The Queen of Wolves, is dead!" His voice carried as all other sound came to a stop. No one spoke or moved, or even breathed. Everything was just quiet as the alpha carefully laid his sister's body at his feet. "I killed her," Byriel stood tall, squaring his shoulders. "I stand before you as your new and rightful King. Love me or hate me, I will do my best to make you proud."

A few alphas stepped up, inspecting the dead Queen, but

the betas stayed pushed up against the side of the road, clearly too scared to come any closer.

"Did you kill her with that dark magic?" Someone yelled above the crowd, making a few turn to find the source. I swore it was the same voice that had taunted the Queen during her speech only a few days ago.

"The red star is gone," Byriel said firmly. "It burned up and disappeared. You don't have to fear it anymore. I am nothing more than an alpha with no extraordinary powers. I'm no better or worse than you, but I will work hard to protect you." He curled his fists tight, holding his head high. "Challenge me for the crown if you must. I welcome it."

There was a shift in the crowd as wolves murmured to themselves. Some where excited at the prospect of a fight, while others just reeked of fear. I knew this was a royal tradition that had survived centuries of Kings, but it was still stupid. How the hell did even more fighting help welcome any new era?

"Byriel!" Jonelle's hard voice cut through the crowd.

The she-alpha's spiky black hair comes into view first. It stuck out in all directions, and her face was covered in sweat. It looked as if she had just run for miles on end, and the army of alphas and betas brandishing weapons behind her made my heart warm.

Byriel rolled his shoulders and popped his neck, readying himself. "Let us fight." He moved around his sister's body, then widened his stance. The crowd moved with him, giving the alphas ample room to brawl.

"This is horrible," Blue whispered, dropping his head on my shoulder.

"I know," I patted his back, praying this would just stop already.

"I ask for my mate's sake that you wound and not kill me," Byriel said to Jonelle, raising his fists.

But instead of engaging, Jonelle stepped right up to Byriel, then bowed low. "King Byriel," she spoke in a loud, clear voice. "I have no intention of fighting you, My King." She dropped to one knee, slamming her fist to her chest. "But I want to be the first to pledge my loyalty to you. If any here wish to fight you for the crown," she turned, glaring at the droves of excited wolves, "then I offer my life in place of yours."

"I do as well," Kenji stepped forward, kneeling beside Jonelle. "Alpha Kenji of Ossory is here to serve you, My King."

"And so is Beta Bracken of Hala," an older beta moved through the throng of wolves that had walked down from the palace. He hobbled, his left leg swollen and his fists bloody, but he still managed to kneel right next to Kenji.

Slowly, more and more wolves moved forward, kneeling all around Byriel.

It was intense and powerful, making tears flood my tired eyes.

There were still a few alphas around the edges of the market that stood with angry snarls and clenched fists, but it was hard to tell if their hatred was for Byriel or just the torment they had endured the last few years at the hands of an unhinged monarchy. This fucking family has killed so many.

"Joon?" Lex's voice was weak, and his form was still gray and soft. "Are you going to kneel too?" The siren asked, with a teasing glint in his eye.

"Hell, no," Joon snorted, but I noticed how soft his voice was, clearly not wanting to offend those that were stepping up to pledge their lives to the new King. "I don't want it to go to Byriel's head. He needs at least one alpha out there who wants to see him dead."

Blue let out a soft laugh, nuzzling my cheek, but there was something so sad in the way he held me. "You're going to leave me," he whispered. "Aren't you?"

I opened my mouth, wanting so badly to tell him I'd never leave his side, but it would have been a bald-faced lie. "I'm so sorry, Blue," I cupped his cheeks, "But I have to get back to my family."

Sadness pulled at the corners of his eyes as he nodded at his feet. "Will you at least write me?"

I placed my hand over my heart. "I will send you a letter every week," I promised.

"And two in the new year?" he asked, hopeful.

"And two in the new year." I reached for his hand, squeezing gently.

"And what about you?" Blue turned to the siren still in Joon's arms. "Will you leave, too?"

"This adventure is over," Lex said softly to the young omega. "It's time for a new one."

A few tears gathered in the corner of Blue's eyes. "Okay."

"Hey," Lex pushed away from Joon, clearly wanting to stand on his own. My mate slowly released him but stayed at the siren's back in case his weak legs gave out. "We should say goodbye with smiles instead of tears." Lex tucked a strand of Blue's dark hair behind his slightly pointed ear. "Don't let it end with so much sorrow."

Blue nodded as tears slipped down his soft cheeks. "I feel like I'm losing my family," he whispered.

"You haven't lost us, pup," I kissed his forehead. "You simply have a whole new reason to visit the villages."

"And we will visit Madra," Byriel stepped up behind Blue, wrapping his arm around his mate's middle. "We will have to visit all the villages to check on our people."

"*Our* people?" Blue asked.

"Yes, my love, Byriel said simply. "You're the King's consort. The Luna of Havre. These people belong to you just as much as me."

Blue's hypnotic eyes widened as he swallowed hard.

"Okay." His voice was a soft squeak, making me snuggle the shocked omega tighter.

"It's going to be okay, Blue," I kissed his cheek. "If anyone deserves to lead the people of Havre, it's the chosen omega that died for them."

Six Months Later

Joon

I BALANCED the large package in my arms, then pushed open the door to our little cabin, grimacing when it slammed against the door, popping back.

"Really?" Tzidal's voice cut from the bedroom. She did not sound amused.

"I'm sorry," I moved into our quiet home, inhaling my mate's beautiful jasmine scent. It covered everything: the chairs, the table, the bedding, and even the pillows. *This was what heaven smelled like.*

"You know," Tzidal appeared in the hallway. She wore one of my oversized shirts over her swollen belly. At six months pregnant, there wasn't much in her wardrobe that fit her anymore. "You won't be able to burst into the house in a few months." She smoothed her hands over her rounded belly.

I sat the package down, then kissed the top of her stomach, "I'm sorry," I whispered to our pup. "Hopefully, I didn't wake you." But a slight bump pushed out at the top of Tzidal's tummy, telling me our babe was wide awake in there.

"How was the village?" Tzidal asked, settling into her favorite chair next to the fireplace. It was mid-summer, too hot to actually enjoy a fire, but since finding out she was with child, Tzidal liked the smell of the cooled, burnt logs. It was weird.

"Your mother wanted me to remind you that you'd be much safer having that pup inside the village borders." I smiled at my fierce mate, watching as she reacted exactly as I expected.

"Why the hell would I live where I'm not allowed to leave by myself?" Tzidal snapped.

Since we arrived on the outskirts of Madra, Tzidal's parents were beside themselves with both happiness and worry about having their daughter home. However, they both hated that we lived outside the village.

"I will never live inside a border ever again," Tzidal said firmly.

"Not even for a few months after the pup is born?" I asked, hopeful. Tzidal narrowed her honey-brown eyes at me, and I quickly held my hands up in surrender. "It's just a suggestion. It's safer—"

"Wolves can be killed inside a village just as easily as outside," she said pointedly. "And not to mention, the gates to the village lock at sundown. Lex would be horrified if he couldn't visit us whenever he wanted."

"That's part of the appeal," I mumbled.

"Stop it," Tzidal smacked my arm. "You love him, and you know it."

"He does keep the rogues away." I glanced out our living room window, admiring the lush summer day. A river was not far off, giving our home a pleasant breeze and the comforting aroma of water lilies and moss. "The siren is excellent pest control."

"What's in the box?" Tzidal pointed to the package at my feet.

I picked it up, carrying it to my mate. "It's from the palace." I pushed one long claw forward, then slipped it over the ties, letting the box spring open. "I assume it's from Blue."

Tzidal let out an excited squeal as she pulled out several baby blankets and pillows---perfect for a tiny nest. "Did I tell you that Byriel found a witch that's half-fae? She's going to help Blue control and understand his powers better."

"You told me." I pressed my lips together, trying to hide a smile. It seemed that Tzidal was constantly forgetting the things she had told me, but her mother assured me it was expected at this stage in pregnancy.

"How cute!" Tzidal held up a baby-sized dressing gown, draping it over her belly. "Oh!" She leaned down and pulled out a tiny dagger secured tight in a matching silver sheath. "And something for the pup to train with." She smiled wide.

I pulled the dagger out of her hand, glaring at it. "My pups will have no need to fight when they're young."

Tzidal pulled a face, clearly judging me. "You are no fun."

I pulled the dressing gown off her stomach, then threw it and the blade back into the box. "How is my pup today?"

"Hungry." Tzidal widened her legs as I settled between them, placing my hands on either side of her belly. I pushed my face against her, feeling our pup wiggle and shift inside my lovely omega.

"What do you think?" I asked. "Boy or Girl?"

"An omega." Tzidal gave me a knowing smirk.

"Yeah?" I smiled, placing a quick kiss just above her popped belly button.

"Yeah," she snarled. "A fierce one, ready for a fight."

THANK YOU FOR READING!

It means so much to me that you read my little book. I hope you enjoyed this story as much as I enjoyed writing it. If you did, it would be so lovely if you could write a short review on your favorite book website. Reviews are so important for authors and even just a single line can make a big difference.

Thank you so much!

Also by Kitt Lynn

The Hund Valley Series

The Casin Series

The Broken Omega Series

About the Author

Kitt lives in Oklahoma with her husband and stacks on stacks on stacks of fantasy books. She writes not-so-exciting technical things in her "real" job but lives for the evenings when she can visit her paper friends in their magical worlds.

She is obsessed with fantasy, folklore, love stories, and horror in general. If you dig these things then you might enjoy her books. You can find pictures of her sweet puppies, her coffee obsession, and the ridiculous things she says to keep herself motivated on her Instagram @kittlynnauthor.

For information on books, signings, and content, please visit www.kittlynn.com